OUR
CUP
IS
BROKEN

OUR CUP IS BROKEN

Florence Crannell Means

1 9 6 9

Houghton Mifflin Company Boston

Books by
FLORENCE CRANNELL MEANS

A Candle in the Mist
Shuttered Windows
The Moved-Outers
Great Day in the Morning
Carvers' George
Knock at the Door, Emmy
Reach for a Star
Borrowed Brother
Emmy and the Blue Door
But I Am Sara
That Girl Andy
Tolliver
It Takes All Kinds
Us Maltbys
Our Cup Is Broken

In the beginning God gave to every people
a cup of clay, and from this cup they
drank their life. They all dipped in the
water, but their cups were different.
Our cup is broken now. It has passed away.

A proverb of the "Digger Indians"

OUR
CUP
IS
BROKEN

1

THE MAIL TRUCK left the railroad early, with Sarah and another Hopi Indian as passengers. It was so early that the morning sun still had its way with buttes and mesas.

"Now if we had whites aboard," said the driver, who was a white himself, "they'd be having fits over the colors. I got to admit the old buttes look good, nights and mornings."

The Hopi boy stared silently at the endless horizon.

Sarah said, "Red."

It was no use hunting words for the buttes. There they stood, their rock and sand melting in color soft and bright as sunset clouds. The sight of them was a sight of home and made Sarah's breath uneven so that she was dizzier than ever.

She had been dizzy when she flagged the mail truck at the edge of town, where the road turned north toward the Painted Desert: dizzy from lack of food and sleep. She was glad there was only one other passenger, so they could all ride on the front seat, which had springs. Though crowded between the men, Sarah would not need to talk. The driver, loquacious and hearty, burned Indian brown by a lifetime of desert sun, knew his Indian riders better than to expect much conversation from them. He talked on and on himself, and that was good. Sarah didn't have to listen. She used his words as a shield against her thinking.

During the first lull in that talk, the boy stared at her appraisingly and asked, "You Hopi?" When Sarah answered "Yes," he loosed a flood of questions in their own tongue.

Sarah sat with downcast eyes and let the talk flow over her. It washed across her lightly, the ends of the phrases curling up in a cadence that was unmistakable. This youth was an Oraibi, then, from the settlement some eighteen miles beyond First Mesa, where Sarah had lived. No one could miss the Oraibi singsong. Sarah sucked in the sounds as a wilting plant sucks in raindrops through all its pores. The sound, not the meaning, for she had lost the unfamiliar thread in the first minute.

"You are riding?" the boy repeated curiously, in the Hopi style of greeting.

Sarah started, jerked out of her dream, and put her answer in English, "To First Mesa." After a moment's silence she added, "For a long time I do not hear or speak anything but English."

"Been to school in Phoenix? No? Albuquerque?"

Sarah shook her head.

"Where?"

"An American man and lady took me to Kansas. Eight years ago. My father and mother, they died when I was twelve."

"Hard lines," said the driver.

The boy blinked ahead of him. "Oh. I remember hearing. Kawasie, she is your aunt, isn't it?"

There were fewer than four thousand Hopis on the mesas and in the settlements that trickled down from the villages on their crests. Almost every Hopi knew almost every Hopi. This boy was of the most usual type, short and stocky, with an Eskimo cast of face. Sarah did not recognize him.

He sucked his teeth thoughtfully. "You going home?"

"Yes."

"Not to stay, kid? Take it from me, there ain't a living thing to do."

Sarah did not answer. Sitting pressed close to her inquisitor, she removed herself from him. The driver made it easier.

"Grey Buttes," he said, nodding toward a trading post, crouching store, house and corrals, tiny on the limitless expanse. "Guess they ain't caught him yet, the fellow that busted in last month. Got a slew of pawned hard goods. Killed the trader. Too darn bad. Hardly seems like an Indian trick. White rubbish, more likely."

He went on talking, and Sarah went on thinking. Going home — home — home. Only to be here, seventy-five miles from First Mesa, gave her wholeness of spirit, in spite of the emptiness that was nauseating her. But the nausea grew. When the truck jolted over a stony patch in the desert road, or shivered through sand or struck a chuckhole, the nausea sharpened to a peak, so that Sarah pressed her handkerchief hard against her mouth.

"Want I should stop, sister?" the driver asked. He was used to carsick Indians. Their systems were not adjusted to automobiles.

Sarah shook her head. She wanted nothing that would delay her homecoming. The Hopi boy hitched sidewise to reach into a back pocket of his jeans, and thrust a stick of foil-wrapped gum toward her.

"Thanks," she said, and chewed it slowly.

Even the purples and chromes and rose of the buttes and mesas were something she had been hungry for, without knowing it. But not as she had been starving for her mother's house. She had always held its picture complete in her mind. During the past months she had escaped to it again and again.

3

It stood high on the Hopi mesa, where every breeze found it, yet its massive flat roof of poles, brush and mud kept it cool under the most scorching sun. It was an old-style Hopi house. Many of them still remained on the mesa, though an increasing number had wood floors and iron bedsteads. Not her mother's house: it would not have looked strange to Coronado. To be sure, its cookstove was of this century and its kerosene lamp and glass windowpanes, and it contained a few store dishes and cooking things, some machine-made clothes, and boards made into a cupboard.

From a higher living room three softly modeled adobe steps led to a lower living room, without partition walls to break the flow of air from one to the other. Another short stair led to a half room, one end for the *piki* baking, one for storage. Twig headdresses hung from pegs and poles, and fox skins with tassels of scarlet wool, and skins of yellow warblers and painted buntings; saddles and stirrups and planting sticks and boomerangs and weaving tools.

The living rooms had no clutter at all, but clear open spaces, swept and still. The rooms were empty, yet supplied with every needful thing: sheepskins for beds and for seats; the grinding bin in the corner; a loom hung from the roof poles at one end. Against the adobe-plastered wall hung objects of use and beauty: bouquets of sharply red chillies, brightly painted *kachina* dolls, and a green-and-white enamel dishpan from the trading post. Clusters of dried beans and garlands of corn lent interest, together with a plaque in the firm coiled basketry of Second Mesa, and one in the bold whirlwind pattern of the Oraibi reedwork.

There was also a flaxen-haired *Bohanna* doll, and the cradle of willow basketry was always a new one. A cradle must be discarded when its baby died, and the babies had all died, some before they were named. Sarah was the only

4

one of her mother's children to live beyond its fourth year. So she was with her mother a great deal, though the whole village was her home, with mothers and fathers, uncles and aunts and clan relations, until most of the few hundred Walpis were of her family.

Sarah huddled close to her mother when she was weaving baskets, sat on her heels near the griddle when her mother baked *piki*, gravely watching and eating the bits of crisp paper bread that her mother handed her fresh from the smooth black stone; pressed close to her mother's side when she ground corn.

Most clearly of all she remembered the grinding, because it took hours of every day. Sometimes, before her cough grew too bad, the mother sang. Sometimes, feeling Sarah a sleepy huddle against her, she would croon a lullaby that was no more than, "Go to sleep, pretty little girl, *bas sonel mana*," over and over in her husky soft voice. It was all quiet and reassuring, the sun in bright patches on the floor, the steady motion of Mother's arms, up, down, up, down, and the meal, fine as sand, as warm, clean sand in a summer field.

Most of her ranch memories were of long, sunny days — days hot at their peak and cool at their ends, with a few summer nights warm enough so that the family climbed to the flat roof and spread their sheepskins there and lay under the piercing-bright stars.

Father was a good farmer. He had a few sheep but no horses, for he and Mother were of poor families. But up through the restless sand of his fields he coaxed a livelihood. He had a sand patch here, another two miles east of it, and a third to the west, and he ran from one to the other with the fine, tireless jog of the Hopi racer. The fields ran, too, but slowly. The sand was all that made the desert arable, so the fields drifted with it. The Mormons had long used irrigating ditches, and the government talked of ditches for the Hopis; but the sand mulch did as well. Father thrust the planting stick through its protective blanket, and into the hole dropped his seeds, sometimes wrapped in moist clay for quicker germination. As he worked he chanted a planting song and made prayers. And many of the seeds came up.

When bugs were prevalent, Father took a bucket of herb medicine and a handleless broom and drenched the infested field, plant by plant. When field mice ate the seed before it came up or the crows gobbled the tender sprouts, Father replanted.

Over near the mesa, every spring, an old man made the proper offering of eggs to the spring winds, so that they would be gentle with the mesas and the fields. Without that offering it was impossible to guess what the winds would have done. Even the tough mesa vegetation was shaped into half globes by their harrying.

Father tended his little peach trees, spading sandy earth over their naked roots, for though they crouched low and gripped the ground with desperate strength, the wind often swept it from under their feet. He made little screens of brush or stone or a tin can for each new plant, or scooped away the sand that smothered it. Sarah could not recall the feeling of wind and sand, but she could see her father working to save his crops from them. And she did not remember when the crops were not saved. When one field yielded little, there were the other fields to depend on. Always there was a harvest.

Throughout the summer Sarah would run along at her mother's side, imitating her as she gathered yucca for utility baskets and bee balm for the paint for her pottery. Like her mother, she gathered wild spinach, and the seeds that they liked to mix with butter, when they had butter, and a small yellow flower for seasoning, and an ice-green plant to drive away the viciously biting chicken bugs. She watched as her mother chopped out the root of the yucca which made copious lather for washing the family's heavy black hair.

Mother worked as hard in summer as in winter. She felt better, out in the sun, though Father complained that she ran all the flesh off her bones. Even when resting in the shade at the doorway, weaving her utility baskets, she breathed hard and short. Sarah, sitting on her heels or with legs sidewise like her mother's, crowded as close to her mother as she could get; and her memory did not reach back to a time when she was not working gravely at crooked little baskets of her own.

From this timeless summer on the desert ranch, the Snake Dance called them back to the mesa every August. Sarah had never fully enjoyed the ceremonial, with the dancers painted black and white and gripping rattlesnakes in their mouths. She always sat breathlessly still when the snakes were put down, after their ritual washing, and went wriggling out over the floor of the court. It would have been a shameful thing to scream and run, as some visiting whites did. Sarah sat close to her mother, her eyes widening whenever a snake came toward her.

Sarah's composite picture of harvest was a sunny one. The year when she could not have been more than six years old she was big enough to help string the beans in small neat bouquets with yucca fiber, to hang on the house walls for drying. The crop of sweet corn was good, and the family held a work party to dig the great room-sized pit and make a roaring fire in it. When the fire had burned long enough to whiten the earth walls, the draft at the bottom was stopped up, and the corn was dumped in — a whole wagon-load. When slabs of stone had been fitted over the top and the crevices caulked with earth, the corn was left to cook slowly through the night.

In the morning, while Mother heated the mutton stew and made hot bread over the ashes, the men uncovered the corn, a great rush of sweet steam veiling them from sight. Always there was a pause while the rain clouds were invited to partake of the feast which they had helped provide. After that, everyone ate as much as he could of the sweet hot corn and of the other good foods, before they loaded the burros with the remainder and carried it to the mesa top. There they prepared it for drying, stripping back the husks and making neat little chaplets of several ears together, as they had done with the beans.

There was *nakaviki* to make from the corn, grinding it coarsely, wrapping it in husks to bake, and finally splitting the packets and spreading them open to dry for winter use. There were peaches to dry, also, and Sarah liked to sit on the housetop, her bare feet tucked under her skirt, and try to cut the peaches as Father and Mother did.

One twist of the wrist divided a freestone and spread it cut sides up in the burning sun. The air grew heavy with the rich smell of peaches and corn and the dry smell of beans, and Sarah could eat all she pleased. Father and Mother laughed and joked with the neighbors who came up the long ladders to the housetop, though Mother coughed rackingly when the peach fuzz stung her nostrils and throat.

It was only now and then that Mother sat for a long time silent with a knife in one hand and a peach in the other, and stared at nothing at all.

2

Sᴀʀᴀʜ's ꜱᴇᴠᴇɴᴛʜ ʏᴇᴀʀ was memorable. Most vivid of all was the incident of Aunt Kawasie and the fetishes.

Aunt Kawasie, short and round like an Eskimo, was a person of influence in the village. She was strong of mind and body, and she was head of her clan. Sarah liked to go to Kawasie's house, where she was as free as in her own.

It was not so tidily kept as her mother's house. It was on the street level, and Aunt Kawasie's swarm of children kept its protective half door on the swing, so that chickens, as well as dogs and cats, ventured in from the street, and added to the confusion. In season basket trays of peaches and apricots stood always on the floor, with children squatting to eat them. The abundant traffic scuffed up the adobe floor so that there was dust on everything. Aunt Kawasie scolded a little and sometimes flapped her apron at her flock and herded them, scuffling and laughing, out the door. Though her temper was quick, her own children seldom felt so much as the weight of her finger. Hopi parents usually left any necessary correction to the aunts and uncles, from whom it came more properly. Until that seventh year Sarah had never required punishment.

Sarah enjoyed the free and easy ways of the house. She enjoyed playing with her cousins. She enjoyed her aunt's cooking. Kawasie was an even better cook than Sarah's mother, and she had more to cook. Her *somiviki* had exactly

9

the right flavor of wood ashes, exactly the right substance in the mouth. Her fried bread crackled with bursting bubbles of crispness; and no one on the mesa could equal her hominy, its great grains luscious and savory with the juices of the mutton stew. So Sarah could often be found sitting with her aunt's family, sharing the food set on an oilcloth on the floor, in pottery bowls and store kettles, basket trays and pie tins. There was talk and laughter and coming and going, and abundance of fragrant food.

One day she came in and found no one, though the door was unlocked and yielded to her hand. Disappointedly she wandered about the two long rooms, helping herself to an ear of boiled corn that someone had left half eaten, and sitting on a ladderlike half stair to finish it, her long skirt wrapped around her bare legs. While she nibbled, her eyes roved around the house. She observed Uncle Mattima's belt, with its silver conchos as big as saucers. She observed, hanging from a trapezelike clothes pole, Aunt Kawasie's best Hopi dress, of heavy handwoven wool, glittering with silver buttons. She observed a small low door set in another wall, a heavy door of gray old planks.

Sarah's small teeth paused in their steady action. Plenty of times she had seen this door, but always closed. Now it was ajar, and on the floor in front of it a pair of woman's moccasins stood toeing in as Aunt Kawasie must have stepped out of them.

Sarah gulped down the kernels already in her mouth and sheared off the remaining row with practiced speed. Then she dropped the cob to the floor and stole softly over to the forbidden door, almost stifled with excitement.

The crack was a narrow one. She flattened her face into it, just above the low-set thumbhole. At first she could distinguish nothing in the dimness. Then her aunt's short, bulky body became apparent. Sarah knew that body; knew the parting straight down the middle of the head, and the coils of black hair disappearing over the shoulders. But the secret room she did not know, nor what Kawasie was doing there. Sarah's eye accustomed itself quickly to the twilight. Aunt Kawasie was offering a plaque of food to something on a low bench of adobe that ran the length of the opposite wall.

Sarah held her breath so hard that her stomach hurt, making out what it was that stood on the bench. One object was a stone deer, with antlers of branching twigs. One was a huge spider, apparently fashioned from bone. Still another was the crude figure of a man, of stone as black and polished as a piki griddle and with head blood red. Clearly he was Masa-u, God of the Underworld, and the sight of him chilled the small intruder and made her turn to steal away.

Unluckily, Aunt Kawasie was also turning, her ritual task finished. As Sarah reached the ladderlike stair, stumbling in her haste over her long dress, her aunt's powerful little hand gripped her shoulder.

Aunt Kawasie whirled Sarah around and stared at her from hot, angry eyes, her jowls puffing and reddening as she tightened her mouth, her fingers biting into Sarah's shoulder as if she were about to shake the child. Sarah, who had never been shaken or beaten, felt her heart jump with fear. Then the woman's eyes cooled, and Kawasie gave Sarah a small shove so that she sat down on a narrow step. The woman closed the forbidden door and balanced herself cumbrously to pull on her moccasins, her breath coming short. She motioned Sarah to go upstairs ahead of her, and the child scampered, drawing in her buttocks protectively.

"To pry into the secret things of the people," Aunt Kawasie said, her words spaced with her gusty breathing, "that is

11

bas kahopi. When children lack respect for the religion, then is the tribe a cornstalk with worms nibbling at its roots. You knew well, Nawamana, that the door was not to be opened."

Her voice was so terrible that Nawamana — Sarah — could only whimper.

"When we open doors that are not to be opened," the scorching voice continued —

This time, Sarah managed to stammer, "I did not open it. Truly I did not open it. Already it was a little open. I only looked through the crack that was already there."

Aunt Kawasie held her eyes steadily, probingly. "There is small difference," she concluded, but more gently. "Remember that we must all be careful, not only the men in the ceremonies, who must make each thought and motion exactly right. And now, so that you may remember, I must whip you."

Sarah stood trembling. She clenched her teeth to keep them from chattering. This was her father's sister, with the right to strike her, since she had first let her wrath cool and would not be striking in anger.

From a crevice in the adobe wall Aunt Kawasie took a length of cord. Using it as a whip, she lashed the child's bare legs, below the hem of her dress. Sarah still trembled, and tears ran down her face. Her skin could hardly feel the stinging cord, because all the hurt went through to the inside.

"Now go," Kawasie ordered, "and tell your father and mother what you have done."

Sarah could not remember what her father and mother said. She did remember that her father took her with him that night when he went to the house of the village chief, the *Kik-Mongwi,* and that she sat still sick with shame while

12

the men talked together. When the *Kik-Mongwi's* small granddaughter sat down on the floor beside her and wanted her to look at the big dog-eared mail-order catalog, Sarah shook her head and folded her hands between her knees.

The chief was telling Father about his recent trip to Canyon de Chelly. A white man had taken him, for though he had lived here all his years — fifty, maybe, or seventy — and his fathers for generations before him, John had never before seen the mystic place some fifty miles across the buttes and mesas and desert.

The deep-set eyes glowed in his aquiline face as he described the visit. The rain had been so heavy, he said, that they could not go down into the canyon as they had expected. A swirling current and quicksand made it too hazardous. They could only walk for miles along its rocky rim.

Before their enemies, the Navajos, had taken possession of it, it had belonged to the Ancestors, that branching gorge, with its lofty walls of vermilion rock and its broad floor where a few Navajos built their hogans and planted their crops. On those sheer walls still hung a few of the Houses of the Dead. The oldest Navajo, the oldest Hopi, had never heard of a day when the living used those dwellings, but the style of them fitted with Hopi legend. The old fashion of laying the stone was different from the new, and John had long desired to see them. Perhaps he could learn some new way with masonry, as the women learned new ways with pottery from the sherds that washed down the watercourses.

Below the finest of the structures, the one which the *Bohannas* called White House, there was also a voice-answering-back. Standing there in the bed of the mighty canyon, a man could shout and hear the whole of his words returning to him, so that you would know by their shape who had

13

spoken them. John could not test the marvel because today he must content himself with his view from the rim.

"And *antsa,* truly," he said, his face shining, "it was well that Old Hornblower chose the time he did" — the Hopi had named this white man Old Hornblower because of the resounding way in which he blew his nose — "for look you: the rain was falling with such volume that it roared over the rim. And, truly, when we came where we could look down upon the White House, a waterfall was pouring down in front of it. More than that, in the waterfall, clear to see, a rainbow with all its colors whole." He gazed at the floor in reverent silence for a moment, and then spoke meditatively. "It is good for the whole tribe that I should have seen this thing. Perhaps it is good even for the whole world."

"But you did not tell Old Hornblower how important," Father said, chuckling.

"No, the whites think they know everything; yet they laugh at what is most important."

"My grandfather used to tell me that we did very well before the whites came," Father said, "but they have spoiled it, somehow. Something is wrong. Maybe we should work harder at the ceremonies. I am sure we should keep our thoughts walking straighter."

Sarah looked soberly at her elders, sitting on stools hand-high. The light from a kerosene lamp fell on John's strongly marked dark face, making it luminous. For the first time Sarah felt herself a member of the tribe. She was part of it. Unconsciously she touched her legs, where this morning the lash had curled. The sting made her feel proud and happy.

Another element that gave her seventh year importance was the government day school on the plain below the mesa. Sarah knew just how she looked on that first day because

14

the new teacher had come up the trail with her camera and had snapped her picture as she dodged shyly behind a boulder. The teacher had given Sarah a print, and Sarah had kept it. Small and brown and thin she was. *Bohanna* shoes made her black-stockinged legs look like spindles between their over-largeness and the hem of her long gingham dress. Little boys were not bothered with clothes on the mesa, but little girls wore a single garment, long enough to keep them well covered. Sarah tied her school stockings above her knobby knees with rags, since there was nothing to fasten them to.

Although the clothes were awkward and ill-fitting, Sarah's face was not bad. Her mother's aquiline bone structure was becoming apparent. Sarah's short nose was delicately arched. Large lids deepened the luster of her eyes under the heavy black bangs. A smile was widening across her thin, dark little face, but she was poised for flight like a desert fox.

The new teacher held out her hand, and Sarah put her small brown fingers into the smooth white ones. Thus she walked down to school, her eyes on the ground or making furtive excursions up the smooth, clean woolen of the teacher's skirt to the crisp blouse and the shiny hair, straw-colored like a Hopi albino's. As they drew near the school Sarah hung back, and the teacher released her hand and let her follow slowly to the strange new place.

Sarah had often come to the group of government buildings. On certain days the women of her village could come down and wash their clothes at the laundry, with water for the turn of a wrist. Sarah had come to the laundry with her mother. She had come with her father or her mother to the little room that was the post office, because once in a great while they got a letter, and, several times during the year

15

the big, bulky, fascinating catalogs of mail-order houses. And once or twice Sarah had come to closing exercises or a Christmas celebration.

Now, for the first time, the government buildings became a part of her own life, though a part that did not match the rest. Sarah dragged her feet as she passed into the green shade of the cottonwoods. A bigger girl saw her lurking behind a tamarisk as the opening bell rang, ran to her briskly and dragged her to the beginners' room. Sarah sat in the seat to which she was led, still as a caught rabbit. She spent that day and many days growing used to the rows of wooden seats and desks, the glare of windows, the dusty-smelling blackboards and, above all, the English language. For here no word of Hopi was permitted.

Sarah could say "Hel-lo" and "good-bye." She could say "Candy" and "Thank you." She could understand when the teacher asked, "What is your name, little girl?" That was a question no Hopi was supposed to answer for himself. A ten-year-old girl who was not shy at all and a twelve-year-old boy waved their hands importantly and said, "Sarah! Sarah!" Sarah slid lower in her seat and examined her hands: slim brown hands with pale nails dark-rimmed and with grimed-in places roughening the knuckles.

"Who are her father and mother?" the teacher asked.

"Tuvenga and Sequapa," they told her.

"Sarah Tuvenga," the teacher said. "Remember, little girl: your name is Sarah Tuvenga."

Those were almost the last words Sarah really understood that day. The remaining hours whirled around her without meaning. Her neighbors boosted her up when she was supposed to rise, or let her stay seated if she clung too tight to be pried loose. They nudged her and nodded her to follow them. Sometimes they whispered a forbidden Hopi word of enlightenment.

Prodded and pulled, she rose and marched and sat. She went through the health inspection, a monitor scrutinizing her about the head, the ears, the neck, the hands. She accepted a handkerchief, which was a square of rag provided by the teacher. At the close of the day all the little rags were washed and hung on a line for next day, though before Sarah was through with that school the rags had yielded to paper tissues. Sarah also ate lunch, for the first time sitting at a table and finding both her dangling legs and the *Bohanna* food disconcerting. The day dragged to its end and Sarah rushed up on top like a small creature let out of a cage.

She soon learned to understand the English for the simplest commands. She liked the smell of the teacher, and even the taste of some of the *Bohanna* food, when she was hungry enough. But the first two years had passed before she could force herself to say more than "I no know," when asked a question, and it was not until the beginning of the fourth year that she passed to second grade. No one had laughed about it, for it was the same with all the other children, except a few whose parents talked English at home. Besides, Sarah was so small and slight that nobody knew she was eleven when she entered third grade.

There was much that the teachers did not know about Sarah. At nine she read aloud, one heavy word at a time, "I — see — a — feesh." With patience worn a little thin the teacher asked, "What is a fish, Sarah?"

Sarah looked sidewise at the strangely curved creature in the illustration and said, "I no know," having never seen a thing like it.

17

"Does it fly?" the teacher asked sardonically. After an instant's hesitation, Sarah whispered, "Yess, it iss fly."

At that the teacher had laughed. Sarah would always remember that teacher, whose face was shaped like an egg, with large pale eyes and a long nose added to the surface. She would always remember her teeth, that showed like a horse's when she laughed. The boys and girls, following Teacher, had hidden their mouths behind their hands and snickered, some with eyes puzzled. Sarah had stood with the book clutched in her hands, turning to fire under that unbearable mockery.

By the time she was in the third grade she understood more English. She began to hide her bewilderment when the lessons told of ferns and moss, of ships upon the sea, of the white world with its endless gadgets. By that time she was a slim, trim, quick-moving little girl, with a responsive smile and a docile manner which endeared her to her teachers. She still looked far younger than her age, even among the small-statured Hopis.

But all the while school was no more than a fringe on her real life. The mission classes were more intelligible than government day school, for the Mission Marys talked Hopi. One of them spoke baby-talk Hopi, but Miss Lundquist spoke as well, say, as Old Nellie, on the mesa, whose brains were touched. The Hopis thought it rather remarkable that a *Bohanna* could speak so well as that, for in all the world there were few but Hopis who knew the language at all. That was doubtless the reason the school people pretended to despise it.

Miss Lundquist respected it. She had been at the mission since Sarah's mother was a child, and Sequapa could remember when she began to write the words in a little book

18

and learn them, working at the task with mind and mouth and tongue and teeth. She did not care when she made a mistake and the Hopis laughed. She laughed with them, throwing herself back and clapping her hands on her knees and shutting her sparkling hazel eyes.

Over and over the Hopis had told the joke about one of the Mission Mary's telling Uncle Abraham that she would pay him yesterday for the eggs he had brought her tomorrow. That had become a part of Sarah's family's vocabulary: "I will pay you yesterday."

The Hopis liked Miss Lundquist all the more because she gave their laughter free course. They were inclined to approve of her God, and many of them would have paid Him tribute if she had not insisted on their casting aside all their old ones as a preliminary. Even with that hurdle to jump, some of them accepted the new religion, Uncle Abraham, for instance.

Sarah had often heard that story. Uncle Abraham was herding the family sheep, when Sarah's father, Tuvenga, heard that the boy was planning to go through the Christian rites of baptism next day. Tuvenga followed the youth at a distance, and found an unexpectedly good opportunity to thwart him. When he was far out on the desert with his flock, Abraham took advantage of a friendly Navajo's sweat bath hogan to give himself a thorough cleansing. Chuckling angrily, Tuvenga rode up and snatched his brother's clothes, threw the grazing pony's rope bridle back over its neck, gave it a cut with a stick, and sent it galloping homeward.

The ruse did not defeat Abraham. Waiting till dark, he ran the twenty miles home to the mesa, crept into his mother's house and put on his best clothes, which he had prudently hidden under the corn in the storeroom. Then he ran

19

the eight miles to Polacca before dawn, and was baptized as planned.

Abraham had been wise enough not to return to the mesa, but when word was brought to him that his old mother wanted to see him he could not disregard her summons. With some forebodings he climbed the two ladders to his mother's house. There he found a dozen men sitting on low stools and sheepskins, and his mother hovering over a fire in the open fireplace. She cast anxious glances at him, her lips working, as he sat down beside Tuvenga.

"He was frightened, the little brother," Sarah's father used to say, "but he had courage. He was only twenty years or maybe twenty-two, and small — as indeed he will always be. But I was very mad. Why should he think he knew better than the rest of us? Why should he take up this religion that said we were no good? The thing he did was dangerous to us all.

"I knew what I had to do," Tuvenga went on. "I had to scare the foolishness out of him. So I pointed my gun right at the young one's heart. Seeing me do this, his clan uncle, Honwi, took out his hunting knife, strong and sharp, and whetted it on a stone. All the while one of the old men was talking to Abraham, telling him how wrong he was, and ordering him to have a ceremony and get the white man's water washed off with sacred cornmeal. But the little brother, he only said he had chosen the white man's way, and would follow it even if we killed him. He got greenish gray, Abraham did, and his voice was thin, like when you have been a long time sick, but he wouldn't change his mind. I got madder and madder, seeing him so stubborn. I got so mad —"

The small Sarah used to shiver at this point in the narrative, and wish that her father would hurry and reassure her,

20

even though she knew that Uncle Abraham was still in the flesh these long years after.

"But his mother must have crept out the back way without our missing her," Tuvenga would go on. "For just then we heard someone call outside, and the voice was the voice of Miss Lundquist. She was still on the ladder, peering across at the open door."

Sarah had needed no help in picturing the scene. She could see the round, anxiously smiling face of the Mission Mary more plainly than the men had seen it that night. She could hear her voice, conciliating yet courageous as she gave them greeting: *"Tai, sikwatsimu? Tai?"*

It was not Father who rushed angrily to the edge of the roof and gave Miss Lundquist a shove, so that she swayed and fell, grabbing at the ladder and missing it. The man who did that un-Hopi act leaned forward to see what had happened to her, his rage already cooling. And then a deeper *Bohanna* voice sounded from the street, growing more distinct as it climbed swiftly toward the frightened group.

"Now, now, what's all this about? Miss Lundquist, you all right? Abraham, you there?"

It was the agent, of all people, his head silver in the dim light. He helped Miss Lundquist to her feet, she maintaining breathlessly that she wasn't hurt a mite, and ascended the upper ladder. By that time Abraham was alone in the house with his old mother who had scurried back after she sent word to the agent.

Abraham had long been a deacon in the little church now, but he had never had an easy time of it. The tribe had made him feel the weight of their displeasure. They had persuaded the *Kik-Mongwi* to take away the good fields that had fallen to him and give him poor ones. Something had poisoned his sheep. His chickens had been stolen.

21

He himself had been threatened more than once. He had courage, Tuvenga admitted, and so had Miss Lundquist.

Unwillingly, Father liked the Mission Mary and so did Sarah, for the Saturday classes were full of enjoyable novelty. There was sewing for the girls, woodwork for the boys, cutting and pasting for the smaller ones. There were unnumbered drinks of water, calling for trips through the mission living room, eyes busy all the way, and into the kitchen and its sink with the magical silver faucets.

The mission bubbled with laughter, and with music. Miss Lundquist had a little box organ that she carried around with her. Sitting on a stool before it, she threw back her shining round face and sang to her own playing, and the children sang with her.

In Sarah's memory those Saturday mornings stood in an even balmier glow than the mesa. That might have been because of the contrast between indoors and outdoors when the weather was bad. At such times Sarah slogged through mud with the others, drenched with rain or hunched inside inadequate shoulder shawls in bitter winter weather, and came into the stove-warmed, dry-floored, window-lighted mission, with its fascinating pictures on the walls. Sarah's time at the mission was warm and bright, but it was short.

3

It was in Sarah's ninth year that Father drove his sheep out to graze on an unforgettable autumn day. She walked with him down to his sheep corral, a loop of stone wall against the side of the mesa. Already in mid-morning the sheep were hunting the shade, for their coats had grown heavy since the May shearing, and the sun baked that eastward slope. When Father released them the flock poured down the trail, a gray-white current flecked with brown-black.

Sarah stood on a high boulder and watched them go, her father behind them. It was so still that her single garment hung straight and limp; so still that her black hair did not blow into her eyes. In that bland stillness Father strode away forever through Sarah's memory. His black hair, warmed with brown, was held back from his face with a red bandanna, and clubbed in a knot behind. His broad shoulders swung smoothly under the ragged plaid of his jacket. His bright blue earrings jerked strongly, and the legs in the faded jeans moved with the ease of the trained runner.

Before the day was done, swift angry clouds had come out of the north and taken the sky. Soft, large snowflakes smacked wetly on the stone streets of the village. The soft large flakes grew small, steady and purposeful. Women grabbed in their sheepskins and quilts and blankets, airing on the housetops, took down the last bouquets of sweet corn and beans, drying on the outer walls. Sheep came tinkling hurriedly up the trail to the corrals, led by the more enterprising goats. The village housed itself against the storm.

Mother ground meal. She baked *piki.* She said, with intense cheerfulness, that if there was enough of this snow the reservoirs here on top would be partly filled. She had Sarah help her carry out their tubs and dishpans, to catch all they could, pausing only long enough to cough herself breathless.

Later in the afternoon a clan uncle breasted the storm and came to Mother's house, snow melting on his steel-gray hair and draggled ribbon *banda.* Shaking himself like a wet dog, he sat down on a low stool near the stove and rubbed his hands in the warmth of the fire. He smiled at Sarah with a great show of teeth. Silently Mother shoved a basket of *piki* toward him. Mother was weaving a flat basket now, her fingers flying fast and her head bent low above her work.

The clan uncle ate a half roll of the paper bread, slowly, as with great relish, before he asked casually whether Father had brought home his sheep.

"He said he would be going far out today, for a better pasture," Mother said in a flat voice. "He said he would camp and let them graze several days, *sene,* perhaps."

"Many hogans off that way," said the clan uncle. "And Five Houses, also. In case tonight should be bad."

His words were almost lost in the howl of the wind around the houses, its shriek down the chimney. He beckoned Sarah to come closer, and she slid across the floor and sat with hands folded on her lap. The clan uncle was much older than Father. He talked to her as if she were a baby, in a kindly, amused way, his eyes bright and his mouth quirking as with an inward joke.

24

"Did I ever tell you the story of the coyote and the little girl doves?" he asked her.

He had told the story a hundred times, and he told it again. Leaning against his knee, Sarah listened and watched the gray-white curtains outside the windows. Once the clan uncle paused to speak to Mother's bowed head. "That one is the best runner on this mesa," he said, "and he always knows what to do."

Mother murmured that she had been having bad dreams. The clan uncle said there were often bad dreams that came to nothing, nothing at all. He went on with the story.

That night Sarah fell asleep early on her sheepskin. Mother had made a bigger fire than usual and kept the coffee and the stew boiling on the stove, so that the air was close and steamy and appetizing with mutton and onion and coffee.

When daylight wakened Sarah, Mother stood peering out of the window, her thin face seeming thinner, the cheekbones sticking out more than they should.

"Did Father — ?" Sarah asked, leaning up on her elbow.

"*Ka-eh,* no," her mother answered.

The sun that morning was a red-hot copper ball at the edge of the earth. Before it was halfway up the sky it had melted the snow, leaving only startling white shadows attached to the west side of every rounded clump of sage and greasewood and saltweed. Still Father did not come.

"Of course not. He would go on with the sheep," said Mother. "Now we shall have clear weather until next new moon, the old men say."

Two nights later a Second Mesa man, driving over to trade with a Hopi who kept a little store here on top, brought news to Mother's door. The word had come only as far as Toreva, the little settlement huddled on the breast of Second Mesa.

It had come there by telephone from the hospital at Keams Canyon.

In the blinding fury of the blizzard Father had stepped into a badger hole and snapped his leg, above and below the knee. He could do nothing that night except keep himself warm among his sheep and wait for the day. He meant to find his burro as soon as morning dawned. Then he could pull himself up into the saddle and get home. But the burro had sought shelter, and it could not be found. Father was ten miles from First Mesa and five from Second Mesa and Toreva. The many hogans with which his clan brother had comforted Mother were none, and Five Houses was farther away than Second Mesa.

Father ordered his dog to keep the sheep, already browsing on saltweed that was poking through the snow, and he set out to drag himself the weary miles to Toreva. Over stony ground, through sand, up and down; wet with the snow, chilled by the snow, scorched by the sun, his hands bruised with stones, and pricked and torn by cactus and yucca, dragging his swollen leg —

On the second day he reached a hogan. The Navajo harnessed his horses, and he and his wife hoisted Tuvenga into the wagon and took him to Toreva. From Toreva, the Mission Mary's car, with the field nurse in attendance, speeded him on to the government hospital at Keams Canyon.

Father would live. They had saved him by taking off the broken and mangled leg, well above the knee.

At that Mother wept and coughed, wept and coughed. "He would rather have died," she whispered huskily.

Kawasie, who had come on the heels of the messenger, scolded Mother for saying it. It was a thing not to be said, that one would rather die.

"If he could have come to one of our own doctors —"

Mother's voice dragged wearily — "The bone doctor, he could make any broken bones like new again —"

"But the green sickness had set in," the Second Mesa man told her, "the poison that creeps upward and kills."

"Not without cause do these things come to pass. We must find out who caused this," Kawasie said harshly, her face set hard as cold tallow.

Weeks later, after Father was brought home from the hospital, the family talked over the cause of the accident. Naturally they thought first of witches. The one who had killed the last boy baby had long since given up and died, but there were still plenty of suspicious characters in the three villages. Father had been too smart. He had known what to do, so that they had not succeeded in killing him.

Kawasie added another possibility. The forces of nature might be angry with Abraham, who paid no attention to them, performed no rites to please them. It was unfortunate to be so closely connected with such as Abraham, she said, her eyes glittering. It might be necessary to punish the rebel.

Father, shifting restlessly and trying not to look at the stump of his leg, said, no, they must not harm Abraham, since they could not be sure he was to blame. There had been misfortunes in their family even before Abraham joined the mission.

Kawasie tapped her teeth thoughtfully. Long ago, she said, there had been an unexplained disappearance of the worship objects of Sequapa's clan. That might have started all the trouble. And it might not. But at any rate they must not have any further dealings with Abraham, Kawasie declared, her eyes hard as obsidian. And Sarah must not go to the mission, either. Come to think of it, Sarah's going to the mission might be at the root of the trouble.

27

Sarah did not go again.

She missed the Saturday classes, with their warmth and brightness and laughter, and their many things to do. And that year she was not allowed to go to the Christmas celebration, where even the clan uncle who chanted so derisively at the Mission Mary, even Aunt Kawasie, would have been welcome to a hearty dinner and a bag of gifts; where the Indian Christians presented a pageant which related the coming of the Christ Child, somewhat as the ceremonials related the coming of the clans to the mesas.

Miss Lundquist sent Sarah her presents anyway: a dress and a doll and candy in fascinating translucent loops and slices. The Hopi trader always gave a tubful of the candy.

The speedy coming of *Powanmnu* comforted Sarah for the loss of the Christmas party. *Powanmnu* was the gayest ceremonial of the Hopi cycle, and it mingled fear with its delight, for it was the occasion when the Natacks, the giants, visited the villages, punishing the children for a year of misdeeds.

Twice during the days of the ceremonial the great creatures with their ravening snouts came parading through Walpi, roaring threats to carry away the bad children and eat them. At their first visit the parents begged time to gather food for the avengers, and at their second appearance this ransom was presented, and the giants went grumbling away, leaving small hearts weak with relief.

Up to this time the fear of the giants had only given edge to Sarah's excitement, to her enjoyment of the dances, the feasting, the gifts. Since she was an only and beloved child, and a docile one, her parents had taken good care that she should not have too severe a dose of terror. When the Giant Mother and her Giant Sons had come hooting up the ladder, Sarah had always been allowed to take refuge. She crowded her small, shaking body between her father's crossed legs and against his broad breast; or into her mother's arms, with only one terrified eye peering out at the grotesque and gorgeous monsters. Father and Mother always assured the giants, in respectful tones that hardly hid the thread of laughter, that their daughter was sorry for everything she had done, and would never do so again, if only they would let her stay in her own home another year. Sarah buried herself as completely as possible in her parents while the giants growled that they were hungry and must have food, and if not Sarah, then what? When her parents offered to collect rich foods, much more tasty than their skinny child, before the giants' next visit, the terrible creatures snarled their consent, gave Sarah's hair a tweak, and stalked to the door. Before they had quite disappeared, Sarah had revived enough to uncover one eye again for a last look at the disappearing horns.

This year was different. The giants came as usual. The *kachina* dances were as usual. But this year Sarah was initiated into the *Kachina* Society.

Throughout the first portion of the ceremonial she waited, with fear and expectancy, for the day of initiation. It was clothed in mystery. None of the old children could be persuaded to tell the new children about the initiation.

Sarah went trembling to the *kiva*, between her ceremonial father, small and thin as Uncle Abraham, and her ceremonial mother, tall and bulky like Aunt Polehongsi, with other boys and girls ranging in age from six to ten. Each was accompanied by ceremonial relations, each carried an ear of white corn, and the little boys were unclothed save for their blankets.

Sarah was too frightened to see clearly what happened in the underground chamber. Under her feet the floor, with its sand painting, rose and fell in waves, so that she was sick to her stomach. She could barely make out that the sand painting pictured the two Tüngwüp, the Flogging *Kachinas*, and their mother, Tümas. When a Supernatural descended the ladder from the hatchway of the *kiva*, the thunder of Sarah's heartbeats almost drowned the long story he chanted, narrating his adventures in coming to their mesa. The Mudhead clowns that followed him ritually around the sand painting were dim, dizzy shapes without meaning.

Unwillingly her eyes sought the ladder, fixed themselves on the white moccasins at its top, followed them to the floor. Moments passed before she could force them upward over the *kachina's* dress to the yucca whips in its hands, and to the crows' wings that flanked its huge turquoise-blue face. From the pitiless Tümas, Sarah looked desperately at her sons, the Floggers, with their horns and their fox skins, with their red horsehair kilts and their cruel yucca whips.

Now a boy was led to the sand painting and the shoulder blanket was lifted from his shrinking brown body. Poli, it was. Sarah knew him well, and he had often pulled her hair and thrown pebbles at her from behind a rock on the trail. Poli tried to stand straight, but his skinny little body arched itself, huddled itself, in spite of him. His ceremonial father told him to shield himself with the hand that did not hold the corn ear.

Down came the green whip of a Tüngwüp. Poli's body jerked and quivered, and a long red line stretched from neck to buttocks. Again the lash fell, crossing the red line with another. Although his body jerked, Poli kept his face stubbornly set, with no lance of appeal to his ceremonial parents, who could take further blows in his stead. Again — again — while the lines oozed redly. Then his foster mother, her face tight, as if this had been hard work for her, too, wrapped his blanket about him and led him over to the other side of the *kiva*. He was sobbing without sound, head erect on taut little neck, lips bitten shut.

Sarah watched with lip hanging. She had not minded the first stroke, because he had teased her so often.

Her ceremonial mother shoved her gently. Her time had come.

Clenching the corn, clenching her free fist, catching her lip hard between her teeth, she tensed her whole small body to receive the blows. They came like running fire through her thin dress: one, two. Then the ceremonial mother interposed her stout body and took two blows, grunting with something like surprise, as if they were harder than she had expected.

Dazed, Sarah was led over to the other side, to wait while the remaining children were whipped. This part was soon over.

Later the initiates were brought again to the *kiva*. This time they came to see an important dance of the *kachinas,* Supernaturals who throughout the whole of Sarah's life had woven gay threads in the drabness of village existence, dancing in their embroidered garments, in their bright paint, in their feathers and fox skins, in their huge and elaborate masks — Supernaturals condescending to human nature.

That night the garments were the same, and the paints and skins and feathers, the turtle shells and beasts' claws and jewels. Not the masks. With amazement the children's eyes sought those magnificent and monstrous masks, and found the great frames petering out into small human heads. More: the human heads were those of the villagers. Father's issued from the magnificent shoulders of a giant. A clan uncle's face looked at Sarah from the body of a Mudhead.

Sarah gazed wildly, while deep shudderings possessed

31

her body. It was minutes before she could take in the meaning of what the *kachinas* were saying. They were explaining that long years ago the Supernaturals themselves had come often to the Hopi villages, to give the strength, the solace, the joy of their presence. They had ceased to do so, displeased by the impiety they found. Now, for centuries, the villagers had taken their places, dressing as they dressed, singing their songs and dancing their dances. This they did to please the Supernaturals and to benefit the tribe. Sarah felt as if the earth had melted under her feet.

Next day she could only enjoy a little the magical bean sprouts which the *kachinas* distributed. She could only enjoy a little the *kachina* doll they gave her, holding it in lax hands. All the time it had been only the men of the village.

That night she turned and tossed restlessly on her sheepskin, and in the morning she was silent and without spirit.

"I go to the house of the *Kik-Mongwi*," her father said, eyeing her thoughtfully. "You shall come with me, little one."

John, the *Kik-Mongwi*, also looked at Sarah thoughtfully, but with the glint of humor that the older man seemed always to have for the little girls. He leaned forward on his low stool and talked to her indulgently. This thing of the *kachinas*, he said, was more than it looked on the outside. Those whom Sarah saw were impersonated by men, true. But while they were going through the ceremonies, the very spirit of the Supernaturals was breathed into them, so that for a while they were the *kachinas*. And so the people came close to touching the fringes of the kilts of the gods. And this was good not only for the Hopis but for the whole of the world, unwilling though it was to receive from the despised handful. Thus, holding together, the chief said, and walking the right Hopi path, the tribe might survive the pitfalls.

Sarah groped solemnly for the meaning.

"Many cannot understand," John went on. "They see only the outer shell of things. So it is that the children who have learned something of the mysteries must not reveal them to the younger children. Else they will be beaten, not with whips of yucca, which wound, but with whips of cactus, which may kill."

Father's face, always sad since his disaster, was turned contemplatively on his child. "Perhaps she understands. Perhaps not."

4

THE NEXT FEW YEARS were not so clear in Sarah's mind. Father continued to try, desperately, to be Tuvenga. He laughed and joked. He teased Mother with the double-talk that Sarah by that time half understood. He had a peg leg, and joked about it with a ferocious humor. It was not bad for stumping around the stone streets of the village, but elsewhere it sank into the sand and impeded him. He would someday get a fine leg with hinges like his own, he told Mother, and then she should see if he couldn't run away from her as fast as ever, and catch as many secret wives.

Once Sarah had a swift realization of her father's actual emotions, and the incident was stamped on her memory. She had gone with her mother to a neighbor's to borrow a sheep's brain for greasing the *piki* griddle and had run home ahead, crossing on soft feet the balconylike roof of the house below theirs. Her father did not hear her, and she found him practicing the steps of a *kachina* dance, his face black with rage and sorrow as his tapping peg refused to follow the intricate measures.

Sarah closed the door inch by inch, stole to the ladder, crept down it. When her mother toiled up its steep length, Sarah was close behind her, laughing with a shrillness that made her mother glance at her in surprise. When the two came in, Father sat on his stool, the peg leg straight out before him, intently drawing together a tear in the knee of his jeans.

Almost as soon as Father had got the peg, Mother had begun to save for the store leg with hinges. She put coins, one by one, into a baking powder can which she kept in the hole in the floor where the hard goods, the silver and turquoise jewelry, were hidden. But whenever she accumulated a dollar, Father's overalls or Sarah's shoes would have reached the point where their patches would no longer hold them together.

Mother did not make many extra dollars with her pottery now. She was always so tired. She was thankful that she had no extra fat to lug around, she told Father: it was hard enough to carry her bones. The field nurse urged her to go to the Sanatorium, but Mother said she would stay in her own home, where she belonged. It did not make any real difference where she was, she told Father, since it was probably the work of the same witch who had tried to kill him. Father brought a Hopi doctor to see her, and he agreed with Mother, after he had found a witch arrow in her chest and pulled it out with prayer and chanting. He said that Mother would get well, now that the arrow was gone, unless the witch was too strong and determined. Father said that if she got well she should be the doctor's ceremonial daughter the rest of her life, and serve him and cook good food for him.

For a while Mother seemed better. Her eyes were very bright, and her thin cheeks red, and she stepped quicker and looked happier . . . But in the end the witch proved too strong.

It was this same year that Sarah was chosen for the flute dance. She would never forget the thrill and exaltation of that ceremonial. The old men dressed the girls for their parts, with especial attention to Sarah, the most important figure. Carefully they combed and adorned her hair, regretting audibly that the *Bohannas* at the day school had cut its shining strands so short that they could not arrange it properly. Though so small, they said that Sarah was good to see in the angular lines of the embroidered garments. And the dance, though at the time she saw it only in a floating blue, afterward cleared, in her memory, into a stately rhythm of color and motion.

Some of the school people witnessed the ceremonial, and after that Sarah was a person of consequence in their eyes. They whispered about her, looking significantly from her to the other girls, those who had not been eligible. The principal and his wife, Mr. and Mrs. Loring, visited Sarah's house and praised Mother for her fine little daughter. Mother sat with head inclined over her work, except when she coughed, and answered in monosyllables, pretending that she did not know what they meant.

But Sarah knew that Sequapa was proud of her. She had always kept her in sight, and given her no chance to loiter on her way to and from school or the spring, even in daylight. And she had explained to her that boys were made as they were made, so that the best of them could not be trusted.

Doubtless Sarah's small size, her slow maturing, had safeguarded her, too. At eleven she might easily have passed for eight, with wide, startled eyes in a small face that showed no sign of ripening.

5

Sᴀʀᴀʜ ʜᴀᴅ ꜰᴏᴜɴᴅ Mrs. Loring better than most whites. The principal's wife never tried to kiss her; and when the little girl came and helped around the house after school, Mrs. Loring left her alone most of the time, which was what most white people seemed unable to do.

Sarah washed dishes according to directions, privately considering all the hot water and soapsuds barbarous. She ran the vacuum cleaner, liking to watch it suck up the dust and scold when it must swallow a hairpin. Everything she did she did silently, slipping through the house like a shadow, listening with all her ears to what was said and observing what was done, but giving no sign that she listened or looked.

It was natural that Mr. and Mrs. Loring should take the child into their home when the need came. During Sarah's twelfth year both her father and her mother died. The remainder of the school term Sarah went on helping Mrs. Loring with the housework, moving more silently than ever, a frightened little ghost of herself. That summer Mr. Loring left the Indian Service, and he and Mrs. Loring returned to the Kansas town where they had been brought up. They took Sarah with them.

She had little to say about going or staying. She was still so small and shy that no one could believe her anything but a child, without a mind of her own. Mr. Loring, bluff and kind, put the matter to the agent, the same one, small, white-

37

haired, blue-eyed, who had been there longer than Sarah could remember. The agent took it up with the Indian Council and the Council with the *Kik-Mongwi* and with Uncle Abraham and Aunt Kawasie, Sarah's nearest relations, both of whom asked to raise Sarah.

Both were poorly situated to add another child to their households. Uncle Abraham's eldest son had brought home from school a Navajo wife and a baby, and the second baby was due any day, filling the box of a house to overflowing. Aunt Kawasie's next-youngest had brought from school not a wife but the shrinking sickness, which the Hopi were learning to call TB. The child was a long time dying, there on a pallet where the life of the household clattered around him, keeping him from the lonesomeness he had known at the Sanatorium.

Mr. Loring agreed soberly that it would have been better for Sarah to stay with her own people if that had been practicable. As it was, the Lorings had room enough for the little girl, and could give her plenty to eat and wear. Yes, the Lorings had more money than they knew what to do with. Some said that his salary as superintendent of schools in the Kansas town would be thousands of dollars, though that was hard to believe.

Over against the splendid bulk of those dollars, Kawasie's and Abraham's cash incomes became still more meager. Abraham had a few dollars a month as interpreter. Kawasie took in maybe fifty a year by the sale of her pottery to tourists, and Uncle Mattima about as much for odd carpentering jobs. The women traded more pottery for groceries at the trading post than they sold for cash; and both families grew most of their food on their little farms, so that they did not starve or go naked. But the Loring opulence was a strong argument.

Even so, the Council might have refused them if they had been like most *Bohannas*. And if not the Council, which had some bumptious young men no more mellow than green apples, then the *Kik-Mongwi*, the same old John of her earlier childhood.

Sarah could see him clearly as he talked to her about the matter, the wide, thin line of his lips bracketed in deep lines of kindly patience, his eyes regarding her intently under wrinkled lids. Had Sarah any objection to going with the Lorings? he asked her gently. The shivering small mouse of a girl could only swallow convulsively and shape her lips to their silent "No."

"They are good people, even if they are whites," John said. "And they do not look at Hopis as if we were pictures in a movie. So, since you have no objection, we will let them take you as their child."

The move to the small Kansas town was like a move to a new world, but the Lorings had softened its strangeness as far as they could. Their home became home to Sarah, a place where she gathered courage for the necessary alien encounters in school, in Sunday school, in the neighborhood, where there was no relief from *Bohanna* faces and *Bohanna* speech.

After two scant years, the period of adjustment ended as abruptly as it had begun. When Sarah was nearly fourteen, the Loring car skidded on a patch of icy road and husband and wife died together.

Mrs. Loring's sister, Mrs. Ramsay, took Sarah into her home at once. Sarah heard her reply to a neighbor, condoling with her for the rude break in their quiet middle-aged home. "I always say to Mr. Ramsay, 'What are we here for if not to lend a helping hand where it is needed?'"

When Sarah first came to the Kansas town, she thought the sisters as alike in appearance as twins. They were of average *Bohanna* height, and therefore tall in the eyes of a Hopi. They had average coloring, between blond and brunette, and average rather nondescript features.

Sarah's two years in Kansas had shown her that *Bohannas* did not all resemble each other as she had thought. Those years had also deepened a difference in the sisters themselves. Now Sarah could see no likeness between them.

There had been a glow about Aunt Lib, an upward curve to the lines that deepened in a weathered face. Sarah, immature at fourteen, wondered at God, that he should have let her and the ruddy, chuckling Uncle Hal die, and left Aunt Carrie and Uncle Guy.

Uncle Guy was kind enough, but without definite form or color, as if strong, thick blotting paper were kept firmly applied to any fresh ink that appeared on his surface. When sometimes Sarah saw him away from home he was different, with hat cocked and shoulders slightly swaggering.

Aunt Carrie did her best to fit Sarah into her dustless, polished house. Both her sons had been gone long enough so that any scars they had left had been healed with wax and enamel and new drapes. It looked as if it had always been an immaculately ordered childless house.

Aunt Carrie had gone to work on the Indian child as energetically, as conscientiously, as on a spring housecleaning. Sarah was not quite so easily handled as an upholstered chair. Sometimes Aunt Carrie was goaded to remonstrate. "I'm trying quite as hard as your Aunt Lib to help you make something of yourself. Only we have different ways of going at it. If my sister had ever had children of her own, I'm sure she — But I know you want to do well and be a credit to her. It's lucky you're so small for your age. I don't suppose anybody realizes that you're so far behind your grade. Most of the children in your room are so overgrown."

Before her marriage Aunt Carrie had been a teacher and an efficient one. She spared neither time nor effort to bring her ward up to her own age group. Unfailingly she devoted to the task an hour a day after school, two hours on Saturday, and as much straight through the hot, heavy months of summer vacation. Sarah used often to regard her curiously, on those July and August days, wondering whether it was only the heat that made Aunt Carrie's face redden and her lips tighten when her pupil was inarticulate.

"But when I think how she was when we first took her," Sarah overheard her complacently telling Uncle Guy. "She was just a little bit of nothing, really —"

"The kid's still like a scared mouse," Uncle Guy protested, "or a shadow. Suppose we'll ever get behind those big black eyes of hers?"

"Well, she'll always be an Indian," his wife conceded, talking in jerky time to the click of her knitting needles. "We can't do anything about that. But here she is, going to graduate from high school at nineteen, for all her slow start. And her grades not too bad. And she looks like the other girls."

Uncle Guy said nothing.

"Nobody could question Lib's kindness," Aunt Carrie said querulously. "But she doesn't seem to have seen Sarah's possibilities. Of course it was simpler to let the girl go her own gait. But there's a time when kindness isn't kind."

Sarah could hear the shift of Uncle Guy's feet.

Sarah did look reasonably like the other girls. Aunt Carrie helped make her clothes that were not only respectable but pretty. She chose good materials, and tried to mask Sarah's skimpy contours by ample cut. Occasionally she invited some of Sarah's classmates, daughters of lifetime acquaintances of hers, to the house for dinner, and she made Sarah accept the return invitations ("My dear Sarah. Cer-

41

tainly you will go. What possible excuse could you have? And you will be much happier if you go about like other young girls, believe me").

Sometimes it seemed to Sarah that she herself had gone underground, shut in deep channels from which she could not emerge. Occasionally she seemed to free herself, talking for a while as loquaciously as the other girls. But oftener she lapsed into stillnesses where no one seemed able to get at her. At such times she would laugh irritatingly, or gaze at nothing with a little smile, so that no one should guess that she couldn't come out. Again, she would look at Aunt Carrie with a sudden cool directness, not pitying her when she flushed and lost track of her crisp sentences.

Sarah could not tell why life had been so completely different during her two years with the Lorings. She had known them when they were a part of her mesa, to be sure. And they had brought to their comfortable, shabby Kansas home a feeling for the desert, as well as Navajo rugs and Hopi pots and baskets for walls and bookcase tops.

Here Sarah was smothered by the trees. They were a different creation from the trees in Hopiland. There a single cottonwood, which had reached through the sand to deep waters, was a world, with flycatchers scolding pleasantly, and a squirrel or two, and each polished leaf precious, helping to make a delicious shade in a thirsty land. The Ramsay trees crowded so close that the grass would hardly grow beneath them. Sarah was often wakened in the night by their pressure, and lay with heart pounding in sick panic. When she could bear no more she would creep from her bed and go to kneel at the open window, staring out. She could not stare far, because of those trees closing around her and hiding the sky. Beyond them she could feel the hidden houses, jailers standing between her and freedom. And the mockingly incessant fiddling of insects, interminable waves of sound that beat on her brain and terrified her by their unshakable complacency.

Sarah would close her eyes and try to imagine herself stepping across the stones, through the sand, in the desert wind with the desert sky immense and free above her and around her. Shut in like this, she could not capture the feeling.

Daytime was not so bad, because she could keep busy. She had learned to follow the routine of housework, and cleaned almost as scrupulously as Aunt Carrie did, and ironed the clothes to almost the same crisp perfection.

Now and then she would break out of her shell disconcertingly. One day — only a few months ago it was — the crash came when she was sitting at the dining table with its glossy damask. She had answered, "No thank you," when Uncle Guy offered her more of the mashed potatoes.

"Oh, just a little more," he urged, smiling at her benevolently across a creamy spoonful.

Sarah said nothing.

"Won't you have a little more, Sarah?" Aunt Carrie put in. "Starches, you know. You need a few more pounds. Just another spoonful?"

Sarah had gritted her teeth until she felt the cords stiffen in her throat, and her eyes had blazed at Aunt Carrie. "No. No. No," she had said hoarsely. "Why do white people have to ask the same questions over and over and over? Isn't one answering enough?"

They had stared at her in open-mouthed astonishment, and then Aunt Carrie's eyes had sharpened. "She's all on edge because I have discouraged this — this friendship with the Torrey boy," Aunt Carrie's eyes seemed to say.

The Torrey boy.

He was the first boy to pay any attention to Sarah. Aunt Carrie had had nothing to say against him; but he was the prized only son of the town's richest banker and the president of the Federated Women's Clubs of Finch.

Sarah had come to the beginning of last summer without dating at all. She knew what the boys said about her: "You can't get to first base with that Sarah. She's a queer one, all right."

A few times she had gone with the other girls to the town's one stuffy movie theater, or to the corner drugstore. Boys always happened to be lounging in the drugstore or in the back seats of the theater, where they stretched long, impeding legs out into the aisles, and snickered or guffawed at the tender scenes in the picture. At the drugstore they usually drifted over toward the girls. Kirk Torrey was one who didn't go steady with anyone, and once he brought his soda over from the fountain and sat at the round table where Sarah and Helen and Irene were already half through. The other two girls tossed back flip answers to his wisecracks, while Sarah sucked steadily at her straw, watching the lusciousness diminish.

"Sarah thinks we're silly nuts," Irene interrupted herself, giggling, and pouted her babyish lips provocatively at Kirk.

"Now, Sarah, come, come!" Kirk Torrey admonished her, with a wink for the other girls and a cock of the head at Sarah, as if she were of another breed than they. "Be your age, Pocahontas. Hi, give us a glance!"

Obligingly Sarah lifted her eyes, her lips still busy with the straw. Kirk was regarding her with indifferent amusement, and Sarah returned the look with one of unsmiling scrutiny. She had hardly thought about him in the nearly eight years she had known him, while he had been growing from a soft little boy into a large, presentable youth. He had thick lashes and a cleft in his chin and a fine head of golden brown hair, crisply curling.

Sarah thought, He thinks he's so smart, with his collar rolled open that way, like some poet or other. And the girls act so silly about him. She lowered her eyes and gave her attention to the soda.

Nothing came of that first encounter, but a little later something did happen. That was when the cast had been chosen for the senior play, and rehearsals began. If the English teacher who was also the dramatics coach had chosen something like *Charley's Aunt* again, or *Seventeen*, Sarah's life might have gone on uninterrupted in its old underground channels. Instead, the teacher decided on a play that featured an Indian maid and her buckskin-clad lover. In its beginnings Finch had been the scene of Indian battles which the years had embellished with romantic legend.

"And we can have something unique. We can have an honest-to-goodness Indian for our heroine," the drama teacher announced with bright enthusiasm to the senior class.

Sarah had studied her small clenched hands, shaking her head. She did not give in until Aunt Carrie stared coldly down her tight cheeks at her and said certainly Sarah would take the part. Wasn't this the first time she had been picked out for anything?

During the first tryout of parts the drama teacher's bright, triumphant smile lost some of its shine. "Sarah's so wooden," she muttered to the principal, who stood with a foot up on a seat, watching and listening. "She says her lines as if she were repeating the alphabet."

"It's something to have her look the part," he encouraged doubtfully. "Besides, she hasn't many lines."

In the play Sarah was a Plains Indian, of course, and someone with an Indian collection had lent the drama teacher a buckskin dress and moccasins. Indian jewelry was popular, and Sarah's schoolmates had an abundance of silver and turquoise to load her neck, wrists, fingers. Sarah used her own beaded campfire headband around her crow-black hair, the entirely inaccurate but inevitable quills stuck in it. When she was fully panoplied, the teachers and the girls burst into a chatter of amazed admiration, and the boys stared as at an astonishing stranger. Kirk Torrey shifted from foot to foot and swallowed visibly.

Kirk Torrey had been cast as the Indian lover.

Sarah knew that she was changed, but not that she was changed so startlingly. She had spent an hour in dressing and making up before her mirror. Everything about her that had been a little queer had in this barbaric garb become exotic. In ordinary dress she looked scrawny, and the shortness of her neck was noticeable, even though she was so slim. In the supple straight-cut buckskin she was all slender grace.

Her face had gained as much charm as her body. The rouge made her lips softer and fuller, gave her sallowness a rich bloom, called attention to her shadowy Oriental eyes. Her eyebrows were irregular and indeterminate, no better than most Indian eyebrows. The teacher had taught her how to pencil them to a winglike contour.

"Not only that," the drama teacher said, as if she had been giving words to her own catalog of Sarah's alterations, "not only that, but she's saying her lines with a spark of life." She spoke in a surprised aside to the principal.

"Trust a woman to know when she's looking like a million," he had answered.

Self-assurance was only a minor factor in Sarah's new manner. From the moment when Kirk first saw her in her costume, his expression altered as sharply as her own. Puzzled inquiry was mingled with actual shock. His lines came alive before Sarah's did, and when, in the action of the play, he decorously seized her hands, his large ones trembled.

"The costumes have something to do with their — their *élan*," the drama teacher commented. "It gets them into the spirit of it, to see their classmates changed into strange personalities. I'm thinking we'll have to have dress rehearsals right through, to keep them up to this level."

Sarah dropped her eyes, her heart pounding at the way Kirk was looking at her. No one had ever had that particular look for Sarah, and in the past six years few had had any look at all. She might as well not have been there. Eyes slid around her, passed through her. Occasionally Uncle Guy's glance rested on her in pitying uncomprehension. Often Aunt Carrie scrutinized her as she scrutinized a layer cake that hadn't risen. Or a teacher studied her with irritated wonder. Sarah did not say all this to herself, but she did think, It's been so long since anybody really liked me. And this was Kirk Torrey, listed in the high school yearbook as Finch High's Most Eligible Bachelor.

At the end of that rehearsal, Kirk walked out onto the street with Helen, Irene and Sarah. He was completely silent as they passed the lighted drugstore, passed a staring group of boys and girls. Helen, glancing sidewise at him, now and then spoke to him with indulgent amusement. Irene's chatter grew shrill. They stopped under a streetlight where Sarah's course diverged from that of the other three. Helen said, "Better run fast, little Injun, so nothing can catch you." Kirk said, "She doesn't need to run. I'm going her way."

Sarah said nothing.

Kirk cupped Sarah's elbow in his warm palm and helped

her down from the curb, tossing his other hand carelessly in the direction of the two girls. Sarah hurried along, head tucked down, slowing her step reluctantly when Kirk's hand tightened on her elbow and his stride slowed to a saunter.

"Gosh," he complained, "it's a swell night, and early. What's the rush?" His voice softened. "When did you get so — so darned pretty, Poky?"

Sarah could not think of anything to say. She wished he would take away his hand. It burned her skin, bared by the short sleeve of the buckskin dress. She felt as if there were people looking out of all the windows and shaking their heads or clucking. She knew there were not, and that they could not have seen the boy and girl if they had been there. Between the small circles of light at the corners the darkness was hardly pierced by the starlight.

"Cold, Poky? You're shivering."

Sarah shook her head. "I'm plenty warm," she disclaimed through stiff lips.

She was angry with herself for shivering. Her thoughts had slid across the years to the mesa. She could hear the old women suck their teeth wisely, see them droop their lids as they watched a woman let a man overtake her, lounge along beside her.

At the same time, there was something about having Kirk's hand cupped under her elbow that mingled pleasure with the discomfort.

Reaching home, Sarah stopped at the front walk, but Kirk marched her on, propelling her to the porch, up the steps.

"Good night," Sarah said dismissingly.

Kirk did not go. He backed away and sat on the railing, dropping his head back against the pillar. "Oh, sit down, Poky, please," he urged.

Unwillingly, Sarah went and stood at the porch railing, well away from Kirk. A big moon was slowly rising at the end of the road. Sarah had never before seen it like this, filmy soft and pink. But she could hear the regular squeak of a rocker on the next porch; could hear from the Ramsay living room a declamatory radio voice cut off in the midst and followed by a listening silence. She was almost glad when a dim figure appeared behind the screen door and Aunt Carrie's surprised voice said, "Oh — is that you, Sarah?"

Sarah moved convulsively toward the voice. Kirk straightened his legs and was standing. "Good evening, Mrs. Ramsay," he said, his voice expectant.

The expectation was not realized. Sarah did not ask him in. "Thank you for bringing me home. Good night," she murmured, and fled past him and Mrs. Ramsay into the safety of the lighted hall.

Mrs. Ramsay stood peering out. "Yes, thank you for looking after our little girl. Good night."

Kirk doubtless took his departure then, Mrs. Ramsay watching him out of sight. By the time she came slowly into the living room, Uncle Guy had turned on the radio again, and Sarah had taken out the tea towels she was embroidering and pretending to listen absorbedly to the program, a favorite with both Uncle Guy and her.

Aunt Carrie sat rocking until it ended on the announcer's indulgent laugh. Then she asked, "Wasn't that Mrs. Torrey's son, Sarah?"

"Yes," Sarah replied, without looking up from her pink and lavender daisies.

The rocking stopped. "But, Sarah," Aunt Carrie's tone was anxious, "have you been seeing him often?"

The blood surged to Sarah's forehead. Mingled with the

anxiety was another feeling, faintly reminiscent of the old Hopi women. Stubbornly the girl misinterpreted the question. "He is in my same class, but we did not see each other much because we never have the same studies. Only now we are in the class play, so I see him when we practice."

Aunt Carrie's rocker moved again, unevenly.

That was Friday. Saturday and Sunday were long, featureless days. The next Monday afternoon before rehearsal Sarah watched Kirk through her lashes as he talked to Helen and Irene and other girls. He was free in his manner with all girls, she thought, but he did not look at them as he looked at Sarah.

The sunlight brought queer gleams of color from his hair, red gleams and gold and copper.

There were five weeks of rehearsal. The drama teacher was relentless in her demands. This production promised to be something more than the usual feeble student affair, she said triumphantly. It was worth all the labor they were giving it.

To Sarah the five weeks passed like a dream. The other players were dream figures. They were cues for Sarah and Kirk, nothing more. They giggled and cavorted so that now and then she could spare a glance of wonder for their childishness. Sarah herself had grown up overnight. The days passed mistily, each one sharpening to reality only during the two hours of rehearsal. Those two hours bulked larger, more significant, than any days had done before. All the other actors seemed only a part of the audience, and sometimes their eyes were uneasy.

Once Irene said, with studied sweetness, "Sarah, I do hope you won't make the mistake of taking Kirk seriously. I don't know how many girls he's made a play for and then dropped." She reddened and flung away when Sarah gave her an uncomprehending smile.

Even on the night when the play was presented, it remained to Sarah only and Kirk moving again through an enchanted hour, and the other players, and the audience, were bodiless. Even the photographer from the *Finch Weekly News,* crouching grotesquely for a candid shot, was bodiless, and his repeated flashbulbs heat lightning amid the blossoms.

Next morning Aunt Carrie frowned at the resultant picture, when Uncle Guy chucklingly handed the paper across the breakfast table. Not all Sarah's gorgeousness had been lost in the black and white of the inky reproduction.

"Never supposed we'd have an actress in the family," Uncle Guy joked, smiling at Sarah. "Watch out, or the movies will be after you, young one. You looked neat."

Aunt Carrie said, "Don't go putting ideas into Sarah's head, Mr. Ramsay." She added, "Kirk Torrey was — effective, wasn't he?"

"When did the boy get so good looking?" Uncle Guy went on. "And he can act! Looked at Sarah as if he could eat her up."

"Now, Guy!" Aunt Carrie said stiffly, and decisively folded the paper with the picture out of sight.

She helped Sarah with the dishes that morning, and talked too pleasantly of many matters. She was working up to something. What would Sarah think about going to the college in the next town?

Sarah preserved a wary silence.

It was small, yes, and some of its equipment old-fashioned. That was only because it was poor, belonging to one of the Dutch and German sects that settled hereabouts in pioneer days. It was good and it was sound, Aunt Carrie continued with deadly cheer, and several members of Sarah's class would be going there. Helen and Irene were already registered, though goodness knows their parents could have sent them East if they chose.

Still Sarah said nothing.

"Wouldn't you like to go to Hermon?" Aunt Carrie put the direct question, her voice unusually soft and even.

Sarah shook her head.

Aunt Carrie stopped in her work with tea towel poised. She had been drying an old willowware platter with the exaggerated care and thoroughness which Sarah always recognized as directed at her. Aunt Carrie's lips tightened and loosened two or three times before she spoke, her tone losing its factitious sweetness. "And what have you against Hermon, pray tell?"

"I don't want to go to school any longer."

"But, Sarah. For years we've been talking about what college you would attend when the time came."

Sarah answered absently, "I am graduating from high school. That is enough schooling."

Aunt Carrie put the platter in place, breathing audibly. Then she said, "Sarah!"

Sarah went on washing dishes.

"Sarah!"

"Yes, ma'am."

"Goodness, how formal. Why don't you say, Yes, Aunt Carrie, as usual?" Aunt Carrie's tone attempted playful lightness.

"Yes, Aunt Carrie."

Aunt Carrie's words hurried, as if to get safely through a swamp. "Boys today are not what they were when I was a

52

girl, Sarah. When I was a girl, they would no more have dared — But in this generation they've changed. So everyone tells me. I hate to say this, Sarah. And don't think for a minute that I don't trust you. Only you might not understand — Most girls, well, a boy like Kirk Torrey would drop her like a hot cake as soon as —" She tightened her lips and breathed noisily again.

Sarah went on washing.

"Of course there isn't any kind of understanding between you and Kirk Torrey?"

Sarah worked with concentration on a knife which she was scouring, rubbing it with a cork dipped in powder.

Mrs. Ramsay's foot tapped the floor. "Is there, Sarah? Is there any kind of understanding?"

As they used to when she was a small girl, Sarah's lips rounded into a silent No, but still she did not look up.

Aunt Carrie's breath hissed through her teeth in an exasperated sigh. "I am exceedingly glad to hear that, Sarah. You have never been in the habit of storying to me. And you surely see that I should have had to discourage any such — as your guardian, Sarah." With apparent effort she lowered her voice, which had risen against Sarah's silence. "For your own sake, Sarah. Kirk Torrey will marry a girl in his own — in his own circle —"

Sarah did look up then.

"As for Hermon," Aunt Carrie's voice was regaining its usual crispness and force, "when you think it over, of course you will agree with me about Hermon." She clipped decisively away.

Methodically Sarah sudsed the tea towels and dishcloth and hung them in the sun. Her spirit had sprung upright from the pressure, and it was shaking loose habits of

53

unquestioning obedience. *If she thinks that way about me — and him — wouldn't she be fit to be tied if he really did propose?*

She paused with a tea towel ready to pin on the line. *Maybe it's for my sake, and maybe it isn't.* "What do I owe the likes of her?" Sarah suddenly murmured aloud to the tea towel. "I've earned my keep, I guess." With the words a wild sense of freedom possessed her.

Next day she penciled her eyebrows as carefully as she had for the play, rouged as carefully. That afternoon Kirk waited to walk home with her. They swung along together, laughing and talking in snatches, until she set a period to their fitful sentences by stopping on the corner a block from home.

"What's the big idea?" he asked, coming up short.

Sarah stood a moment silent, contemplating the sky, already hot and dry with early summer. "Aunt Carrie —" she began. "Well, she doesn't approve."

Kirk stared, his mouth dropping with astonishment. "Old lady doesn't approve? Of me?" Naïvely he thrust a finger toward his chest.

"She thinks you are bad medicine," Sarah said demurely.

"But —" he stammered, his shock touched with gratification, like a little boy in Wild West costume being tapped by a policeman's forefinger.

"Quite a reputation you're getting," Sarah murmured, noticing that she was speaking almost as other girls did.

"Well, what's the old lady going to do? Shut you up in a convent?" Kirk blustered.

"Send me to Hermon."

"Hermon! Good gosh! And I'm going to K.U. She can't do this to me."

54

"Well, goodbye," Sarah murmured, moving decisively away.

She did not turn to look, but she knew that he did not at once move from the corner. Before she was out of range, he shouted defiantly, "Poky, listen! I'm not licked yet! You're driving me goofy, Poky," he muttered. "Do you realize how little I see you? Realize how little I've ever seen you, except during rehearsal? If you could even meet me tomorrow night — we could figure something, maybe —"

Sarah's mouth formed it's almost inaudible "No," but Sarah's eyes lifted to him as she denied him, and she flushed at the look he bent on that soft-speaking mouth. "Someone would tell Aunt Carrie."

"Couldn't you be going to Helen's? Irene's? I'd be waiting halfway up the next block. Sarah, we could anyway walk and talk — plan —"

She was long silent. "Helen's," she whispered at last. "Irene doesn't like me. It would have to be when I came home from Helen's. Daylight saving time — it gets dark so late."

"Gosh," Kirk mumbled, his chest rising and falling with a deep breath, "gosh, Poky."

Sarah, with the slightest shrug of the shoulders, went on stepping softly down the street. Her mind could see him there behind her, staring and at length turning and striding away, the sun shining on his head.

For Sarah the next day stretched endlessly long, and momentous, as if it were the first reality she had ever known. At Helen's house that night she was by turns talkative and silent, so that the girls stared at her, puzzled and resentful.

She was gauging the oncoming of the dark, probing its thickness while her heartbeats stifled her. Now. Now.

She was hurrying down the dim street, wondering what she had said in getting away, wondering whether it had made sense. The evening was as soft as fingers stroking a kitten's fur. All up and down the dark streets insects fiddled in the arching maples and elms, fiddled in long, languorous waves of sound that died out to a sibilant sigh only to begin again. Sarah's small feet sank into the heat-softened asphalt as she crossed one street, two. Her eyes pushed into the shadows. As she passed a deep-shadowed maple she found herself no longer alone. A warm hand possessed hers and the two were walking slowly through the shadows, laughing softly, jerkily, as they tried to match their steps.

"Littlest!" Kirk said huskily, and pretended to nibble at the smooth fingers he had carried to his lips.

"Such a funny way!" she whispered, her laughter catching in her throat.

"How is it with Indian boys?" he demanded jealously.

"How should I know? I was twelve years old when I came away from there. And my mother took very good care of me." She added soberly, "I am pretty sure they are not so polite."

Even at twelve she had caught glimpses of what went on in the shadows on the mesa. She had seen quick skirmishes, with small finesse. She had partly understood her mother's warnings. All she had known of love made her value Kirk's gentleness the more. She could have sauntered on forever at his side, hands clasped in that deep intimacy, palms kissing.

But presently she made him stop under a streetlight, after a swift survey to make sure no one was near, and turn his watch so that she could see it.

"But it's only ten," Kirk protested.

"Aunt Carrie — soon she would telephone to Helen's house. Hurry, Kirk, hurry."

Reaching the house, she smoothed down her breath and her hair before she went in. Aunt Carrie and Aunt Guy turned from the radio, Aunt Carrie's eyes sharp above her crocheted tablecloth, Uncle Guy blinking sleepily.

"I don't like your being alone on the streets so late, Sarah," Aunt Carrie complained. "You were alone?" The question pounced at Sarah.

Something in the girl purred silkily. Aunt Carrie could question, could forbid forever and what good would it do? Poor Aunt Carrie. Had she ever known anything so sweet as that walk in the darkness?

"No," Sarah said clearly, "Helen's little brother asked to take me home."

"Why didn't you invite him in?" Aunt Carrie reproved.

Sarah only smiled vaguely and went on up the stairs.

That was the first of a procession of tranced evenings. Evenings beyond price, when Sarah was able to escape from the house, dead evenings, when no escape could be contrived and the minutes clumped past on lame feet. Then the stars burned in vain, and the crickets strummed in vain, and the fragrance of roses went to waste as Sarah sat working lavender and pink daisies with stiff, automatic fingers.

It was a drought summer, and sickeningly hot, so that in Kansas people left their living quarters and moved down into their basements, setting fans whirring there, and hanging before the half windows sheets with their ends dipping into tubs of ice. Sarah did not notice the heat. She felt well. Small and stunted by early malnutrition, she had been late in maturing, but now womanhood had come full tide, deep and strong.

Life with Aunt Carrie and Uncle Guy continued to dwindle in importance as Kirk filled Sarah's world. When the clasp of hands was followed by the close pressure of lips, in kisses that disturbed the hardness of Sarah's body, she felt at last essential and almost whole. Then the years behind her stretched like a Limbo where Sarah was a leaf forever blown by the wind. Now she was rooted, and life came alive.

This flowering was perfected by the seemliness of this love affair. Kirk did not treat her lightly, like a waif from a lesser civilization; his attitude was as it would have been to Helen, she thought exultantly. Once when he held her too close, so she felt dissolved in his ardor, she struggled weakly away and his arms dropped from about her. "Sarah," he stammered, "I'm sorry. Sarah, you will forgive me?"

Aunt Carrie had often warned her about the relationship of men and women, tasting her words with shocked eyes and prurient tongue. She explained that it was mortal sin when indulged outside marriage, and even when so sanctified a piece of inexplicable bad taste on the part of God, and to be suffered stoically by the wife. Sarah had not taken much stock in Aunt Carrie's ideas, but the years in the small town, with its insistence on a straitlaced virtue, had had their effect on her Indian mores.

And even on the mesas, Sarah had established a bent toward chastity. Her father and mother had cherished virginity as a rare and beautiful crown. Now it was strengthened by a knowledge that her situation was directly opposite to what it would have been on the mesas. Here among the *Bohannas* her maidenhood was her strongest hope of becoming Kirk's wife, in satin and orange blossoms.

The longed-for declaration came after they had met no more than a dozen times in the tender June dusk, hardly even glimpsing one another in common daylight.

They were walking slowly along the outskirts of town, as they usually did.

Tonight Kirk lost patience. "Poky," he groaned, peering at her in the strange light and shadow of a carbon streetlamp, "now that school is out I don't even see you. This once let's walk through the park —"

Sarah's laugh was a shaken murmur. "Even if we sat on one of the benches that has a light right over it, we wouldn't see each other any plainer than right here."

The park was too remote, she felt with a rush of fear and longing, its shadows too deep.

Kirk had no laughter. "I want to kiss you," he begged. "Just kiss you, Poky, for an hour without stopping. You're so — so sweet and little. Please, Poky."

Sarah drew a quick, shivering breath, and he bent his head sharply toward her.

"You're afraid!" he challenged her, mastery in his voice. Then it softened. "I won't let anything hurt you, princess. Not even me. I promise you."

They did go to the park. They sat side by side on one of the wire seats Sarah had mentioned, with a lamp relentlessly chaperoning them. They sat close, with Kirk's arm across Sarah's shoulders, so that they could kiss when there was absolutely no one near.

After one such embrace, Kirk sat with head bowed, gripping Sarah's hand in his. When he spoke, his voice was ragged and almost inaudible, yet Sarah heard, with a triumphant leap of the pulses, "Sarah, we have to be married. We have to."

Her answer waited till she could quiet the flutter in her throat. "Kirk — your mother. Your father. And you aren't old enough."

Kirk laughed excitedly. "We'd go to K.C. and be married by a justice of the peace. Think I couldn't swear to being two years older than I am?" He was leaning close, looking into her eyes in the dimness.

"I—don't like running away," she said faintly. "I — don't like lies, either." Her pride rose in feeble rebellion. "I don't like your parents being ashamed of me. I'd rather have a — a church wedding."

She was feeling the white satin and the floating veil. She was hearing the *Lohengrin* march. Most clearly of all she was seeing Helen's and Irene's faces, with every trace of patronage wiped off for once.

Recent footsteps had died away. Kirk was catching her close, crushing her against him so that her body was bruised and her breath stopped. Her joy swelled above the pain and made it desirable. "Poky — oh, Poky!" he was whispering hoarsely. "We'd have to wait so long — so long, to bring them round. Say you'll come to K.C. next week — say it! We could be married in church later, after I'd coaxed the folks around. Don't you see, darling? No one would need to know that we were already married."

Sarah was thinking as well as she could, drunken with his nearness, his urgency. His plan would be good, very good. They would belong to each other, and still the triumph and the glory need not be lost. She would not admit even to herself that she would have him, then, against all comers; would not admit any fear of his strength and steadiness.

"Darling, you will?"

Darling. Darling. Like the glint in his hair; like the blue of his eyes; these endearing terms were new and wonderful.

"You will?" he said roughly, holding her away to look at her.

"Yes, yes, I will," Sarah stammered, struggling free and reaching up to smooth her hair with shaking hands. "Kirk! Someone's coming!"

He sat back with a sigh that mingled intolerable aggrava-
tion and relief. "Oh, think when we won't have to listen for
footsteps — think —"

"But now we've got to go," Sarah said in a small voice
which she tried to keep practical. She was on her feet, and
he rose, slowly, reluctantly, and followed her.

The next evening at the Ramsay dinner table the three
were listlessly eating their desert of sherbet and iced coffee
when Uncle Guy spoke out of the silence. "Everybody who
can is making tracks to some place cooler than this Hades."

"Oh? Well, with all of us sleeping in the basement — and
this house so well insulated —" Aunt Carrie's tone was uneasy, and it's uneasiness sharpened Sarah's attention.

"Someone — someone new going away?" she asked, unable to lift her eyes.

"Mrs. Torrey. Had a heat stroke, I judge. Torrey packed
her and the boy off on an air-cooled train this afternoon.
Colorado."

Sarah sat and stirred her sherbet till it was melted; dripped
it a drop at a time from her spoon back into the dish, was still
sitting when the cup was gone from before her and Aunt
Carrie had washed the dishes and was sitting with Uncle
Guy listening to the radio, as if she wanted to avoid any
conversation with Sarah.

The night was another sleepless one. Sarah lay in the
slightly dank atmosphere of the basement, wrung and
beaten with emotion, unable even to cry. Uncle Guy, apparently with a vague idea that something more than heat
exhaustion was wrong, murmured in gruff undertones to his
wife, who returned short answers, till he gave up and set to
snoring his distinctive choking snore. Aunt Carrie's treble
did not join it, and Sarah hoped that she was suffering for
what she had done. Of course there was a faint possibility

that she had not gone to the Torreys and told them, that Mrs. Torrey might really have fallen ill, so critically that Kirk could not even take time to get word to Sarah. But in that case there would be a letter, a special-delivery letter or a telegram in the morning, even.

In the morning no words passed between the two women until the hour of the postman's coming drew near. Then Sarah deliberately left her chores and sat in the porch swing, waiting. Mrs. Ramsay came and watered the plants in the porch urns. They did not look at each other.

But when the postman approached, dragging his feet wearily and stopping at their front walk to mop his face and neck interminably with a limp handkerchief, Mrs. Ramsay broke the silence. "There won't be anything, Sarah," she said, almost pleadingly. "Believe me, this could end only one way, and it's for your own good that it should be now and not —"

Sarah could hardly hear the words above the drumbeat in her ears. She pushed past Mrs. Ramsay and stood with hand outstretched, waiting for the carrier.

"Well, young lady, looks as if you were expecting it," he joked. "Sign right here. Registered, and return card requested. Somebody's mighty keen to see you get it. Gosh, not out of town twenty-four hours yet, and —"

He was looking at her with quizzical and measuring eyes as Sarah signed with a writing that was hardly recognizable, and he had not finished his sally when the girl again pushed past Mrs. Ramsay and disappeared in the house. She went up to the stifling room under the eaves, sat down on her bed, ripped open the envelope. The page went black before her, but it was the blackness of relief. "My own little darling," Kirk began.

Gradually she was able to read the whole of the letter, in

his copybook hand that was so boyish. He was pretty sure it was an act, but there was just the chance that his mother was really seriously sick. She was always talking about her heart trouble. And they sure had sewed him up tight. They hadn't given him a minute to get away and telephone Sarah, though he thought it would drive him nuts. And she understood, didn't she, that it was she he was thinking of, as much as his folks? No sense in cutting her off from having things nice and easy one of these days, just by flying the coop now and giving it away to his parents. Just give him time. He could always bring the old folks around. And the minute he could get back to Finch, he and Sarah would make that trip to K.C. His postscript added that he was sending this registered from the post office car. If there had been dirty work at the crossroads, as he bet there was, it must have been her sweet Aunt Carrie that poured the poison, the old so-and-so, and he wouldn't put it past her to hold up Uncle Sam's mail.

During the endlessly dragging days of July and August, Sarah lived on Kirk's letters, reading and rereading them. He could not get away yet, he wrote. His father had taken a vacation and come out, and old folks could make it gosh awful hard for a man — Sarah smiled at the word, touching it tenderly with her finger, and gazing down at it through misted eyes. A man. The smile lost positiveness and the tears thickened. He was such a boy. At twenty she was a woman, but at nineteen he . . . This handwriting of his, like a schoolboy's. Even in the mousy-smelling heat of her room Sarah grew cold.

She had given up her opposition to Hermon. Better there than here, with Kirk at K.U. When September brought a slight relief from the lifeless heat, Aunt Carrie began to bestir herself to help get Sarah's wardrobe ready for college.

Sarah had never known Aunt Carrie to be so indecisive as she had been during these summer months. She had had a middle-aged solidity; now she was old and flaccid.

Even the moderation of the heat wave did not bring Mrs. Torrey back, nor Kirk. Kirk's letters continued. You could not expect letters to remain for ten endless weeks at the same peak of intensity, Sarah told herself. Her own were inexpressive, she knew: "Dear Kirk, It gets to seeming too long"; and then a little news of the town, and the ending, "I love you. Always your Sarah."

It seemed impossible that his mother should keep him away till after Sarah had gone to Hermon, especially since K.U. was opening at the same time. And it was impossible. On the night before her departure, while Sarah and Aunt Carrie were washing the dinner dishes, the doorbell rang.

Sarah could hear Uncle Guy mutter a protest, because he was listening to a newscast; could hear his feet pounding across the floor. Her heart stumbled and she eased down the dish she was putting away, straining her ears. Uncle Guy padded back and thrust his head inside the swinging door.

"It's Sarah that's wanted," he told them with a chuckle. Uncle Guy had been kept in the dark about the whole matter, Sarah was sure. As she passed him, not even pausing to take off her apron, he smiled at her genially. "It's that young Torrey," he said, and went back to his newscast.

Kirk was waiting just inside the door, and he took her at once into his arms. "Gosh. Gosh. Do you know how long this has seemed to me?" he muttered into her hair. He was kissing her when Sarah heard the swinging door creak and pulled away from him. She had never resented Aunt Carrie as she did now.

"Why, Kirk!" Aunt Carrie said. "How is your dear

64

mother?" Her voice was plushy, the voice she kept for the Torreys, and her eyes avoided Sarah. "Do come in, dear boy! Tell us all about the summer."

He was in a chair in the living room. Sarah was in a chair across the room from him. Aunt Carrie was on the other side, her face set in a smile which did not touch her eyes. As the evening limped on, Sarah felt herself shrinking and growing colder, as if there were no blood in her veins. When at last she — and Aunt Carrie — went with Kirk to the door, she saw herself in the mirror, and furtively loosened the hair that was too tight around her pinched face. She had not thought how unbecoming this print dress was.

Kirk made a final desperate stand. "You are really going to Hermon tomorrow, Sarah?" he asked stiffly.

"Yes."

"I will be at the depot," he said, his shoulders squaring with the effort of speaking before Aunt Carrie.

That next morning Sarah dressed carefully. She gave passionate thought to her choice of a becoming dress. She put on lipstick and a little rouge, and penciled her eyebrows. The red and black stood out garishly, and she rubbed them almost off. The summer had been hard on her and she had lost weight. Otherwise, she assured herself, she looked as she had always looked.

Kirk himself showed signs of wear when she saw him at the depot in the full light of day. He was gaunt and troubled looking.

It was not much good, his being there, since Aunt Carrie and Uncle Guy were there also.

On the train Sarah sat staring out of the window at the unrolling landscape of rich southern Kansas farmland, so that she need not talk to Helen or Irene or any of the other girls from her class who were also entering Hermon. She was explaining Kirk's goodbye to herself. He couldn't have said anything important, under the circumstances. He couldn't. Was that why his eyes had been the eyes of a puzzled little boy?

The first letter she received from him at Hermon deepened the fear that had touched her. She read it over and over, explaining it away, reading into it the things his words did not say.

October went by in a vague haze of blue sky, a vague fragrance of fallen leaves. November crept into the air with a chill that matched the growing chill of her spirit. She went to classes. She studied, not thinking but memorizing. She was a woman in a dream, a woman walking amid feckless children, a person apart.

She did not go back to Finch until the Thanksgiving vacation. During the two weeks before the holiday there was no letter from Kirk.

Still, letters did not mean much. Generations of her forebears had done without letters. If Kirk were to judge her feeling for him by the words she wrote — she could never express what he was to her.

Kirk would come home for Thanksgiving and all would be right once more. When he held her in his arms there would be no need of words.

Her trip home was as unreal as a movie. Arriving at Finch, she found even the station strange and dreamlike, and the Ramsays as unsubstantial as everything else.

At sight of Sarah, descending from the train, Aunt Carrie put on a smile over her look of shocked surprise. Uncle Guy did not try to hide his.

"Good gosh, Sarah," he protested, "haven't they been feeding you at that darn school?"

She smiled at him politely, watching the holiday throngs

for the one person whose absence left the place empty and useless. She went on smiling politely as the three of them rode home.

Uncle Guy drove into the garage, and they went into the house from the kitchen. The turkey was evidently roasting in the shining automatic range. The house was stuffed with the fragrance of its celery, onion and oysters. Without pausing, Sarah went on through those substantial odors, her eyes reaching for the hall table. She shuffled through the few letters with hands that dropped them. All for Uncle Guy.

So Thanksgiving Day also was held in the half world of waiting. It was followed by a night measured out by the quarter hours on the chimes downstairs.

Without apology or explanation the next morning she went to the telephone in the kitchen and called the Torreys' number. Though she had never before called it, she did not need to look it up in the thin small-town directory.

Aunt Carrie went on with her task of making a molded salad from Thanksgiving leftovers. Her silence was intense and listening.

The brisk trill of the telephone sounded in Sarah's ear, again and again. Then came a voice, but not his. "Yes?" Before Sarah could get a sound from her dry throat, a word from her dry lips, it repeated, "Yes?"

"Is Kirk Torrey there, please?"

"No, Kirk is not in," the voice replied, all its vowels round and all its consonants clipped.

Sarah steadied herself against the wall. "When — when do you expect him?"

The voice tinkled in laughter. "When do we expect Kirk? Perhaps at Christmas. My son has gone East with a classmate for the Thanksgiving holiday. Who is this speaking, please?"

Sarah's knees buckled and she closed her eyes.

"Who is this speaking, please?"

Aunt Carrie was across the room in a scurry of clicking heels. Sarah opened her eyes and stared ahead of her.

"Oh, Sarah. Oh, poor little Sarah," Aunt Carrie whimpered. "You'll get over this, Sarah. You're young. But think what it would have been to marry a man who would let you down like this. He is still only a boy, Sarah. There is more difference than the actual two years."

"One year and five months." The words were as mechanical as a phonograph, etched in her mind by frequent repetition. Even while she spoke them, she was crying, in sudden bitter clarity, *It is true. He is a boy and I am a woman.*

It was like leaning in the darkness on a strong support and feeling it crumple like a straw and leave nothing.

Aunt Carrie had gone on. "You were something so different, Sarah. I noticed it myself. When you were acting in the play — Sarah, you were beautiful —"

Were beautiful. Were beautiful. Were.

"Mrs. Ramsay, let me go home!" The plea was wrenched from Sarah without her expecting it. "Let me go home!" she moaned.

"Home? What home have you but this, Sarah?" Mrs. Ramsay's voice sharpened from incredulity to querulousness.

Sarah shook her head dumbly, drawing a breath like a gasp. This was prison. Only the mesas stood clear and serene and welcoming and real. "Let me go home."

Mrs. Ramsay said, "Certainly not. What an insane thing to ask. You will return to Hermon Sunday, Sarah, and get yourself back to normal as quickly as possible. Girls don't die of unhappy love affairs."

No, they only want to die.

Sarah said no more, recognizing the finality in Mrs. Ramsay's tone, gaining in firmness as Sarah crumpled before her. She sat a long time with eyes shut. Her tense body gradually relaxed. Home. She would go home. Nobody could prevent her.

Mrs. Ramsay went back to her work. She clicked to and fro between table and refrigerator. The teakettle piped up its thin, high whistle and the heels clicked from stove to sink.

"There," Mrs. Ramsay said decisively, "that's done. Come, Sarah, there's a good girl. Let's go in and see if we can get any news on the radio."

Obediently Sarah rose and followed her. She had it almost worked out. A bus ticket to Winslow, Arizona, would be less than the train fare. It used to be twenty dollars. And if she had to go out from the railroad on the mail truck, that used to be eight. Uncle Guy was pretty sure to slip her ten for pocket money when she started back to college. And she had about twenty saved.

If she returned to Hermon, and then was sick and said that she had to go home, at Hermon they would suppose of course she meant Finch and the Ramsay home, and they would not make inquiries about her at once. Neither would Aunt Carrie be making inquiries, since she would suppose her safe at Hermon. With any sort of good fortune she could be at the mesas before they had any idea of it. Home.

The plans worked with the exactitude of blueprints. "I think you should go to the infirmary instead of home," the dean of women said, when Sarah went to her office.

Sarah's knuckles whitened as she clung to the desk for support. "No. Please. I got to go home," she whispered.

The dean came swiftly around her desk and led the girl to a chair. "Why, you really are ill. If you feel that you must go home, Sarah, I'll telephone them to meet you at the train."

"No. No, please," Sarah pleaded desperately. "Aunt Carrie would be scared. I'll be — I'll be fine."

The dean had already perched on the corner of her desk and picked up the telephone. Reluctantly she set it down, nibbling her lip and studying Sarah with a frown. "Well," she conceded. "If Dr. Bennet says it's safe for you to go alone."

That was the first hurdle, and Sarah passed it safely. Helen and Irene went to the train with her, subdued before her muteness and pallor. In the dusty coach they lifted her bags to the overhead rack and stayed talking spasmodically until Sarah thought she could not endure another minute.

"Please don't risk the train's starting," she begged them, pulling her mouth into a smile.

They did at last lay a little package of malted milk tablets in her lap and go, looking back at her from the vestibule. Helen even ran back, leaned over, and kissed her, her untouched girl's face troubled. She had never kissed Sarah before.

They would stand outside the window, with hopeful glances toward the locomotive for signs of activity that would end the paralysis of waiting. They would put on bright laughter, and would mouth messages which she could not understand, until the endless minutes were cut short by the conductor's long call, "All aboarrrd!" snapping with blessed decisiveness at the end.

Sarah could not stand any more. She shut her eyes and left them shut until the conductor's shout sounded, until the train jerked and buckled, jerked once more and slipped into its clacking rhythm. Helen and Irene could do nothing about it. And she would never see them again.

She opened her eyes and looked around the coach, fearful of what she might see. There was no one whom she knew.

Now if she got through Finch without being seen, all would be well.

As the train approached Finch, she went into the washroom and washed her hands again and again; took off her hat and made pretense of combing her hair. Only when the train had stopped and started again did she go out to her seat, and huddle against the stale plush with eyes shut.

She heard the conductor's feet approaching, heard his gusty breathing as he stopped to peer at the paper stub he had stuck in the window beside her, felt his hand on her shoulder.

"Young lady! Young lady! Wake up! Don't you know you've passed your station?"

Sarah blinked up into the eyes that were regarding her with consternation through his slid-down glasses. "Now what?" he scolded paternally. "Now what am I to do with you?"

Sarah sat erect and looked out of the window. "If I get off at Linden — " she suggested huskily.

"We don't stop at Linden, but —" the conductor stretched up a pudgy arm and jerked the bell-cord.

The train jangled to a perturbed stop, while he heaved down Sarah's bags and went puffing to the vestibule with them. In another minute Sarah stood on the platform alone and watched the train gather speed and hoot away into the distance.

Weak from gratitude and relief she staggered feebly under the weight of her bags, and had to put them down and sit on them twice before she reached the bus station across the street. The bus was due in a half hour, another stroke of good luck. She knew now that she was hungry, faint from hunger, yet she did not dare hunt a place to eat, lest she meet someone she knew. She ate malted milk tablets, one by one, till the bus zoomed up to the station, with passengers looking down condescendingly from seats already pushed back for the night's rest.

When Sarah woke from her intermittent doze, the darkened bus was streaking through the gray dawn past farmhouses still inert with sleep or sending up tentative smoky breaths from their chimneys. Sarah straightened her aching body; watched in the driver's mirror the color streaking the East; watched the woman beside her, who had her corset off and comfortably across her knees, her stockinged toes sticking straight up on the footrest, her close-netted head tilted back and her upper teeth clicking up, clicking down, with her resonant breathing. In the opposite seat a little girl's scuffed shoe stuck out into the aisle and her cheek, exquisite with sleep, was pressed tight against the armrest. Sarah could see only one other traveler awake. The driver's mirror reflected an old man's face, his coat collar turned up, his cap visor pulled down, his pink old face curving with the pleased interest of a child as he watched the countryside streak toward him. The driver caught Sarah's eye in the glass and winked at her with the camaraderie of the young and waking amid the old and sleeping. He was almost as young as Kirk.

At last the sky grew bright and flooded the bus with uncompromising daylight. People began to stir, stare with sleep-glazed eyes, sit straight in their seats, clear their throats, blow their noses, put on their shoes. The little girl yawned and stretched deliciously, stared about her in wild astonishment, and pulled at her mother, still sleeping. They came into a town, and the driver drew up before a café with a BUS STOP sign sticking out from its door. He pulled at brakes, hitched himself out of his seat, flexed his back, opened the mechanical door.

"A half hour here for eats, folks," he announced.

Coffee and a roll. It was not nearly enough, but its price was as much as Sarah dared spend. She perched on the stool at the end of the lunch counter and placed a wall of silence between herself and the old man, who sat down beside her. She ate the roll slowly, took the coffee by spoonfuls, filled the cup with cream when she had drunk half the beverage, and spooned down the brownish, tepid mixture while the old man's amiable chirpings died out from lack of response.

At noon Sarah bought a Coke and a candy bar. During the afternoon she was able to forget her hunger in the excitement of seeing buttes and mesas again, seeing Indian villages. They were not the pueblos of her people, but they were of related tribes, and she gazed at the natural camouflage of their adobe houses among the rocks, gazed as if she must fill her eyes with the sight. The first hogan they passed was beautiful to her, though she had never liked the Navajos. The first flock of sheep and goats, with a full-skirted Navajo shepherdess, dragged tears into Sarah's eyes. The great sky, the illimitable desert wastes, the place where long, regularly formed red rock mesas stood at right angles to the highway for miles, like vast headless animals all facing blindly toward the passing vehicles — all these Sarah knew well. As familiar were the arborlike booths where the Indians sat with their merchandise of pottery, blankets and beads, in the tourist season, and the Indians now waiting hopefully with their wares at every small station.

These were parts of the approach to home, and they passed with alternations of swift speed and dragging slowness. The bus stopped at Holbrook. It passed the great meteorite crater. It drew into Winslow. Sarah made her way out in the slow procession about to eat at the station there. She watched the driver open up the belly of the bus and deliver her bags. She staggered with them over to the

73

railway station where she must wait for morning and the mail truck.

Her head whirled with excitement, joy, weakness. But she was no longer hungry, and that was lucky, since she had so little money left. She would have liked to walk around and feast her eyes on sky and distant buttes. But after she had heaved her bags up on a seat where the ticket seller could plainly see them through his wicket, she found herself too unsteady. She curled up beside her baggage, to doze and wake throughout the long night.

As soon as she could make out by the dimmed lights that the station clock said six, Sarah washed and tidied herself in the empty twilight of the rest room, with its smell of train smoke and soap and disinfectants. Then she counted her money once more. The result was the same as the last time, eight dollars and fifteen cents. She fished about in the depths of the handbag, hoping that a dime, or even a nickel, might have slipped out of the coin purse. She sat down on a bench there in the rest room and took out the contents of the bag piece by piece and laid them on the bench beside her, but the emptied bag disclosed no stray coin. She replaced everything, shaking a notebook by its spine to be sure. She opened the billfold and looked in all the compartments, and closed it hastily because Kirk's face smiled out at her from one of those pockets. There was just twenty-five cents that could be spent for breakfast.

She made her way stiffly, like an old woman, to a small, sleepy restaurant she had known years before. Indian boys sat on stools drinking coffee, and a waitress served Sarah coffee and two doughnuts, patting her yawn with the back of her hand.

Before the sun was up, Sarah stood shivering at the fork in the road, waiting. When she could not stand any longer, she sat on a suitcase, which tilted uncomfortably. She had waited for an hour when the mail truck came to a stop beside her. She got up so slowly that the driver called above the idling of his motor, "Got to step lively, young lady, if you want to ride with us."

6

By the time the mail truck, consuming much time in detours to trading posts, had approached the Hopi villages, the mesas had assumed their most familiar aspect.

To the left of the road was Second Mesa, crowned with ancient villages that looked like tiny blocks grouped on its summit. Sticking up like a thumb from its shoulder was Corn Rock, and near it the dark green crayon scrawl where school and other government buildings stood amid dusty tamarisk and shining green cottonwood. On the horizon First Mesa was outlined.

The truck passed in sight of Five Houses, and Sarah counted them with rapt eyes. Yes, still five, no more, no less. The relentless drift of the sand had half buried one. Only the tops of the windows looked out over the scalloped waves.

On the other side the great rock mass of the Giant's Armchair rose solitary from the desert. Here if nowhere else the men found rattlesnakes for the Snake Dance, whirring and buzzing amid the purple mariposas and rosy mallow and scarlet paintbrush and sickening-sweet snowball.

They passed in sight of Second Mesa church and mission and the small Christian settlement, dropped like a handful of pebbles at the foot of the mesa. Sarah craned her neck to see the new stone building between missionaries' house and church.

In another half hour the truck was chugging patiently toward Polacca, at the foot of First Mesa. It passed Red Earth, with its long, low house where one family had always lived. It dipped through the government compound, with children pouring out upon the grounds in a shrieking recess flood. It came out again, and Sarah registered a new house here, another there, the post office —

At the post office Sarah clambered out, stiff from long sitting. The Hopi boy handed down her suitcases. "You staying here?" the driver asked. She nodded, moistened her lips and said, "I do not know any more what is the fare." The driver winked and replied, "Maybe next trip, sister. It's all in the family." And Sarah said, "Thank you," smiling with pleasure because it was an unexpected good, to be coming home with eight dollars in her purse.

She stood in front of the little post office, her bags at her feet, and looked around her. Off to her right and before her rose the prow of the great stone ship that was First Mesa. Sarah's eyes fastened hungrily on the cut-out squares of the villages "On Top." There was Walpi, Place of the Gap, the figurehead of the ship, compactly modeled and comely, irresistibly drawing painters and etchers. Sichumovi followed it, with a little space between, and after another space Hano or Tewa.

Sarah's eyes started at the Gap and traveled through Hano, Sichumovi and Walpi, set like three cars on a railway track. Only then did she come to the place where her mother's house should be.

She came with fearful expectancy; and there it was; during the years of her absence it had not crumbled away. She was trembling. Against all that she knew perfectly well, it seemed to her that she would find her mother waiting for her behind those translucent-looking amber walls and bright blue shadows.

Three short-legged mongrel dogs rolled almost at her feet in a snapping, snarling, yellow and brindle ball. An old woman trudged past her, toward the post office door. She peered at Sarah with filmed eyes, through a gray fringe like a sheep dog's, her feet noiseless in their high, silver-buttoned moccasins, her dark winter blanket clasped close around her chilly old body. "You are walking, my friend?" she asked in a high, cracked voice, peering at Sarah as if to make out her identity. Sarah flushed with pleasure at the salutation. "You are walking, grandmother?" she responded politely. She wondered if it wasn't Numpeyo, the Toad, greatest of Hopi potters. Yet Numpeyo had seemed to the little girl Sarah already too ancient to live.

A round, shave-headed child in overalls and bare feet romped by, and a little girl chased him, her plaid winter shawl dragging. Her dress was shorter than Sarah's used to be, but otherwise she was much the same. She smiled shyly at Sarah and stared back at her as she ran, and Sarah felt tolerant even of the children's crusted wet noses.

Her gaze traveled on to the Hill-Where-We-Spread-Our-Rabbit-Skins-to-Dry. On those sandy, sunny slopes the people had staked out their rabbit skins to make the blankets they so prized, weaving them loosely of the twisted ropes of furry hide. Back and back went the story of her people, to the days when they wandered down from the dizzy cliff dwellings hung in Mesa Verde canyons, in what is now Colorado, or on the beetling crags of Pu-Ye in New Mexico, or in the walls of deep-slashed Canyon de Chelly in Arizona, or on numberless other massive cliffs. Harried by drought or by fierce plains Indians, or by both, they had wandered down, seeking food and safety, and here they had stayed through the centuries.

Something of all this Sarah knew, piecing together the

stories the old men had told, with the history that Mr. and Mrs. Loring had narrated. The past seemed to reach from the sand and the rock and lay hold on Sarah. She had come home.

There was all the time in the world. Sarah could not recall any clocks in her mother's house, or any calendars. There was no hurry, but she might as well be getting on. Her feet remembered the feel of the sand, how you stepped in and pulled out, stepped in and pulled out. They remembered and were glad.

Here to the right Numpeyo had lived, with some of her daughters who were coming up to be good potters themselves, though without their mother's fame. Farther on was the mission, of Indian masonry, with a few trees coaxed up out of the sand for shade; and the church; and the Mexican-style house with its shaded patio. Here the field matron had lived, and the Water Witch and his wife, he who was sent by Washindon to find water on the desert and put up tall windmills and concrete watering troughs. Here were the shops and garages which belonged to the Water Witch and the government, and where many Hopis ambled about in grease-smeared overalls, the beaks of their caps knowingly over their ears.

And settled solidly in a hollow was the house of Uncle Abraham. Since it was so near, Sarah would go to see Uncle Abraham and Aunt Polehongsi first. Her mouth filled suddenly with water, thinking that it was sun-high and they might be eating. When she had eaten and rested she would catch a ride up on top. She would see her mother's house, even if someone else were living there, and she would go to Aunt Kawasie.

Smoke rose from Uncle Abraham's chimney, but there was no one in sight. Sarah knocked at the closed door, forgetting that knocking was not Hopi custom. Before she could correct her mistake and turn the knob, calling aloud to those within, it was turned from inside and the door opened. Sarah looked into the round, wide eyes of Miss Lundquist, hardly higher than her own.

Miss Lundquist gazed at Sarah with a puzzled smile. "Will you come in?" she asked. "There is sickness here, but —" She peered closer. She met so few Hopis who were strange to her.

"I guess you don't remember me. I am Abraham's niece," Sarah said shyly. "I was just a little small girl when the Lorings took me away."

Chuckling, Miss Lundquist caught her by both hands. "Oh, this will do your uncle more good than a medicine!" The laughter ran through her voice and crinkled her round face, with the fine lines around eyes and mouth and under the chin. "Here, let me take your satchels. We'll surprise them." She drew Sarah inside.

Sarah shut her eyes and took a deep breath. Throughout the past eight years that complex of odors had been waiting to rush into her nostrils and fill her lungs and stomach. She had forgotten it, but now it was as familiar as if she had never breathed any other air. It was made up of the adobe which plastered walls and floor, the fine dust that filtered through the pole and brush ceiling, the cornmeal forever being ground on the inclined millstones in the corner, the coffee forever brewing on the stove, and the mutton which had cooked here ever since the house was built. Mutton steam had permeated the adobe, the brush, the blankets. It had permeated the people.

Sarah opened her eyes, only a moment closed. Miss Lundquist was holding her out like a new doll, saying,

"Abraham! Polehongsi! You have company!" and then waiting, expectant.

An iron bed stood in a corner, a brass-trimmed iron bed. It was neatly made, with a clean spread, bright pink, and it had a real mattress under the bedding, instead of the bare springs: Sarah could tell by the thickness. But it was the same bedstead. Sarah had always admired the brass balls, and her reflection in them, distorted to absurdity.

Uncle Abraham was not in the bed. He lay fully clothed on the smooth adobe floor, his head and shoulders up against the wall. The eight years had aged him little. He was still smaller, and his bright, kind eyes had retreated farther in their cavernous sockets. The lines of patience about his mouth were as Sarah remembered them; but his hair, like a child's Dutch bob in length, had been shining black when Sarah went away, and now it glinted with sharp silver under the bright silk band that held it out of his eyes.

Always tall and corpulent, Aunt Polehongsi had grown larger rather than smaller. She was a mountain of a woman, a full salt sack set on a full sugar sack set on a full meal sack. She had been stirring something in an enamel saucepan on the small iron range, and she twisted the salt sack and the sugar sack around and gazed at Sarah with spoon suspended.

Uncle Abraham smiled up with dawning recognition, and Aunt Polehongsi's eyes looked out from their dark, smooth folds of flesh, lids blinking. After a long minute Uncle Abraham pulled himself to a sitting position and stretched out both hands, crying joyfully, "Sarah! Little daughter! *Uhpitu lolama!* God be thanked I see you once more upon this earth!"

Aunt Polehongsi's spoon splashed into the saucepan and she was upon Sarah with surprising agility. She pushed for-

81

ward a chair, and Sarah shook her head and sat down on the floor beside Uncle Abraham, her legs moving stiffly sidewise at the well-remembered angle, the only proper way for a Hopi woman to sit. Miss Lundquist dropped into the chair and sat forward, hands clasped between knees, round face shining with shared delight. They talked, running from Hopi to English and back again, while Sarah's tongue found itself as a cyclist's feet find long unused pedals.

They asked if she had come home for a visit. Sarah spread her small dark hands and surveyed them intently as she answered, No, *Kaeh,* she was come home to stay. She was not a very good *Bohanna,* white woman, she added: she was a Hopi from the skin in. Uncle Abraham asked if the *Bohanna* had not been good to her, and Sarah answered, warily, that Mrs. Ramsay had been all right. Uncle Abraham knew that Mrs. Loring had died long ago? Sarah's bright dark eyes misted unexpectedly as she spoke Aunt Lib's name. Yes, they had heard. Miss Lundquist had heard, and that her foster-mother's sister had taken Sarah, as a Hopi mother's sister would do.

"Beautiful clothes the Ramsays gave you," Miss Lundquist commented, admiring the fine fur coat-collar from which Sarah's face emerged small and darkly bloodless.

"Nice clothes," Sarah assented. "I could not bring near all. She did not want me to come away."

That was all the explanation she need give, she thought. But she did add, "They sent me to college. High school was enough. I had had enough school."

"College!" Miss Lundquist cried, "and you such a child."

"Twenty," Sarah corrected her.

"Scrawny like your uncle," Aunt Polehongsi said with friendly candor.

Miss Lundquist studied her more closely. "You don't

82

look too well," she scolded. "You're peaked. A cup of hot tea and some dinner, that's what you need. I'll take her home, Polehongsi. I'll feed her some dinner and then tuck her up on the sofa for a nap. The child is all tuckered out."

Sarah looked toward the saucepan bubbling on the stove, and her mouth watered for the remembered flavors, but Miss Lundquist was urging her up from the floor, smiling and nodding at her, at Aunt Polehongsi, knowingly, as if they were in a friendly, three-cornered conspiracy. Sarah found herself emerging from the muttony interior, into the bright, light outdoors, sharp with the smell of burning piñon wood.

"Your uncle is better; but they had such a broken night," Miss Lundquist explained, as she led the way across to the mission doorstep, where she stamped the sand from her feet before pushing in.

Sarah followed, lugging one suitcase while Miss Lundquist carried the other. Childish tears of disappointment were boiling up into Sarah's nose. She was through being a white. She had been hungry, beyond any food hunger she could remember, for dripping spoonfuls of Aunt Polehongsi's stew. She had been tasting the luscious kernels of hominy, brown with meat juice, and the slippery rings of onion, and the large golden brown beans, and the fat mutton with its sagey tang because of the sheep's browse.

Well, she could be patient. Just once more this *Bohanna* food, and then not again. She sat in the wonderful rocker she remembered, with its high golden oak back and its cretonne cushions neatly attached with tapes. She sat stiffly, without rocking, and murmured replies to Miss Lundquist. who called out to her from the kitchen, smiled at her radiantly as she pattered in to set something more on the dining room table. With her first mouthful Sarah reluctantly admitted to herself that the luncheon was good.

"It's nothing but a pickup lunch, Sarah," Miss Lundquist was apologizing. "Still, if you don't mind its being scrappy, I always say there's something about a pickup meal. These cupcakes, though: the oven was too slow; or maybe a speck too much baking powder and flour." She held the plate out at arm's length and laughed gayly at the cone-shaped frosted cakes. "I call them Delectable Mountains."

Sarah remembered how Miss Lundquist had eased a hard road with such jokes. Once when crossing one of the larger washes on her way to the railroad she was almost caught in the flash flood which swept away her suitcase and all her best clothes. Afterward Miss Lundquist wrote funny verses about the adventure. Another time she climbed up to mend a leak in the plaster of her bedroom ceiling. She stepped up on a chair which she had set on a table, and she fell. That accident had brought out pages of comical jingles, especially since she could not get a doctor to brave the storm and the impassable roads, and the broken arm had set crooked. Miss Lundquist had said wryly that now it matched the other arm. She had broken that one during a flu epidemic when the Hopi were dying like flies and Miss Lundquist nursed them day and night on the mesa, till, blind with fatigue, she slipped in crossing a snowy roof to a ladder—

"Such fat bacon this time," Miss Lundquist was scolding vigorously. "There's only one good point to that: the drippings. I always did like drippings for warming up cold victuals."

By this time Sarah had forgotten Aunt Polehongsi's stew. The potatoes were cut fine and crisped to a golden brown, with just enough salt, just enough good black pepper, and Miss Lundquist had whisked together a batch of biscuits. "Good butter, Sarah," she assured her. "The Water

84

Witch just fetched me a pound from the railroad. And try a
little honey. Wild sage honey from Moencopi. I declare.
I forgot the cold meat. Do you object to cold meat, Sarah?
I'd be tickled if you could help me out with it. Samuel
brought me a whole arm of mutton."

Dimly Sarah thought that Miss Lundquist used not to
talk so much about the food: it crossed her mind that perhaps the missionary had noticed how avidly she was eating.
With that thought, she tried to pick at the food uninterest-
edly, but the rich full savors together with her fast, broken
only by coffee and snacks, were too much for her.

"Oh, I have a dish of dried peach sauce in the refrigerator," her hostess remembered. Bringing it in, she spooned
out large darkly golden spoonfuls into a sauce dish for
Sarah. "That's one thing I don't have to apologize for," she
said, beaming. "I warrant you didn't get anything better
than Hopi peaches."

True, the Hopi peaches had a flavor unknown to the large
blushing tissue-wrapped fruits in bright-labeled boxes.
Distant descendants of the peach trees which Coronado's
men had brought to the mesas, they had fought drought,
sand, wind, through the centuries, and had gathered into
their fruits the rich, deep mellowness of desert suns, the
tang of this land of sagebrush and juniper.

"Now suppose you stretch out on the sofa," Miss Lundquist said when Sarah sat back from the emptied table. "I'll
just scrape these dishes and pile them in the dishpan. This
is the day for women's sewing class, but you're much too
tired to meet a crowd like that. I know what traveling's
like."

Sarah felt herself urged along to the old sofa behind
the heating stove. Miss Lundquist pulled up a quilt made
of bright flannel pieces, and tucked it snugly around her.

85

Then for a minute she studied Sarah's face, her eyes a little anxious.

"Is it just that you are so tired, Sarah child? Or have you been sick?"

"Just tired. And then it was so hot in Kansas. I've always been well, up to this summer."

Miss Lundquist patted her. "We'll have the doctor take a look at you," she concluded. "But now you take a nap. Don't worry about a thing. Just take a little nap."

Sarah lay blinking at the empty room. On in the kitchen she could see the cold white china shine of a small electric refrigerator, new since she was last here. Sarah remembered meat and butter wrapped in wet cloths in the window, and often spoiling in spite of Miss Lundquist's care. New electric lights dangled on cords: formerly there had been imposing Coleman lamps, to be pumped up every night. The Delco which made possible the new luxuries was throbbing fussily in the cellar directly below Sarah. It was very fine but subject, she knew, to spells of temperament.

She thought with wonder that this plain, bare room once seemed to her very grand, and Miss Lundquist a wealthy woman. Wasn't she living a life of luxury, with water at the turn of a handle, and wooden floors, and chairs and tables and dishes and all the food she could eat?

Sarah's eyes went drowsily around the room — Navajo blankets over the holes in the linoleum, a little organ, the high-backed rocker, and a smaller rocker, and oak dining chairs with machine carving. There was nothing inviting to settle down into, Sarah realized. Except this sofa, with thick pads of old comforts to cover the protruding springs. But then, Miss Lundquist never had time to settle down. Always on the jump, not walking if she could run, and perching on the edge of a chair if she did give in and sit.

There was a low fire in the heater, and Sarah had been chilled. This lassitude, this weariness invaded every part of her body and lay heaviest on head and eyes.

The Hopi room, adjoining this one, was noisy with the scuff of feet, the opening and closing of the door, the squeak and bang of the doors of cupboards where the quilt supplies were stored. Sarah remembered it well. The women's voices were only a little muffled, high and crooning, like the talk of hens in the sun, and punctuated with laughter. And once, when the door into the dining room was briefly opened, that smell of wool and mutton rushed in upon Sarah. She tried to struggle away from the deep sweetness of sleep in order to savor the sounds and the odor, but in that basking warmth sleep was too strong for her.

Dusk had fallen when she woke. Miss Lundquist had not turned on the lights, but she stood beside Sarah, looking down at her, a funny little felt hat pulled down stoutly over her gray hair. She was yanking on her good, serviceable tweed coat. There was no longer any sound of contented voices from the next room. The women had gone back to their houses and their supper work. But through wall and closed door came crying.

"I hate to waken you, Sarah," Miss Lundquist said. "But I have to go on top, and there's a chance for us to ride. My little Henry's on the blink — did you know I had a car now? But there's always something out of kilter. I couldn't leave you alone, and it would be a good chance to see your aunt."

Sarah struggled to a sitting position, sleep clinging like the folds of the woolen comfort. "Yes," she said, with an inquiring glance toward the Hopi room.

"Mona and her husband," Miss Lundquist explained, while Sarah got into her wraps. Miss Lundquist darted here and there as she talked. Her voice came muffled from the bedroom, was cut off when she banged down the bedroom window and locked it, grew clear when she returned to snap on one light to leave. "It's Mona's last baby. Born while Jerry was off in Nevada on a job. He was on that job two years," she continued matter-of-factly, "and this baby was born just after he came home. But he was fond of it all the same, after he got over feeling someway. And it was the sweetest baby. Smart as a whip. I think its father was a Navajo, and our Navahopi babies are usually smarter than the full bloods."

"Do Mona and Jerry come to church now?"

Resignedly Miss Lundquist shook her head. "But they want a Christian burial."

Mona's long face was dark and despairing and she nodded without interest when Miss Lundquist said, "You remember Tuvenga's little Sarah."

Mona was another of those who had lost one baby after another through the years. In contrast to her long, haggard face, her body was bulky with bearing. She was not young. Sarah thought, curiously, how late passion seemed to burn in the Hopi, the passion of parenthood along with the rest. Even to old age. Jerry's grief was shut behind his broad russet features, and his eyes were opaque.

But coming out into the early dark to the trader's long car which awaited them, Sarah forgot Mona and her problems. Here was another of the components of her own life. She had not brought it into her consciousness for years, yet it had remained a part of her.

The air was sharp, now that the sun had set, and it was edged with the smell of burning juniper, so that Sarah's nostrils flared avidly, and she opened her mouth to gulp in the strong, keen aroma. A trace of sunset color still shone clear along the western horizon, and against it loomed First

Mesa, with a frail new moon and a star hung above it, as keen to the eye as the burning wood to the nose.

"Andy," Miss Lundquist said, as the man in the car leaned over to open the door, "do you remember Sarah, Tuvenga's little girl?"

Andy studied her interestedly. "Oh, sure, sure thing," he said heartily. "Well, what do you know!"

Sarah's heart gave a surprising leap. Wavy hair. She'd completely forgotten the wavy hair with a warmth of brown in its black. The color had won him the nickname Yellow Hair, and the wave had plagued him by the innumerable ribald jokes it had called forth. The child Sarah had not admired his hair, but the woman looked at it with nostalgic pleasure, her palms burning with memory.

He was a few years older than she, and had been one of the lounging boys her mother had warned her against. His American name, Andrew, had been given him by Miss Lundquist during the brief period when his father had been a member of the church and she had hoped great things from his leadership. A powerful Hopi, Jake, though spidery small like Abraham. It had been long since he had entered the meetinghouse, yet his regard for Miss Lundquist and her more transitory co-workers had never faltered. He was always ready to take them here and there, from the time when he was the only Hopi to own a pleasure car. And again and again through the years Miss Lundquist went hurrying at his call: when Star, his wife, could not bear her baby; when this Andy coasted down the Gap in his father's car and the wheels locked —

Now Andy tooled the car up the road, an ancient cart track worn in the living rock, scrawled like a baby's first writing on the side of the mesa. Twisting and turning, it climbed to where the villages hung in the darkening sky.

"We'll drop Sarah at her Aunt Kawasie's," Miss Lundquist told Andy. "Just wait while I make sure Kawasie's there."

Sarah stumbled from the car, trembling with eagerness. There was the half door she remembered so clearly, now swung back against the wall because the whole door was shut for the autumn night. And here was —

For an instant Sarah stopped short. Here was the smell. It was not the pungence of burning desert wood, though the smoke smell lay beneath it. It was not the pervasive odor of mutton steam. It was a scent which she had probably never noticed before she went away, because it had always been a part of the air she breathed. It was the smell of the Hopi villages, innocent of plumbing, innocent of outhouse, from pre-Coronado days to this. Even in the autumn chill, without the livening heat of the sun, it made Sarah cover her nose.

Then she almost forgot the fetor, for Miss Lundquist was calling a salutation in Hopi and pushing open the door.

On the floor, in the light of a kerosene lamp, an oilcloth was spread with Hopi bowls and a frypan and a few cracked plates and cups and a graniteware coffeepot. Around these the family were gathered, Aunt Kawasie with her back to the door. Sarah saw with emotion the neat parting down the middle of her black hair, which lay in coils like long curls over her cushiony gingham shoulders. She could see the rag-stuffed pillow which her aunt always wadded under one hip, to ease her weight on the side away from her folded-back knees, and to balance her.

Aunt Kawasie twisted her bulk about, smiling at Miss Lundquist. "*Hakami* Miss Lundquist!" she welcomed her warmly. "You hungry, *sene?* You come taste our *nakaviki,* is it? Or we got canned tomatoes from the store. Frances, you get a plate for Miss Lundquist and — who is it you got with you, Miss Lundquist? My glasses don't work so good. I guess the *Bohanna* girl at the Dime Store didn't fit me right last time I go to the railroad." She cackled with laughter at her own wit, but the laughter died on her lips when Miss Lundquist pushed Sarah into the circle of lamplight.

Her breath shook her lips and her coppery face grew gray. *"Okiway!"* she whispered. "My sister Sequapa — no, it cannot be —"

"It is Sarah of course," Miss Lundquist said practically, pushing her hardy hat back from her round forehead and then jamming it down again. "She does look like her mother, doesn't she? I'll stop by, in an hour or so, and take her home with me for the night. I must go on with Mona now. You knew that Mona's baby died, Kawasie?"

Kawasie mechanically murmured, *"Owi — okiway — okiway —"* but she did not take her eyes from Sarah's face.

"Well, for goodness sake, Sarah," said Frances, Kawasie's daughter, "come along in and have something to eat. Too bad you can't stop and visit, too, Miss Lundquist."

Old memories of *nakaviki* came up to meet the flavor of the actual food, when Sarah had taken off her coat and hat and sat down and bitten off her first mouthful of the sweet corn tamale. When she praised it diffidently Aunt Kawasie bounced up and fetched a dish from a blue-painted cupboard, smiling and widening her eyes at this newfound niece. It was peach meal, which Sarah had always loved.

Sarah talked little. She shot shielded glances at the family as she ate, or gazed more openly around the well-remembered rooms in the soft half light. Frances was about Sarah's age, a sulky looking girl and untidy, with her hair awkwardly clubbed at her neck. It was growing out from its schoolgirl bob and had attained a ragged stiffness, and

91

not enough length to be put up in the glossy squash-blossom whorls. Cecil was a wiry, unattractive twelve. Uncle Mattima was wiry, too, and undersized. He was under Aunt Kawasie's thumb, Sarah recalled, and asserted himself only by making acid jokes, when his usual refuge of easy humor was not enough.

Except for the addition of two iron bedsteads, the house had changed little since the day when Sarah had peered into its forbidden room. She could not now see the rough plank door of that chamber, for her view extended only into the near end of the storeroom; but her mind reconstructed the entrance with certainty.

On the walls Aunt Kawasie was using a whiter plaster than Sarah remembered. A newer style of enamelware hung amid the *potas* from Second Mesa and Oraibi. Cecil's crayon pictures, now proudly pinned up between *kachina* dolls, were of a bolder design than Frances' used to be.

Aunt Kawasie stretched out pudgy arms and began to clatter the dishes together, looking out under the Dime Store spectacles or tilting her head to peer over them. Uncle Mattima sat back, clasping his knees with one arm and automatically pulling the scanty hairs from his chin with a fold of tin from a can. He studied Sarah with kindly pondering eyes.

Sarah cleared her throat. "My mother's house?" she asked.

Before anyone had answered, the door opened and another woman came in, solid and large-waisted, with a child on her back, its head hanging back in sleep against the sustaining blanket wrapped around its mother and itself. Two other children followed her. Wide-eyed with pleasurable horror at sight of a stranger, they made a scampering detour around her and plunged upon Uncle Mattima.

Bessie, Aunt Kawasie's Bessie. Incredible that she should be thus settled and plain. She must be well past thirty, though, and by that age many Hopi women had grown shape-less and had lost all look of youth.

In her turn Bessie wondered at Sarah. *"Okiway, okiway!"* she squealed, after a candid scrutiny of Sarah's college-girl dress, her well-cut, glossy hair, her shoes, showing their qual-ity through the dust. *"Okiway,* Sarah! You would not make two bites for a hungry man!" The others joined her uproari-ous laughter.

With a grunt Bessie sat down beside her cousin, shifting the yearling around to her high-stomached lap and stifling its waking murmur by suckling it. She asked a few ques-tions and vouchsafed much information. Three more children she had; no, four: she had lost five. Luke? When Sarah asked her how was Luke, her husband, Bessie spoke in a startled tone, as of one who had almost slipped her mind. Luke? Oh, Luke was fine. Ornery as ever. He was married to Dolly; did Sarah remember Dolly? Skinny as Sarah, Dolly was.

Somewhat hesitantly, Sarah asked who was Bessie's hus-band now; who was this child's father? Bessie looked down at the child, who was alternately dozing off and losing the nipple, and waking enough to grab it again. She had mar-ried Harry after Luke, she said; and then Stanton. But that Stanton was no good; she hadn't seen hide nor hair of him for a long time — oh, for a year or two, she said vaguely.

The other two children sprawled against Uncle Mattima, their lustrous eyes peering through tangles of hair at the stranger. Their grandfather caressed them silently, and Aunt Kawasie focused her attention upon the dishes she was picking up. Sarah sensed that they were a little embarrassed before her.

Without clear-cut relevance, Sarah suddenly envisioned the new white bathtub at the mission, the shiny white toilet with its varnished seat. It would be good to be clean again, after her dusty, clothes-rumpling trip. She put the thought away resolutely.

"My mother's house?" she asked.

Bessie said beamingly, "My house is what she ought to see. Isn't that so, Mother?"

"Oh, *bas lolama, bas lolama*," Aunt Kawasie chimed in, as if glad she could be proud of something of Bessie's. "Did you hear, Sarah? Bessie got the prize for her house last time. Such a set of dishes you never saw."

Sarah, listening hard to follow the Hopi speech, remembered those contests. They had been instituted by the field matrons appointed by Washindon. Once a year a committee, field matron, field nurse, agent, made a tour of the mesa and chose the best houses, the cleanest, the most modern. And always the ugliest, the artists said.

"And my mother's house?" Sarah persisted.

"I guess it's yours now," Kawasie answered. "There is nobody else. The key, I keep it." She padded across the room, stood on a low stool made of planking and two-by-fours, reached up and clawed a rag-wrapped bundle out of a niche in the adobe, unwrapped it to disclose a key. Sarah's eyes clung to that key. "Some things were stolen," Aunt Kawasie warned her. "Boys — *kahopi*. In the morning we go see."

"And then I show you my house, too," Bessie assured her complacently.

Again a voice at the door. Again Miss Lundquist smiling in. "You ready to come home, Sarah? Well, Bessie! Where have you been keeping yourself? This young one of yours was only a month old, the last time I saw him."

Miss Lundquist trotted in to peer beamingly at the baby, clucking at him, creep-mousing up his plump stomach. "I do believe, Bessie, he's one of the prettiest babies you've ever

94

had," she said with no reproof in her voice. "Get your things, Sarah, child. Andy's waiting for us."

The bathtub had receded. Her mother's house filled Sarah's mind. She could not wait to dress and eat and climb the mesa next morning before seeing her mother's house. "Miss Lundquist, thank you, but I think I sleep here tonight."

Miss Lundquist did not urge her, though her round face sobered. "Oh, Sarah, I was counting on you to try out my new waffle recipe. Someone sent a waffle iron in a barrel. I thought, Now Sarah will be company."

"I would like to, but I must see my mother's house," Sarah explained.

Miss Lundquist waved to them from the door. A moment later Andy poked in his head and said, "Want for me to fetch up your suitcases tomorrow, Sarah? Or will you be down?" His black eyes flickered between Frances, washing dishes in a pan on the stove, and Sarah.

Sarah thought she would never capture sleep, that night. At first she welcomed her wakefulness. She could lie there, on a sheepskin on the floor because there were not enough beds, and feel a oneness with her aunt's family and thus with the tribe. She could gaze up at the pole and brush ceiling and at the prayer feathers hanging still and gray, her eyes shaping themselves to the dark. She could rise cautiously on an elbow and look through a peephole upon the plain, vast and still under the stars.

She would get used to the lack of mattress and smooth sheets. But she was not so sure how she could learn to do without a clean nightgown on a bathed body.

When she had stood the adobe floor as long as she could, she inched herself quietly into another position. At first it seemed exquisitely comfortable, and then, little by little, she discovered new points where the floor reached up and prodded an elbow, an angular hipbone, making them ache in a crescendo of discomfort until she shifted again. Exhaustion brought late sleep, but when the movements of the family roused her in the early morning light, and she pulled her stiff, aching body upright, she felt as if she had not slept at all.

"Gee," Frances said, studying her, "you sure look a wreck, Sarah. I mean you really do."

Sarah had to see Bessie's house first, in spite of her impatience. It had plank floors instead of adobe, and it always took time to get over the habit of the clay, which took to itself the tracked mud and hid it from the casual eye, and which was charitable toward greasy spatters, as well. Bessie dismissed the maculacy of her planks with nonchalance. "Before they inspect it I scrub it good with lye."

A golden oak china closet demanded attention, its wood shiny and its glass doors curved. Bessie had got it at a second-hand store at the railroad, to make a place for the prize dishes, lush with pink roses and gold scroll work. "One hundred pieces," Bessie repeated proudly, "with the lids of the sugar bowl and vegetable dish counting."

She had bought the bed new, from a mail-order house, the chest of drawers with it. Stanton had had a good price for his wool that fall, and she was able to pay cash for the splendid objects. The mattress was fine and thick, though growing soiled. Bessie had made it down at the government community building. Washindon had provided the cotton and the ticking, and had taught just how to compress small mountains of piled bats into their stout covers.

Bessie scolded at her second from the youngest child when he climbed to the top of the chest and sat among the miscellany kicking his heels against the half-open drawers. He went on kicking, for the scolding was perfunctory. Bare heels did no more than smear the veneered wood; and, besides, harsh scholding of one's children was *kahopi*.

Sarah admired and admired, poised for the moment when, as she phrased it to herself, she could get away without making her cousin mad. It was punishment, to be so delayed as she neared the goal of this whole journey, the refuge of her thought throughout the years. Even after they had turned their steps toward her mother's house, villagers thrust themselves in the way, delaying her still more.

Aunt Kawasie sailed along the stone streets, through the stone courts. Her back was straight and her round stomach well out ahead, and her bright-bordered Pendleton shawl covered her prosperously from the sheared wife-locks fanning out on her cheeks almost to the tops of her high moccasins. She nodded and laughed and exchanged greetings in the high Hopi singsong, and explained Sarah proudly.

An old man came out on a housetop and looked down at them, keen eyes probing Sarah. "You come on a visit?" he asked courteously. And when Sarah said that she had come to stay, he peered closer and spoke thoughtfully. "For some," he said, "it is hard to leave the shiny waterspouts and sinks of the *Bohannas,* and their lamps that you light by pulling a string or turning a button. And so often we Hopis choose the wrong things to bring back to the mesas. Our schoolgirls sometimes put big *Bohanna* windows in their houses up on top, forgetting how hard it is to keep out the winter winds. May you choose well, granddaughter."

"Who is he?" Sarah asked Kawasie.

"You know him well. It is John, the *Kik-Mongwi.*"

An old woman came padding out on bare feet at the sound of their voices. Uselessly she lifted her opaque eyes, and then she ran her fingers over Sarah's face, while Sarah stood still and endured the stale smell and feel of the horny tips.

In a low voice Sarah asked her aunt whether this was the one called Kuna because the Tewa word for thank you dwelt on her lips so constantly. The round face looked much like Kuna's, withered like a russet apple, and the coils of frowsy hair over her shawl-wrapped shoulder. No, Aunt Kawasie said, Kuna had died years ago. This was Sehepmana, a clan relation of Sarah's.

At last they had run the gauntlet and reached the front end of the mesa, where the houses were not so crowded together. At last they had reached the house which was most withdrawn of them all.

Sarah's legs trembled as she followed Aunt Kawasie up the ladder, and across the housetop, littered with debris. She waited, tense, while her aunt bowed her chunky body to fit the key in the padlock. The plank door creaked open. Sarah's breath hissed softly between her teeth as she followed Aunt Kawasie in, Bessie and Frances and a few children behind them.

"Cold," Aunt Kawasie commented.

Sarah shrugged her coat closer and nodded. Both movements were automatic, for she felt no chill. She stood rooted on the threshold while her cousins pushed past her and the little ones went hopping and scurrying up and down the steps between upper room and lower room. She stood rooted and filled her eyes.

Seven years — eight years — of dust had driven in, sifted in. It lay thick on everything. The children's feet were patterning it. It rounded the corners. It coated the cobwebbed windows and let the light through only dimly. At one corner the roof had leaked. The adobe plaster had been eaten away and the wall on that side was beginning to crumble. "*Okiway!*" Aunt Kawasie lamented, sucking in the word on

98

an indrawn breath as she looked at the light that thrust its fingers between the stones.

Certainly almost everything had been taken away. A chest in the storeroom gaped open, with a few rags trailing out of it. The adobe walls were empty of the baskets and *kachinas* which Sarah remembered. There had never been much furniture. The tall pottery jar which had always held drinking water still sat in a corner. Sarah tiptoed across the room and peered into it. The skeleton of a mouse lay in the litter inside. Tuvenga's loom still hung from the roof poles at one end, dangled askew, with a blanket barely begun at the bottom. The grinding bin still stood below its peephole, the *manos* lying in dust instead of cornmeal.

It was not hard to see it exactly as it had been, with her father at the loom and her mother at the grinding stones. Sarah could picture Sequapa sitting back on her heels and brushing the hair from her eyes with the back of a floury hand while she smiled at Sarah.

Aunt Kawasie and her daughters had been talking and laughing together and the children racing through the empty rooms, the little girls clutching their shawls tight against the chill. Frances at length broke in on the silence of this strange cousin.

"Well, what do you think of it? Is it like you remembered it?" she asked, her eyes probing Sarah's closed face curiously. "Gee, but it's lonesome and quiet. You'd think you weren't in the village at all."

"It wouldn't take much to make it just like it always was," Sarah replied. "I will sweep it out and clean the windows and build a fire in the stove — And do you suppose the women would help me mend the roof and the wall?"

Thoughtfully, Aunt Kawasie sucked her teeth, "You could

have a work party," she said. "But the food costs more now, and you would have to buy everything. But it is true that it will all fall away quickly, once it has started."

"I must get work," Sarah said in a small voice. "With an education in the white schools maybe there would be something in the agent's office. I had typing and shorthand in high school. I want to keep my mother's house whole. I want to live in it."

Aunt Kawasie sucked her teeth more sibilantly, the sound significant. Frances and Bessie snickered.

"You can't live here, an unmarried girl," Aunt Kawasie said, uneasy question in her eyes.

"Maybe you don't remember how the Hopi young men are," Frances said.

"Or maybe she does," Bessie muttered.

Sarah thought she had remembered. But she had remembered with the mind of a child. She had not thought what it would be when she returned, twenty years old and in fine store clothes, and got a job working for Miss Dayton, the field nurse. She had not seen herself running the gauntlet of boys idling around the villages at the end of the day when she returned from work to Aunt Kawasie's house up on top. She had not felt their hard, knowing stares when she went into the trading post, had not remembered the words spoken mockingly, insinuatingly.

Sometimes she considered staying at Uncle Abraham's house, so that she need not endure the evening ordeal. His house was more convenient to the field nurse's, and Sarah could have made its location an excuse for leaving Aunt Kawasie. The outhouse swayed Sarah more strongly than the boys. She had almost forgotten the ledges at different quarters of the village, jocularly referred to as "the men's toilet," "the ladies' toilet." It was easier to manage the bathing. Miss Dayton, the nurse, was glad to let Sarah bathe daily in her porcelain tub. The Water Witch had put down an artesian well, so that the Hill-Where-We-Spread-Our-Rabbit-Skins, and the government buildings were never too short of water for a reasonable indulgence in cleanliness.

Since more money would be coming in, Sarah used her eight dollars to buy food for the work party which would repair her mother's house. The town crier called the news from the top of the tallest house in the village. "All you in your houses listen to this: Work party tomorrow! House of Sarah Tuvenga. All come and help mend the plaster and clean. Dinner at sun-high for everyone. Let us go and be happy."

Miss Dayton gave Sarah the day off, and she served coffee with plenty of sugar and canned milk; plenty of store bread; canned tomatoes, canned peaches, and canned corned beef hash, which the Indians loved.

At early twilight the place had emptied of its gay swarms. They left the wall whole again, the refuse swept away, the windows clean. Sarah locked the door and followed Aunt Kawasie and Frances home, Bessie's children cavorting around them. She knew now that it was impossible for her to live there alone, and marriage to any of the Hopi boys she had seen seemed as impossible, after her romance with Kirk.

Even though his love had been short-lived, it had always been, as she put it to herself, so polite and the memory of his gentleness remained with her. When she had come away from the town of Finch, she thought she had put Kirk also behind her, and for a while she was glad. Very soon the thought of him crept back and pervaded her.

She found herself thumping the electric iron furiously on Miss Dayton's ironing board as she whispered to herself, *It can't be. It can't be. He can't have forgotten me.* As she

101

used the vacuum cleaner she brought out Kirk's little petting phrases and names, as she had done when she swept Mrs. Ramsay's house, and the desolate tears stung her eyes.

When she had been on the mesa only a few days she wrote to him, as if her rusty pen were pushed by a compelling force, against her determination to cut herself off from everything outside Hopiland. She told him that she had come back to her own people. She told him that she had found her mother's house waiting for her, and had had it put in order. She told him that the snows had begun and that they made the desert pretty. She wrote and rewrote her final sentence, and was not satisfied with the version she finally sent: "I suppose you have changed and do not feel like you used to feel. About me. I am not one who changes easily."

She sent the letter to the university. On the day when it should have reached Kirk she went about shaken with a wild hope. Perhaps he had missed her increasingly as the weeks went by. Perhaps he had written to her at the Ramsays', and Aunt Carrie had burned the letters. Perhaps he had telephoned to the Ramsays', and Aunt Carrie had said she did not know where Sarah had gone. Perhaps — Perhaps.

No letter came. No mail at all came for Sarah, until at last there was a kind, anxious letter from Mr. Ramsay. Would Sarah please tell him if she was there? Was she all right? Was her Uncle Abraham still living, or that aunt of hers? Her Aunt Carrie was too badly hurt to speak of her at all, but her Uncle Guy did know that Aunt Carrie could be hard to understand.

The phrase was written on a fuzzy stretch that made the ink blur slightly, and Sarah could see Uncle Guy carefully scraping out with his penknife the words he had written first.

If Sarah ever needed anything, she was to let him know.

It might be quicker to write to him at the store, marking it personal. He enclosed a ten dollar bill, fresh and new.

Sarah settled into her work in Miss Dayton's house and in the clinic. It was good to have her days filled with routine, so that time did pass, though like a mechanical conveyor belt whose machinery needed oil, so that it creaked with painful slowness.

Once in a great while when she had free time, she went over to Uncle Abraham's and sat and listened to their new little radio, run erratically by a rotor like a two-bladed windmill atop their low stone house, and gossiped with Aunt Polehongsi and with her daughter and her sons' wives. The sons had been almost as casual in their relationships as Aunt Kawasie's Bessie, but they were all back in the little mission church now, and one of them had built a new stone house in the nearest sandy hollow. It was much easier to follow the ways of the church if one were living near the missionaries.

Miss Lundquist sometimes came to her door and invited Sarah to come in. Otherwise Sarah did not go. Now that she was a Hopi again, she wanted to be all Hopi, not identifying herself with anything *Bohanna,* even the *Bohanna* religion.

The Christians were themselves unacceptable to the tribe. Since the first American missionaries had come to the mesas, the group had grown with painful slowness. The work had begun about the turn of the century. Sarah had heard Aunt Kawasie tell of her earliest memories of it.

Kawasie said that the villages were not very different then. Only there were no cookstoves, and no oil lamps, and no glass for the windows. Some window openings had sheets of mica, to let in a murky light, and some were tiny and uncovered, like the peephole above Sarah's mother's grinding bin. After Washindon became aware of these *"Moquis"* on the distant desert, he had sent them stoves, lamps, glass, and also chairs and tables which were fine for firewood.

Aunt Kawasie said that the Mission Marys began to come soon after the window glass and stoves. They didn't have it much easier than the Hopis in those days, Kawasie said with relish. They not only did not know how to do the simplest things, but they did not even know how to talk. They had to learn, and it did not come to them naturally, as to a baby. At that time the Hopi language had not been written down, either, and the Mission Marys had to pry it out of the Hopis, a word at a time, and put it into writing themselves. Their mistakes were ludicrous, and gave both the Hostiles and the Friendlies fine cause for laughter, though the flavor of the laughter was different.

Many of the Hostiles had learned to hide their dislike for the sake of the rich gifts the Mission Marys had to offer. Boxes and barrels came across the desert to them from the world outside, and any ragged Hopi could go and ask for warm clothing and receive it; any new mother could come and carry home little nightgowns as soft as mouse fur and tiny shirts and hemmed squares of cloth which were supposed to be washed each time the baby used them.

And with all their laughter and sneering, most of the Hopis soon realized a thing about these Mission Marys. No child could approach their door with eyes inflamed and suppurating, that they would not stop to put in the red medicine. No old old blind man could come knocking, his trousers or shirt torn, that they would not find him a whole garment or get needle and thread and help him mend the one he was wearing. Some said that Washindon sent the Mission Marys, just as he sent the Water Witch and the agent, and that

104

they had to mind. However it was, the mesas had come to rely on them in all sorts of emergencies, most of all on Miss Lundquist, who had been the second to arrive and who had stayed for an ordinary lifetime.

For a long time the Hopi priests had told their people, as they began to do in the days of the Spanish friars, that the white religion would in the end sweep the Hopi religion from the face of the earth, but that the gods would fearfully punish any Hopi who did not resist that invincible onsweep. At that time, Aunt Kawasie said, they took it for granted that all the *Bohannas* had the same religion. Now that they had learned the truth of it, they were much more comfortable.

Sarah was not entirely at ease about it. She did take strength from Miss Dayton, however. Miss Dayton was an educated person, and capable. Her blond hair always looked as if she had just stepped out of a beauty parlor, her oval nails were always perfect and her fair skin as soft and bright as the desert would allow.

"Why can't they let the poor people alone about their souls?" Miss Dayton would inquire, shaking her shining head in bewilderment. "Give them sanitation, yes. Give them an education, yes. But let them keep their own worship."

Sarah fumbled with the question whether they could go on making prayer sticks and dressing like the *kachinas* after they were educated, but she could not put it clearly even to herself, and would not for anything have tried to say it to Miss Dayton.

Perhaps if they were educated and sanitary they would discard the things that had gradually gathered around their observances. Perhaps she herself could do that, she thought. Certainly God would see into her mind and know that she still believed in him. God had made her a Hopi, hadn't he? He'd understand, then, that a Hopi needed to be a part of the tribe, as a sheep needed to be part of the flock, and would die if separated from it. And she could even help her people more, if she were wholly one with them —

That oneness was more difficult than she had expected. The Hopis were pleasant enough to her. They did not shut her out of their observances. They were too polite. And she felt dimly that some of the trouble lay in herself, that she couldn't feel her oneness with them as she had done when she was in Finch.

Every morning she came hurrying down from the mesa, catching a ride if she could, or walking down the long trail, down the gigantic uneven staircase of stones that was a part of the foot trail. She walked past the eagle graveyard, where every year the captive birds were buried after they had been ceremonially smothered, so that their home-going spirits could carry good reports to the gods, and prayers from the Hopi. She walked past the inscription rock, now fallen from its place, where the Hopi had rudely incised the count of slain Apaches in the last great battle, when the Tewas had helped the Hopi vanquish their tormentors. She walked upon rocks that had felt the feet of her ancestors for five hundred years. And it all stayed outside her. She was still Sarah, and no more a part of Hopiland than she had been a part of Kansas.

One bright Sunday afternoon when she felt her life empty like a dried gourd, she went up alone to her mother's house. She worked only half a day on Sunday. Though it was January, the day was mild and glowing, almost like Indian summer. When Sarah walked across the ancient stone causeway there was no one about, and she stopped and turned silently to take in the whole sweep of the scene, the huddled villages held up in the sky, and the windswept, sun-drenched expanse of desert.

Walpi was really like the paintings of it which the Lorings had hung on their walls: cubes piled one, two, three high. Cubes that looked pale clear yellow in the sunshine, as if melting in amber. Shadows clear and cool like lilac blossoms. Slender poles of ladders cutting a different blue shadow across the dazzling brightness. The odors bothered her less now; less and less. She could see with her eyes alone and know that it was beautiful. She ached with longing for it. She must be patient. Perhaps in a few more months it would come into her and flood her instead of staying so bafflingly outside.

Days were still short, and she must go on to her mother's house. She went swiftly up the ladders to its roof, thankful that there was no one around to stop her for talk. She examined the adobe for any breaks, and peered into the chimneys, the large pottery jars with their bottoms broken out, to make sure that nothing had fallen into them. Then she climbed down the uppermost ladder and up the few adobe steps to her door; quickly, so that she should be unobserved. She closed the door behind her and was at home. This at least, was hers, she told herself insistently. It was really hers.

But it was cold. With the few bits of paper, brush and wood that she had piled in a corner of the storeroom, Sarah built a fire in the stove. She was not used to wood stoves, and the blaze went roaring up the pipe without much softening the chill. Sarah sat on the floor close beside it, her coat-collar turned up, and gave herself to her dream. She tried to be Nawamana, little daughter of Tuvenga and Sequapa, but Nawamana never used to be alone here, and so it was hard to make it come right. The outdoor sounds were muffled by the thickness of the walls and came dreamily to her ears. Perhaps in a minute she would get the old feeling —

Through those muted dream sounds her own ladder

107

creaked hesitantly. It would be Aunt Kawasie, probably, or Frances, or some of Bessie's children. She leaned sidewise to see and her heart sucked downward into her stomach. Across the housetop which was her dooryard, rising above the edge with the setting sun full upon and brightening its color and wave, a man's head. For one instant she thought that it was Kirk, and a joy so keen that it was unbearable broke forth in a cry.

At that welcome, the man on the ladder swung himself up and strode quickly across the roof, his smile cutting a white gash in his coppery face. He stepped inside while Sarah gazed unable to speak. He closed the door.

At that she scrambled to her feet and instinctively backed away. "I was just going," she stammered. "It will be dark. I have to go —"

Andy grinned down at her arrogantly, head high. "Don't say you aren't glad to see me come. I heard you cry to me when first you see me. On the ladder. I say to myself, Sarah will be lonesome. A pretty girl like that without no boy-friend."

He was looking at her as if she were a Hopi, but Sarah could find nothing but fear before that look. Her eyes darted past him to the door. His strong bulk blocked it off.

"Cold here," he said, looking around him curiously, and shrugging his sheepskin-lined coat closer.

"Too cold," Sarah agreed, her teeth chattering. "We mustn't stay here. We must —" She made a hopeless move to dart past him.

Andy, laughing lazily, barred the way. "You don' want to run away from Andy," he teased her, and clasped her small, icy hand in his. "You are really cold. You catch the pneumonia. See, I put my coat around you; around us both. Don't fight so, you little wildcat — I said, don't fight me."

Sarah's free hand shot up and clawed in silent desperation that took the indolent smile from the face so close to hers. He twisted the arm he held, so that her fighting body relaxed with the pain of it.

"I don't want to hurt you," he snarled.

It was early dark when he went away, opening the door a little and standing leaning negligently against the wall, looking out to be sure no one was around. Now that he was too late, Sarah could see through swollen eyes the *Kik-Mongwi* walking below them with the measured step of age.

Andy came back and stooped above her. "Now you are my secret wife," he said. "You will like me, too. But don't try no more tricks, biting and scratching."

"I hate you," Sarah muttered, her voice choked with sobs.

He laughed confidently, and she could do nothing but glare up at him like a beaten animal.

"Next time I bring wood and make it nice and warm for us. When you are here, light a little fire — like you did today — and I will see the smoke and come."

"I don't want ever to look at you again," she whispered furiously.

Andy said, "I will be watching for the smoke." Cat-footed he crossed the roof and was gone.

During the next days Sarah seemed to meet Andy at every turn in the trail. She set her face stonily ahead when he whistled at her out of a crowd of young men, went on as if she neither heard nor saw him when he lounged along possessively at her side. He came to the clinic to have a hurt dressed, holding out his open hand toward Miss Dayton.

"I pet a little cat and it bite me," he explained, insolent laughter in the glance he directed toward Sarah.

109

"Infected," Miss Dayton said shortly. "I suppose the same — cat — scratched your face."

It was soon after the encounter in the clinic that Sarah ceased seeing Andy waiting to waylay her; ceased hearing his piercing and insinuating whistle. For a while she was relieved.

It was January, and there was much snow. The little houses were warm and steamy, their smell of wool and mutton and people overpowering. Snow was soon churned to mud on the mesa and the mud tracked in on the floors.

It was the season when old men, if there were old men, sat comfortably cross-legged on the floor and told stories, since now the snakes and horned toads and lizards were not around to hear and to carry the news to the gods, who disapproved of idle tales. Aunt Kawasie's house had no old man, and it was a gloomy place. Frances was evidently pregnant, and while her mother said very little to her about it, she was cross. Her usual high cackle of laughter was silent. She banged things as she worked, and the pear shape of her face was accentuated by the sour droop of her lips. Frances was cross, too, and muttered under her breath, hugging the fire and doing nothing. Uncle Mattima withdrew into a somber silence, mouth straight and thin.

Before January was over, Sarah went silently to her mother's house in the latening dusk and built a fire in the small iron cookstove. She sat silent in the chill room, drawing into herself as her body drew into her coat, hardly listening for sounds outside, hardly noting the clink of bells on sheep pattering up from the plain.

The last red faded from the light-plastered adobe walls. Sarah stirred uneasily. He was in the village. She had seen him at a distance, his broad shoulders, his high-crowned Stetson. She went outside and scooped up snow which had remained in the shadow of an unused chimney pot, dabbled paper in it, crowded the paper in on the fire to make a denser smoke, waited again. It was late when she went home, walking heavily, her shoulders stooping.

Aunt Kawasie was clattering the evening's dishes in a dishpan on the stove. She stared hard at Sarah as the girl crept in. "You should not walk up alone after dark," she scolded. "You do not understand these boys. If you are not more careful you'll be finding yourself in a fix like hers — " She shot out scornful lips toward Frances.

Frances was studying Sarah with a glance that had momentarily lost its sulkiness. Sarah thought heavily that Frances would be glad.

Three nights she built her little fires in her mother's house. On the third night Andy came.

Sarah would always remember the austere beauty of the sky as it was that night. Pale violet banded the skyline as far as she could see, immeasurably cool and aloof, and above it an icy blue and a cold primrose. She was watching it from the window when Andy stood silhouetted against the ineffably pure color. He closed the door, and stood silent.

"I see your smoke," he said at length, in a voice strangely awkward.

The coldness of the sky ran in Sarah's veins. She leaned forward, fingering the hem of her coat, not to look at him, and her voice creaked, like a windlass bringing water painfully from a deep dark well. "I did not want to call you. But I have to."

Andy's breath hissed through his teeth. "What you mean?" There was something like fear in his bluster.

"I think you know what I mean," Sarah said thinly. "I told you I am not that kind of girl. Now what will you do?"

Andy stood still and gathered together, as if straining his

111

ears for some faint faraway sound. "How do I know it's me?" he asked with another feeble attempt at a bullying tone.

"I think you know," Sarah said coldly. "We marry now, and divorce as soon as it is born."

Andy did not speak, and Sarah lifted her head and questioned him in sudden fright. "You are not married already?"

Andy said, "Married? Me? No, I never been married yet."

"We needn't stay together at all. There's nothing I want less. But I won't be shamed like this."

To her astonishment, Andy dropped down on the floor and hid his face in his hands. "Honest, Sarah," he croaked, "I'd like to marry you. I sure wisht I could."

Sarah moistened dry lips. "But — but —"

"You're my clan aunt."

Her childhood memories crowded back upon Sarah and made the words bleakly explanatory. "Did you know it? When you —"

Andy shook his head. "My mother tell me. She hear me whistle to you. You ought to known it yourself," he said, with another attempt at bluster.

Sarah's mind was running in dizzy circles. His clan aunt — "You Bear clan?" she asked huskily.

"Yess."

"But when already a child is started — Is it worse to marry in the clan than to do that to me? And to the child?"

He shook his head groggily. "My folks, they never let me."

No. Marriage inside the clan was unthinkable; incest; one of the few unforgivable crimes.

"The missionary at Keams Canyon would marry us."

112

"The whole mesa would be mad with me. No, and you cannot prove nothing."

It was useless to argue. Sarah knew that it was useless. Andy might pretend that it was only the wrath of the people that he feared. In truth he feared the marriage itself, the incestuous marriage: feared death or blindness or madness from the avenging gods.

When Sarah went to the clinic next day she looked covertly in the medical dictionary Miss Dayton had. She could find nothing to help her.

That evening she asked Frances, as casually as she could, whether she had ever tried to rid herself of the child she was carrying.

Frances shrugged angrily. "What kind of fool do you take me for?" she snapped. "Of course I've tried." Her face changed. "You find out something good, there at the clinic?" she asked eagerly.

Sarah shook her head. "It wasn't — Andy?"

Frances twitched her shoulders impatiently. "Andy is the same clan. Didn't you know that?" she asked with sudden alertness.

Sarah turned the talk. "What have you tried?" she asked. "Maybe I look in Miss Dayton's books. For you."

"It's too late now, I guess."

"But I thought some of the old women had herbs —"

"Oh, yes. But they sure didn't work for me, no more than a cup of tea would."

Sarah tried the herbs. She was carefully careless in going down the giant staircase of the mesa trail, and fell heavily. The only result was skinned knees and angry purple bruises.

Miss Dayton was the first to suspect. Sarah clapped a

113

medical book shut one day when the nurse unexpectedly came into the room. "Increasing your education?" she asked.

Then she looked attentively at Sarah, stopped by the intensity of the girl's quiet. "Sarah. Is anything wrong?"

Sarah said nothing. She gazed sidewise, with an inturned look, pushing back the cuticle around her nails, one finger after another, mechanically.

"Oh, heavens and earth," Miss Dayton said under her breath, "if I didn't have enough grief without this."

Something in Sarah's face seemed to change her tone of annoyance. "Was it someone here? It must have been, of course. Oh, Sarah. Surely you were warned what to expect. It seems to be a regular custom. The boys — just one girl after another —"

Sarah's lips writhed out of control. "I was alone in my mother's house," she said jerkily. "He came in before I knew. I — didn't want it. I fought him, but — " She shook her head hopelessly, the tears creeping down her cheeks.

Miss Dayton's blue eyes searched the girl's face. "Well, then," she said at length, "there's one of two things, Sarah. Either you get him to marry you or you make charges against him. These Hopi boys think they're the lords of creation, and I must say the girls don't do anything to knock their ears down."

"I guess it's always been like that," Sarah said lifelessly. "They don't see anything very bad about it. But when you've got used to other ways — But he can't marry me."

"Already married?"

Sarah rounded her lips in their old, silent "No." "No. He is my clan nephew."

Miss Dayton's teeth showed in a sharp grimace. "No blood kin, though?"

114

Again the softly rounded negative.

"That clan business. It's tommyrot. Sarah, surely you know it's tommyrot."

Sarah went on edging back the cuticle from her lacquered nails. Tommyrot to the whites, but to the old Hopis, to any but the educated Hopis, solid as the mesas. It was hard to tell how many of the young Hopis really believed the clans important. The practical effect was the same as if they did, for the approval of the tribe remained powerful.

Miss Dayton's sigh was exasperated, but her voice was husky when she spoke. "You poor kid. I've got pretty hard-boiled since I've been here. So many things happening all the time. But, honest, Sarah, this makes me feel like the dickens."

Sarah raised hopeful eyes. "Aren't there ways?"

"Oh, but, Sarah! I couldn't be a party to anything like that. After all, I'm a representative of the government. And it's wrong."

"But when — when it was like an accident you couldn't help. Is that just the same?"

Miss Dayton shook her head. "That's hairsplitting, if you know what I mean. Besides, it's dangerous. To you, I mean."

"I wouldn't care how dangerous," Sarah whispered, her lips twitching out of control again.

"Nothing doing," Miss Dayton said with finality. "Not along that line, Sarah."

Sarah felt herself shriveling.

"When?" Miss Dayton asked after a moment.

"September, I think. Do you have to fire me?"

The nurse's laugh was short and harsh. "Like to see them make me. No. You work here as long as you are able. Then we'll take you to Keams Canyon." The government hospital

115

was at Keams Canyon. "But first, Sarah, let us go to the agent with this."

Sarah shook her head. What good? If she brought charges, wouldn't the agent make inquiries in Finch about her life there? She could hear the murmurs that would run through the Kansas town — Aunt Carrie — Helen and Irene — the Torreys —

Miss Dayton argued the case with vigor, with growing annoyance, but Sarah retreated into herself and remained impervious to all her reasoning.

It was a long, hard spring. Miss Dayton took the best care of Sarah that she could without exciting comment. Sarah's health was better. Her throat rounded out and her eyes grew more lustrous. The Hopi boys increased their whistles and their insinuating remarks when she appeared, but she passed them as if they were not there.

Miss Lundquist called to her from the mission porch as she sailed by a tormenting group one evening. "Come in and have a cup of tea and a spice cake with me," the missionary said, a chuckle running through her voice. "I'm just finishing supper. And it certainly does tickle me to see one girl give those fool boys their comeuppance. I had a letter from Finch the other day, Sarah."

The girl stopped short at the name, and then turned and went into the mission.

"I declare, Sarah, you walk as if you had a baby on your back," Miss Lundquist said, still chuckling. "Tired?"

Sarah did not smile. "A little bit tired."

"The letter was from Mr. Ramsay," Miss Lundquist went on, getting a cup and plate. Sarah dropped down on the edge of a chair. "He wanted to know if you were all right, Sarah. Said he hadn't heard from you."

Sarah's knees stopped shaking.

"I wrote back that you looked a hundred percent better than when you landed here last fall. Cream and sugar in your tea, Sarah? Only the cream's milk. I told him you were a grand girl — passed up those rowdy Hopi boys like a queen."

The spice cake stuck in Sarah's throat.

"All the same, Sarah, you're young. You ought to be thinking of getting married, don't you think?" Miss Lundquist stirred her tea with a vigorous spoon and popped a morsel of cake into the pink pucker of her mouth. When she had swallowed it, washing it down with a draft of tea, and Sarah continued to play silently with her food, the missionary went on.

"I know what you're thinking. But there are nice, progressive boys among the Hopis, just as there are among any other group. From what I read, the white boys aren't any great shakes themselves; not these days."

"The — boys — I knew at Finch were — were very polite," Sarah said protestingly.

Miss Lundquist's hazel eyes had left off contemplating Sarah and were evidently making a survey. "There's Bennie," she said. "I've seen Bennie watching you as if you were the Crown Jewels, Sarah. And Bennie's a nice boy. Oh, he's got his faults. Who hasn't? But if Bennie married a bright, educated girl like you — and a good girl —"

Sarah choked on a cake crumb, and the tea she swallowed made the spasm more acute. If only she could get away without looking at Miss Lundquist again. How would the Mission Mary feel when she found out? As if Sarah had lied to her, pretending to be what she was not?

She was so virginal, Miss Lundquist. With all the fatherless babies she had helped into the world, with all the name-

117

less sin she touched, she remained virginal. She was like an apple that had bloomed and fruited and ripened among its fellows, and now was withering a little but still unblemished.

As Sarah continued to choke, Miss Lundquist ran, laughing, to take her slopping cup, lift her arms, smite her on the back. "My, but a choking spell like that can get the best of you! Brings the tears, doesn't it?"

Sarah's brimming eyes overflowed.

Miss Lundquist stopped laughing, scrutinized the girl with shocked attention. "Oh, Sarah!" she whispered. "Oh, Sarah, no."

It was all to be told over again. Over and over again. Miss Lundquist believed her. Sarah was sure she believed her. She had seen her when she did not believe. "Mmmm," she had heard her say, on a strange, withdrawn note, her round hazel eyes sorrowfully puzzled, and watchful of the liar. Sarah had seen her foot tap the floor, her crooked hand tap the arm of her chair, unconsciously. But now Miss Lundquist took Sarah's incomplete, staccato story for truth, as Miss Dayton had done. Aunt Kawasie would not, nor Frances.

When Sarah had finished the tale, lengthened by long pauses when she blew her nose and caught back her sobs, Miss Lundquist smacked balled fist into palm, angrily.

"This clan business, Sarah. It's at the root of so much of the trouble here, the devilment. I'd tear it out, root, stock and barrel. All the old Hopi ways — you've got to get rid of them all, if you ever —"

Yes, Miss Lundquist didn't even want to speak of them; wouldn't even look at a *kachina* as he came up from Five Houses way toward the mesa.

The Mission Mary had stopped herself abruptly. "Now

118

won't you stay here with me, Sarah? I've got the spare room."

Sarah looked involuntarily through a half-open door. The spare room was almost sacred. Miss Lundquist's best old Navajo blankets lay on its floor, hung from its wall. Photographs jostled each other on the dresser: past missionaries, nephews and nieces, the Hopi girls who had gone on for further education. The bed wore Miss Lundquist's best rayon coverlet over plumped pillows, her best Pendleton blanket folded across the foot. The small bathroom lay between it and Miss Lundquist's room, with a furious little black coal stove to make hot water for tub and lavatory when needed.

Regretfully Sarah shook her head, rubbing at her eyes with a balled wet handkerchief. To stay here would make the reunion with her people impossible. "Thank you," she said, "but I guess it is better for me to stay with my aunt."

She wished she could find words to say it better. The white people's thanks flowed so freely, so sweetly. Even in her own ears her stark words sounded ungrateful, but she could do nothing about it.

With the spring came the incessant wind. It dried up the mud, and there was some comfort in that. It was tiring to accumulate more and more of the sticky clay wherever one went, until one was lifting a peck of it on each galosh. But that wind drove sand through any wall, it twitched coats and shawls, it twisted them in tight folds around laboring legs. It lifted the debris of the mesa and flung it about in bitter whirling eddies that stung eyes and nostrils with dried filth. Sarah struggled through it all like an automaton, head down. Even before the warmer weather forced her to go coatless everyone knew about her.

Frances said crossly, "My land, don't go moping around

like you're — like you're — Folks are all alike. It's only that some of them get caught and some of them don't. I suppose that old Uncle Abraham tries to tell you different. But if we was white girls, do you know what'd happen? We'd just go to the hospital and the hospital would sell the kid for us, and nobody'd ever be the wiser."

There was only one ray of light in Sarah's darkness. Her mishap might bring her closer to her people. She would not be superior to them any longer; and they liked babies.

Frances went to the hospital at Keams Canyon and came home with her child. He was a big boy baby, and Aunt Kawasie made a great fuss over him. Neighbors ran in and out, admiring him, and Miss Lundquist brought him a furry white kimono with pink bindings.

It was a busy time on the mesa, for the people were making ready for the Snake Dance. Now the men were furbishing up their dance costumes. The women sat on their heels before their grinding stones for additional long hours, making an extra supply of cornmeal. Or they sat before the *piki* griddles in the *piki* house or in the corner of their living rooms, spreading the gray film of corn batter over the hot black stone with swift small palms. Children stood around, as Sarah used to do, waiting for a tidbit crackling sweet and corn-flavored. The folded packets of blue tissue, of white and red tissue were piled high on one flat basket after another. A great quantity must be ready, if the ceremonial were to be carried out properly.

Miss Lundquist, bringing her present to Frances's baby, said, "You're all so dreadfully busy —" and her eyes, bright as sunny spring water, were clouded with an eternal wonder.

And Sarah thought, "Yes, it is true. Our women, our men,

too, are no more than through one ceremonial than they begin to get ready for another.

Even Washindon had given up the attempt to end the dances. They had never been successful in their prohibitions; but now that they had said, Go right ahead! the observances boiled over.

The old men went about their tasks with dignity, on their shoulders responsibility for the welfare of the tribe, for the coming of rain which should ensure a harvest. Only if they carried out every requirement with exactitude, could the rites which had preserved their small people from the bright mists of antiquity down to the dusty present continue to preserve them.

The old men carried also the burden of keeping in line the irreverent young. And the irreverent young were not too unwilling. The wild, gay sociability was worth a little trouble.

Sarah was too heavy and awkward to help with grinding, even if she had had time for it. She was still helping Miss Dayton, moving cumbrously and waiting for a lift up the mesa trail. The regular light work kept her muscles strong and ready, Miss Dayton said, and she could, besides, take the treatments that Miss Dayton had given her regularly, since the first blood tests had been made.

"But you can have a little holiday," Miss Dayton told her on an August day. "I find I must make a quick trip home. My mother. We'll close the clinic for a week, and the doctor and the field matron will have to make out without me. You can stay up on top and see the Snake Dance. It's a good six weeks before you're due, maybe two months, the way we've reckoned it."

So it came about that Sarah was all day immersed in the

feverish activity of the mesa. She welcomed the opportunity, like a person chilled and trying to warm herself at a wind-quickened fire.

She was watching some of the preliminary races not far from her own house, when she had her first premonition of immediacy. The color, the rhythm of racing feet, the dust, beat upon her dizzyingly, so that she drew a little away from the onlookers whom she knew, and found a place where she could hoist herself up on a low wall far enough away so that she need not talk. She laughed when there was anything very funny, and she fastened an expression of eager attention on her face, so that anyone glancing her way should see her enjoyment. The eager smile froze to a grimace. A pain that had been coming frequently and without result had gripped her mightily.

Sarah clutched her summer shawl tightly about her, as if the rose-printed cashmere could give her support, and sat with all her thoughts and feelings turned inward. She sat with fixed face, as if listening.

"Look, Sarah, you feelin' someway?" a woman asked her with casual kindliness.

Sarah came back with a start. The pain had let go. "No. I'm OK," she said. "I just remembered something."

She let herself down from the wall, cautiously, and began to make her way to her mother's house. It was closer than Aunt Kawasie's, and she was afraid of what would happen if another of those tearing pains should come before she reached shelter. One came, and she dropped down on a bench before a house and sat clenching her palms together under her shawl. At a little distance now, the shouting and the laughter eddied away and were almost lost.

After a timeless effort, she had toiled up the ladder,

crossed the housetop, unlocked the padlock with the key she always carried around her neck. She was panting. Her clothes clung wetly to her body, her hair to her forehead.

Between the pains she did what she could. She could not make things sterile, but generations of Hopi babies had been born without benefit of boiling water and aseptic gauze. She was sorry that she hadn't the silver nitrate for its eyes, but the minute anyone came in she would send for it.

She felt a certain pride. She was an Indian, and it was good to be an Indian. A white girl could not face this alone.

As afternoon shadows softened the light she began to understand that the task was too big for her, Indian though she was. If she could rest a while betweentimes, long enough to gain strength for the next onslaught. But each fresh attack found her unready. Inexorably they marched on, without pity, accomplishing nothing but exhaustion. It was an eternity before her door opened and Aunt Kawasie looked down at her, eyes round with alarm.

"*Okiway, okiway!*" Kawasie gasped. "Dolly told me you looked someway —"

Other people entered, then or hours later, their bodies, their faces, passing through each other's. A fire crackled and a kettle squealed. Hands laid hold of her. Voices told her how to move and what to do. Hands pressed and kneaded, agonizingly. Pain rent her so there was nothing of her left to hold in the scream that tore at her clenched teeth.

When she came out of her strange half-world, the room was dark and quiet. In the street below children shrieked and splashed.

"The — dance?" Sarah whispered, as her aunt bent above her.

"Over two days ago. And it brought rain."

"Two days? Oh, no!"

"Your soul went away," Aunt Kawasie explained. "We feared it would not come back."

"My — baby?"

Aunt Kawasie held up a small, tight, yelling bundle. "A girl. Good wind. Much hair. The ceremonial ashes will take off what is too much."

All the right Hopi ways had been followed, Aunt Kawasie said. The umbilical cord had been fastened among the ceiling poles as soon as it was severed, and the Mother Corn laid beside the child.

Sarah, drifting between slumber and waking, drowsily said, "The silver nitrate, of course."

"Of course." Aunt Kawasie's strong, comfortable nod dropped Sarah into immediate deep sleep. "Of course," Aunt Kawasie repeated. "First thing in the morning I send down for it."

Sarah wanted to stay in her mother's house, and it was decided that she should be allowed to stay. Aunt Kawasie would come and take care of her there. It was better so. The child should not, by Hopi tradition, see the sun during her first twenty days. Tradition had to be broken when the birth took place in a hospital, but now it need not be.

Aunt Kawasie made the House of Life on the walls, on each of four walls a line of cornmeal for each five days of the twenty. She set up a screen at the door to keep the sun from the child. Every five days there would be special bathings. Every five days Sarah would rub off the top line on each wall.

Before the fourth day was done Miss Lundquist had heard, and had brought the usual gift. It was more than the usual gift. It was two of the tiny wrappers like silken fur, white with white satin bindings. Miss Lundquist handled them tenderly. "My old rough fingers! We never had quite such pretty ones sent in, and right off I thought, Now Sarah is the one who will appreciate them."

Her bright, round eyes flinched slightly from the baby as she spoke. The child was bound on a board because no willow cradle had been woven for her, and the cloths with which Aunt Kawasie had swaddled her under the crisscross lacings were nothing more than cloths, faded to drab.

"She is a dear little thing," Miss Lundquist said. She hesitated. "Sarah, her eyes aren't sore? You did use the silver nitrate?"

Sarah nodded. "Yess. She cried like everything." She frowned anxiously at her daughter. "I think the ashes inflamed her lids a little."

Miss Lundquist touched the child with those gentle, crooked fingers of hers. "It was a shame you didn't have time to get to the hospital. I wish Miss Dayton had been with you, at least. Sarah, why not come down with me now to the mission? I'd like nothing better than to have a baby in the house again. I've got a new clothes basket," she went on, her face sparkling with eagerness, "and the women would help me fix it up pretty and dainty for her —"

Sarah held her voice steady with an effort. Dimly she sensed the generosity of the offer, with Miss Lundquist alone at the mission just now, and the program and the needs of the people already consuming all her hours. Nor did the invitation fail to tempt her. She could see the baby nestling down in the soft fragrant bassinet, in clothes like these silky wisps, and after a daily bath.

"I guess I must stay here in my own place," she said. "Miss Lundquist, do you think Kirkina would sound all right for her American name?"

125

"Kir — what was that again? Kirkina? We-ell. But anyway there wouldn't be another one like it on the mesa."

"I thought maybe Kirkina Melissa," Sarah said diffidently. Melissa was Miss Lundquist's name.

"Oh, mercy me!" the Mission Mary cried in pretended horror, clapping hands on knees and throwing back her head in a gurgle of laughter. "You might as well drown the poor little kitten and be done with it." Her soft, faintly wrinkled face flushed with pleasure, to her throat, to her forehead.

A few days after Miss Lundquist's visit, Miss Dayton's trim coupe clipped across the rock causeway as near as possible to Sarah's house. She came hurrying in the door, fanning herself with her handkerchief. It was hot, even there on the mesa, seven thousand feet above sea level.

"Just the minute my back was turned," she accused, half laughingly. Yet her fair face, with its careful accents of rouge, was troubled. "Oh, Sarah, couldn't you have got to the hospital?"

"I couldn't," Sarah defended herself. "I had no idea it could be yet. And then it came so hard I could only just get here —"

"Well, now I want to see how everything is. I'll want some boiling water, Kawasie — She's wonderfully big and strong for a seven-months' baby, Sarah. The little wuzzums, she *is* a baby — " Her voice trailed off in an absent-minded clucking and cooing, as she carried the child over to the window and stood gazing down into its face.

Sarah was leaning up on her elbow. "She is all right, isn't she, Miss Dayton? She is a fine, perfect baby?"

"Weighs about five pounds, I'd guess," Miss Dayton said briskly. "I can tell better when I get her off this board and heft her." Briskly still, she unlaced the bundle of baby and blankets, and lifted her out of her bed of fine-shredded cliff-rose bark, grimacing because she was soiled.

Sarah watched intently as the nurse turned over the petal hands, inspected the soles of the crumpled feet, peered at the eyes. "The ashes," Sarah explained, speaking like a Hopi, on an indrawn breath.

Miss Dayton turned in her lower lip and ran her tongue around it in a way peculiar to her when she was uncertain of anything, but her voice was casual when she said, "Of course you did get the silver nitrate drops into her eyes right away. You knew all about that, so I needn't ask."

Sarah made a little gesture toward her aunt. "Aunt Kawasie did. She tended to everything."

"We'll wash out her eyes with a good antiseptic solution," Miss Dayton said brightly, "and get rid of any infection from those dirty ashes —"

Sarah lay opening and closing her hands and trying to speak. "You don't think it could be — anything —?" she asked hoarsely.

"Don't let's borrow trouble," Miss Dayton advised. "There's nothing that couldn't be explained another way."

"But do you think she can — see?" Sarah asked tensely.

"Oh. See. At this age they don't really see anyway. At least, they don't coordinate. And especially not a premature infant."

She bathed the child, while Aunt Kawasie's plump arms, folded across her plump abdomen, unmistakably disapproved. She anointed the satiny brown body with sweet-smelling oil, rubbing the furry black hair into peaks and swirls that made Sarah catch her breath. "Gosh, she's got a mess of cowlicks," Miss Dayton observed. "Or else her hair's kind of curly." She dropped more dark medicine into the eyes, and the baby loosed a thin but vehement wail, and sneezed, and clenched her aimlessly waving pinky tan hands and feet.

"I brought her a present," Miss Dayton went on, still in her talk-making tone. She slipped a soft shirt over the oiled head, applied diapers, replaced the soiled and soaked bark with thick folds of diaper, laid the baby upon it and covered her with a fluffy blanket, all pink bears and ducks. Her chin doubled itself as she worked over the child, giving her whole profile a more substantial maturity under the excessively bright curled hair. "You lace her in," she concluded, laying the board down beside Sarah.

The baby was like pictures of the Holy Child, its arms by its sides, its swaddlings compact like a mummy case.

"What will you name her?" Miss Dayton asked.

"Her name — her American name — is Kirkina Melissa," Sarah said, eyes clinging to the child.

"Heavens! Where on earth did you get such a whopping big mouthful as that?"

"The Kirkina is for a white friend in Finch." Sarah had that explanation ready, so that it would come without telltale hesitancy. "The Melissa is after Miss Lundquist. I like it better than the Tabitha part. Her Hopi names will not be yet till two weeks."

When all the cornmeal lines forming the house of birth had been torn down, then came the great day, the naming, one of the big events of every Hopi's personal life, though he could never himself remember it. Early in the morning its activities began, with the mother roused in the gray dawn, bathed, and robed in her wedding finery, its white made snowier again with white clay. Then came the father's family, bearing in their hands gifts of food and in their minds names for the child. For although the child was of its moth-

128

er's clan, its name should stem from the father's, or from the namers: either source was allowed. When all the names had been given, the child must be carried to the housetop or the mesa edge by mother and grandmother, and there given to the rising sun. Since the sun would wait for no one, all must be done swiftly, in unerring order.

For the Naming Day of Kirkina Melissa there was no father's family. There was no wedding garment. When they asked Sarah for the father's name, she shook her head, retiring to herself with a quiet, unmovable obstinacy.

Aunt Kawasie sucked her teeth thoughtfully. "When the father's mother is dead," she said at length, "and the mother's mother, then the mother's aunt —"

So it was.

With the mesa somewhat relaxed after the feverish activity of the Snake Dance, the Naming Party was well attended. Sunrise came still so early, at the beginning of September, that Sarah was wakened in the small hours, to be prepared for the inexorable schedule.

Now her mother's house was ghostly, the sky still black through its windows, the lamps sending weird shadows to the pole and brush ceilings. Sarah thought, *Everything has happened here in my mother's house: everything.* She did not know whether the fact was comforting or desolating.

She thought, *How would it be if she were being christened in Finch, instead of being named here?* She pictured herself and Kirk standing at the altar of the Episcopal church while a young rector with a fine-drawn, burning face touched wetted fingers to the baby's head and said with grave gentleness, "I baptize thee Kirkina —"

And then the dream was swept away in the swift activity of the day. There were the endless ceremonial washings of the hair in yucca suds — the washing of the mother corn

129

that had lain on the adobe floor beside Sarah ever since the birth — the enumeration of the names: Flute Maiden, Yellow Flower Opening Out, Maiden Who Rides Behind the Men at the Rabbit Hunt and others. Finally there was the climbing of the ladder to the housetop where the child should first look upon the sun. Mona had been keeping watch there in the cool of dawn. Just as the first small fresh breeze of morning ran in at the door, reached a finger through the peephole above the grinding bin, she hurried in to tell them that the moment was come. Her long somber face was greedy as she looked at Sarah's child.

With Aunt Kawasie carrying the child and Sarah the ear of corn, they climbed the long ladder, Sarah moving in tremulous haste.

Below her on the mesa the sheep were milling about in their rock swallow nests. A rock wren was singing over and over its song, always the same, always fresh as dew. A cock in the village was answered by others in Polacca. Mesa, village and limitless plain stood in waiting solemnity. Sarah felt herself uplifted. This child — her heart ached with love for it. She would do anything in the world to make its way good. She would die for it.

She and Aunt Kawasie reached the edge of the housetop just before the first sharp rim of the sun cut the skyline. Quickly they went through the prayers, through the prescribed movements with the sacred cornmeal. Quickly each placed meal on the small mouth puckered hopefully for sucking. Quickly, while the tentative tongue reached for it, they blew it away toward the east. The sun stood round on the earth's edge when Sarah prayed her final prayer for the little one's long life. Prompted in an undertone by Aunt Kawasie, who checked them off on pudgy fingers, she called out to the sun the long list of names her daughter had been given, so that he should recognize her, whichever name might be used. It was done.

Sarah looked tenderly into the child's face, hoping that Nuvensi Nawamana Kirkina, might be smiling. She was so good, Sarah thought with a swelling heart. She had not once cried or squirmed when Aunt Kawasie uncovered her face. No, she did not smile. Neither did she whimper at the dazzle of the blazing ball. Placidly she seemed to gaze straight into its incandescence.

Aunt Kawasie also looked closer at the baby. *"Okiway!"* she whispered. "Oh, the poor little one."

Sarah's house was redolent with freshly cooked delicacies, corn marbles and corn pudding and stew. The heavy fragrance sickened Sarah as she stepped down into it from the cool calm freshness. She dropped down on the floor and hid her heavy sickness of soul and body by changing the baby's diapers and binding her again on her board. She put over her head the little twig canopy she had made, and threw a clean towel across it. The flies were beginning to stir, and they made a sufficient excuse. Sarah could not bear to have the people looking at her child, staring at its eyes. All these days she herself had been arguing about them, denying them. There on the housetop all her arguments had been stilled.

Aunt Kawasie spoke in a compassionate undertone. "Sit and rest, my daughter. When you have had a dozen babies, you will take what comes. Look at that Frances, now," she added, as if she had not been referring to eyes at all. "She is as good as new. And twice as much of her as there used to be."

For the present Sarah continued to live alone with her daughter, locking her door as soon as darkness fell, if none of her relations were with her. Until she had had a few more treatments she could not go back to working at the clinic. Before that time came, the eye specialist returned from his vacation and Miss Dayton took her over to Keams Canyon and had him examine the baby.

Sarah sat on one of the benches in the entrance, waiting. There was much to see. Dimly she could remember how grand and important it used to be in her child eyes. It had shrubbery outside, and grass, scraggly and dusty, but wonderful in a grassless world. Inside, nurses slipped along the corridors, their uniforms like white porcelain. Some of them were Indian, and some of the Hopi girl orderlies Sarah knew.

Navajoes came in, the women in their long, full skirts walking high-headed and queenly, the men soft-footed, easily arrogant. Little girls were copies of their mothers, in voluminous skirts and velvet shirts, their scanty hair screwed into a knot and tied with sacred cord.

A Navajo man hitched along the floor, sitting. Crippled with arthritis, he even tended his cornfield so, Sarah's Hopi neighbor told her. Comfortable, square Hopis came, bringing children who needed the new and wonderful sulfa drugs for their trachoma. Maybe it was only trachoma, Sarah thought with stubborn hopefulness. Navajo babies came, riding in wooden cradles on their mother's backs, babies still undernourished because the past winter had been a hard one and there had been little but coffee to keep them alive, together with morsels of meat chewed for them by anxious elders. These babies were all eyes, great indignant eyes. Dark bright clear eyes.

Usually Sarah could have entertained herself here for hours, watching the busy and varied life. Today its hundred sounds and movements beat feverishly upon her brain, while her mind kept struggling away from them to the room where they had taken her baby. Perhaps it was nothing very wrong. Perhaps it was because the child was premature and her vision slow in developing. Perhaps she had congenital cataract. Cataract could usually be rectified by surgery. Sarah had been poring over the pages about eyes in Miss Dayton's books.

But when an orderly came and summoned Sarah to the office, all the stubborn hopes dropped away.

Miss Dayton was holding the baby, who was crying, comforting her against her shoulder. Miss Dayton's face held its aquiline, double-chinned look of somber maturity. The doctor was making notes on a card.

Without looking at Sarah, he said, "According to our records, you were to come to the hospital for this birth? Why didn't you?"

Sarah had entered the office as her mother might have done, with the flat step and drooping shoulders of the burden-bearer. Standing with hanging head before the desk, she said, "There was not time."

Her intonation, with less than the usual spacing of words and hissing of s's, lifted the doctor's gaze to her face. "Sit down, sit down," he said, impatiently compassionate. "Is she undernourished?" he asked Miss Dayton. "Any TB?"

Miss Dayton said, "No TB, Doctor. She's taken it harder than most. The unfortunate circumstances, I mean. I told you her story, Doctor Danovitz."

The doctor cast an uneasy pitying glance at Sarah. Above the starched white smock his swarthy face was impassive, but his eyes were vulnerable. Beyond him, in a mirror, Sarah could see her own face, with shadows like bruises beneath the eyes.

"Take it easy, sister," the doctor advised. "If you couldn't

133

help it, you couldn't help it. Period. Only it's a rotten deal for you and this kid of yours — what is her name?"

"Melissa," Sarah whispered. "Doctor Danovitz, do you mean that — that my baby — ?" She could not speak the word.

The doctor thumped a paper weight down hard on his desk. "We will make more tests later, but — "

"An operation?" she pleaded.

He shook his head. "If the infection had not yet reached the cornea. But it had. Don't feel too bad. We can put her in a school where they will teach her. She won't ever know what she has lost."

Sarah still stood in that pose of complete submissiveness. She did not even clench her hands. They hung at her sides, small and brown and helpless.

The doctor busily piled up letters. "Maybe you'd like to leave her here at the hospital," he said. "Under all the circumstances, we could look after her and put her in school as soon as she was old enough. It might be better all around."

"No," said Sarah, the monosyllable almost silent as it had used to be. "No. But thank you."

"We will try treatments," the doctor added soberly. "I have given Miss Dayton instructions.

7

Sarah lived on quietly with Missy in her mother's house. She had saved enough money to get along for a while without working, and Miss Dayton said that she should wait until she was stronger.

Sometimes she went down to the Mission Mary's house and made little wrappers and diapers on the sewing machine, feeling moderately comfortable when Miss Lundquist was there alone. When other women came in, Sarah gathered up the baby and hurried away. Cheerful high voices and the scraping and stamping of feet at the entrance always gave warning of their approach. More rain had followed the Snake Dance, as it usually did. Scarcely had the captive eagles been buried when heavy downpours began. The skies which for a while had been empty of everything but wind now poured out endless gray floods. The arroyos ran brimful, swirling, churning, fetid. Every shortest walk was a plowing through mud.

So the scraping and scuffing of muddy shoes gave Sarah time to flee with her baby. She felt herself withering under the glances, the spitefully triumphant glances, even the kindly, sympathetic ones. She found her own four walls a needed shelter.

On the many fair days she took Missy outside her own door, spread a blanket on the swept adobe, let the child lie in the sun, Sarah beside her, inexpertly weaving a cradle.

Together she and Aunt Kawasie had gathered the necessary materials, the right kind of bent juniper for the frame and lemonberry and willow for the weaving. Aunt Kawasie started the basketry and Sarah finished it, working high on the housetop at her mother's door, with the plains limitless around and below her, dappled by purple cloud shadows. The cradle was imperfect, not quite symmetrical, earnestly though Sarah tried for perfection. Yet it had beauty. It was like a great basketwork sandal, its sole curving up to make a central band that met the arch of the bow. Sarah tore up a red dress to make the lacings, which zigzagged across the front, over the swaddled baby.

"It is pretty," she told the child, when first she laced her in. "It is pretty. And so are you, Missy."

Missy. After the day in Dr. Danovitz's office Sarah never again called her daughter Kirkina. She was always Missy.

The girl in the house below caught her soundlessly weeping. The girl came up the ladder with her own baby's large black eyes, lustrous like ripe chokecherries, staring solemnly over her shawled shoulder. After one glance at Sarah's wet face, she said, "Sarah, can't you come down to my place for a while? I've got bread in the stove and I got to watch so's it don't burn."

Rubbing away her tears with a covert sleeve, Sarah bent over Missy, picked up the cradle, followed Maude down the ladder. She did not want to go, but she could think of no good excuse. She liked Maude, who was used to white ways and did not think Sarah queer. Maude had gone all the way through one of the government's off-reservation boarding schools. She had stayed at school and worked through most of her summers, so that she had been away from the mesa almost as long as Sarah had. When she married, her mother let her wall up one end of the maternal house and make a

136

tiny apartment of her own, there on the level of the mesa's rock street.

Now she opened the half door which kept out wandering animals, and led the way in. "You haven't been in my cupboard before," she said. Her tone was half apologetic, half proud, as she looked around its boxlike smallness.

While Sarah dropped down on a low stool Maude spread a blanket on the floor, slid her baby around from her back with a sinuous shrug, and deposited him on the clean expanse. He looked out of place, sitting there placidly in immaculate blue rompers, knitted sacque and store shoes. The walls were Hopi walls and hung with Hopi handicraft. The ceiling was the Hopi ceiling, with prayer feathers hanging from the poles and brush and drifting languidly in the breeze. An iron bedstead almost filled the remaining space, though a small wooden table had been crowded up against one wall. The metal grinder clamped on the table and the smell of *Bohanna* bread were the only signs of modern America in the room. Except the baby, so fat and scrubbed.

"You have just done your floor," Sarah commented, hunting a topic of conversation. The clay was still dark, and palm marks showed on it. "Your place is so clean. And that cute cradle, up out of the way."

"It's got to be out of the way. There isn't no room to turn around here." Maude had squatted to open the oven, and now she paused to look up at the cradle, hung by cords from the roof poles. It had been made ingeniously from a wooden box. Both girls looked at it thoughtfully, Sarah wondering whether Missy would enjoy a bed like that. At the same time she imagined the cords breaking or Missy freeing herself, and the mother's whole body leaped in protest, her eyes squeezing shut as if the imagined crash were real.

Maude opened the oven door and slid out the fragrant

loaves, dimpled with fork pricks and beginning to brown. "Not quite done," she said, sliding them back. "Conrad, he made the cradle," she said wistfully. Sarah had seen Conrad, Maude's husband. He was a small, agile youth with a self-confident swagger of the shoulders and a jaunty way of tying his neck scarf inside the open collar of his shirt.

Maude sat back on her heels, looking up at the hanging cradle. "It's sure hard to get use' to things all over again," she said abruptly. "Why did you come back here, kid?"

"Well, why did you?" Sarah countered.

Maude screwed around and played absently with her baby's toes, huddling protectively an inch back from the tips of his tan kid shoes. "I guess I thought most anything would be better than the kind of places I'd of had to live in town. Nasty cheap places. Nastier because one family after another had lived in them, and they were all beat up and filthy. I can stand our own dirt better than that kind," she said, laughing half-heartedly. When Sarah made no comment, Maude went on, "When I married Conrad I thought, well, there isn't no reason why we can't live nice, even up here on top. I'd miss the running water and the electricity and gas, but what the heck."

"You really do keep everything clean and neat," Sarah murmured politely.

"Like to lay myself out, just keeping it clean," Maude said with a sniff, "and what's it get you? Your folks think you're stuck up."

Sarah made a protesting noise in her throat and leaned close to suckle Missy, whose cradle lay across her knees.

Maude's expression was divided between laughter for her baby and dissatisfaction with the world. "That's what makes you get my goat, Sarah. I mean, you got no cause to act ashamed. Gosh, you only got to look around you once —"

Sarah's head drooped lower above the cradle.

Maude clicked an impatient tongue. "What's the matter with you, anyway? You weren't in love with her daddy, were you?"

Sarah shook her head. "I hated him," she said in a strangled voice.

"Well, then, what the heck? Honest, Sarah, I don't know but our folks got more sense about such things."

"How do you mean?"

"Well, they say, live natural. Have a good time. Be nice to people. Don't get mad at nobody." Maude tossed back her glossy curled hair angrily. "A fat lot of good it done me to be so particular." She spatted the baby without reason, as if she were seeing Conrad in him, but when he puckered up his face in astonishment she seized him and hugged him close. When all was quiet again, Maude returned to her starting point. "What I really was getting at, Sarah, you got no call to hang your head."

Sarah smiled stiffly. "I'm all mixed up," she admitted.

Sarah had argued the same point, during long, lonesome nights, with Missy's cradle pulled up close beside her sheepskin on the floor. The Hopi way did seem reasonaable. True, there were too many Hopi babies with syphilis and gonorrhea, but she knew that there was plenty of syphilis in the white cities, too, in spite of their pulling such long faces over sex. And the Christians, in their houses down around the mission, fought an endless long battle with the lusts of the flesh. Again and again they came before the deacons and confessed, the difficult tears wrung from them as they accepted discipline. And all but a few of the Christians wept with them. Chastity was a strange thing; maybe an alien thing; yet it was like a jewel for which they fought. The non-Christian Hopis laughed, Gargantuan laughter, and played out the episodes of sin, confession, discipline, at the next ceremonial, in broad but recognizable burlesque.

Sarah sometimes thought about it, during those long nights. If the Mission Marys could only be a little reasonable — Christianity was certainly a good thing. Sarah had always liked the cleanness that seemed to go with it, the children's noses cleaner, and their fingernails. Though to be sure even the pagan noses were cleaner than they had been eight years ago. And Sarah preferred the Christian God to Masau'u, the Bloody-Headed.

But here again she drew back from the ideas of the Mission Marys, who called Masau'u the Devil and the Hopi Devil-Worshipers. Masau'u might have some malicious qualities, but fundamentally he was merely the god of the Underworld, Sarah knew. And when Miss Lundquist turned indignantly away from even the sight of a *kachina* mask, she dealt a wound, since the *kachinas* were precious to the Hopis. It was confusing. She could be certain of only one thing: tying herself up with the mission would cut her off from the Hopi as a whole. She told herself that a great and magnanimous God would not hold it against her if she seemed to go along with her own people; especially since he had not concerned himself enough to keep her and Melissa from misfortune. And she felt the stain of that misfortune less when she was with the pagans.

Uncle Abraham and Aunt Polehongsi had come to her as soon as they heard of Missy's birth, bringing fresh stew for Sarah and for Missy a little silver bracelet with a turquoise. They had come again when they heard of Missy's blindness, and Uncle Abraham's face had worked with violent emotion while he held the cradle board across his knees and clucked at Missy. Sarah had never felt so close to him as she did then. With all his small stature, Uncle Abraham was a

140

man of dignity. Only the deepest feeling could have done away with that quiet poise. Sarah had looked away from him as one who intrudes, but not before she had seen his eyes widen angrily against his own tears, and his mouth, trying to smile, writhe into the contortions of weeping.

Sarah could not refuse when Uncle Abraham invited Sarah and Missy out to his desert ranch for corn harvest. And she found it piercingly sweet in its reminder of corn harvests long past, when the world was good.

So many women were busy with the food, there in the small stone ranch house, that Sarah wandered outside with Missy's cradle clasped in her arms. She stood watching the big sunset; stood watching one of Uncle Abraham's boys drive home the flock.

Here the desert had no bounds, and the small house crouching low beneath the flamboyant sky appeared to be the only human abode in the measureless expanse. Doubtless hogans were hidden behind every gentle rise of ground, but Uncle Abraham's house seemed completely alone.

Behind it stood the stockade, like a Navajo corral, of saplings set on end in an irregular circle. And coming up from behind a knoll, as if pouring out of the sunset, was the flock. They spilled over the edge, a mass of white and black, and flowed down the gentle slope. Behind them their shepherd was for a moment silhouetted, a black twig against the gigantic splendor of sky. That sky was savage flame and red and purple, and from it like smoke billowed clouds of saffron lighted with fire and edged with molten metal. More consciously than ever before, Sarah gazed at the spectacle. She, Missy's mother, had eyes to see it.

The flock came swiftly; they were coming home. The late lambs, which had been kept in the corral, set up a shrill blatting at sight or sound of them, and their mothers ran heav-

141

ily, bleating an answer. A youth ran out from the ranch house to help Uncle Abraham's boy Mark, and Sarah guessed that he had been waiting for an excuse to come out where she was. He was the Bennie whom Miss Lundquist had held out to her as a proper husband.

He did not look at Sarah. His eyes were completely focused on the flock and the corral. As soon as the first animals reached it, he pulled open with a flourish the rude gate of wires and poles and helped Mark let the animals in, one at a time. Mark counted them, as he always did, to make sure none had been seized by sly coyotes, or had wandered during the long day of grazing. The dog, a woolly mongrel, leaped from side to side, barking and nipping at careless heels when the sheep massed or scattered.

Stephen, one of the youngest of Uncle Abraham's sons, sauntered from behind the house to help sort the mothers and children. Already the waiting lambs and kids were bunting the firstcomers with frantic little heads, nuzzling for their delayed dinners. Some of the ewes were stubborn, and slow to own their lawful progeny, and Sarah's young cousin bestrode one of them and then another, holding them still until their nurselings could get a firm grip.

Sarah, the cradle balanced on her hip, laughed with enjoyment of the sight, and came closer, step by step, till she could get a clear view between the crooked posts of the corral. The lambs dropped devotionally on their knees and stretched up blunt noses to suckle. The spaniel-eared kids waved their brief tails faster and faster in their exuberant satisfaction. They looked like windshield wipers upside down, Sarah thought.

Bennie lifted a shoulder to reach into a pocket of his tight Levis and pull out something which he held through the openings for the sheep. They came crowding to seize it, and he opened his hands as if to show them that he had no more, and then turned to smile at Sarah, whom he had shown no sign of seeing before.

"What was that you were feeding them?" she asked, his shyness putting her at ease.

"I no know. Not exackly. I find it always on the junipers. It grows there, like flowers made out of straw. They eat it as if it was candy, the sheep."

You could see that he liked the creatures. Stephen came up to him as he talked with Sarah, thrusting a tousled, sunfaded head under the older boy's arm, which automatically admitted it. Sarah had seen him carrying Uncle Abraham's grandchildren on his shoulders. Sarah ostentatiously cooed at Missy, tickled her under her soft brown chin until her toothless mouth twitched sidewise in a vague, delicious smile. Sarah darted a glance at Bennie. He was not looking at Missy.

Sarah turned and went back into the ranch house without another word.

She was still pointedly ignoring Bennie when she had put Missy to sleep and sat down to supper. Nevertheless, he dropped down beside her when she seated herself at the table. Without looking at him Sarah knew that he had turned a deep red, and she was unwilling to increase his embarrassment by making an excuse to move, as was her first angry impulse.

The table was spread on the floor, a long oilcloth set out with Hopi bowls and baskets of food and with enamelware pans and coffeepot. When they were all seated, Uncle Abraham came in, his copper-colored face a mass of curved-up lines of pleasure, bearing in both hands the latest addition to the meal. He had pulled fresh onions and washed them at the windmill tank. He laid them along the edge of the oilcloth, bouquets of fresh, wet white and green. Sarah had lifted one of hers to bite into its succulence when Uncle Abraham's words arrested her: "Our Father, we thank thee for food and for life," he said. "We thank thee for the gift of thyself. Amen."

Sarah glanced sidewise under her thick lashes at Bennie, to see if he had noticed that she was not used to blessing before meals. She felt uneasy, because everyone here was of the Christian group. She felt uneasy and resentful of Bennie, because both Uncle Abraham and Miss Lundquist had tried before to get them together, with invitations which Sarah had evaded.

She slid another glance at him. He had a face that trembled between laughter and frowns. His head was well-shaped, except that it was flat in the back, and it was set on the typical short neck of the Hopi. The flat head was all right. The Hopis said that it indicated a well loved child, who had been kept long on the cradle. They were sure that the cradle built straight backs, and that the binding of the hands not only kept a child from scratching its face, but cultivated placidity and control by their enforced stillness. Sarah thought he might not have turned Christian if his father and mother had lived. The whole family was strongly pagan.

Well, Uncle Abraham and the Mission Mary would have their trouble for their pains. There was nothing about this quick-moving youth that appealed to Sarah. His face, square at the jaw, was very dark, and he was hardly taller than Sarah herself. She thought he was probably a year or two younger, also.

In spite of Bennie's nearness, the evening grew pleasant. The food was good: the luscious mutton stew of which she never tired and the crisply crackling blue *piki,* which looked like hornets' nest paper and tasted like fresh corn flakes, but with a sweeter flavor. There was blue pudding, too, baked long in an underground oven, in a kettle lined with corn husks to deepen the taste. It looked, she thought, exactly like the blue-gray modeling clay they had used in the schools at Finch. She had taken a hungry bite of that clay when she was twelve. Basket trays were heaped with bread-that-bubbles-up, large puffy cakes fried crisp. Other *potas* were piled with fresh corn, sweet and milky. The coffee was not so delicious as the other foods, and Sarah diluted hers with much milk. It was canned milk, and always the same kind, with a flower on its label. It was the brand the Hopi had first learned to use, and they insisted on it, as the Navajos did. Only the milk with the flower was right for their babies, they said.

The assemblage ate slowly, with typical decorum. Without putting the idea into words, Sarah thought that only a Hopi could dip his *piki* roll into the common dish of stew and bring it, richly laden, to his mouth without unseemliness. Outside, half the great sky still blazed with color, which shone through the small windows and stained the white walls pink. When the flames cooled and went out, Aunt Polehongsi lighted lamps and set them on the floor at each end of the oilcloth, so that the shadows of the people stretched up and bent over, to lose themselves on the ceiling amid the poles and brush. It was dark and the stars were piercing bright, sharp as steel points, when the meal was finished and the women had washed the few dishes and put things to rights.

Sarah slept on the housetop with Uncle Abraham's daughters, Missy close beside her. She chose the place farthest from

145

the ladder, thinking of Bennie, wrapped in his blanket somewhere below, but there was no sign of him till the next morning.

It had been years since Sarah had slept on a housetop, with nothing between her and the sky. After her cousins had stopped chattering, she lay long awake, gazing up at the dazzling sweep of the Milky Way across the starry blue deep. Once later Missy woke and cried, and Sarah raised up and suckled her, and then mechanically tilted the cradle up and down with a muffled thud to send her off to sleep again.

It was new moon, and the stars remained brilliant. The aroma of sage and other desert herbage was keen in the cool air. There were no sounds at all except the restless stirring of horses in a shelter nearby, and the hoot of an owl, and the wild laughter of coyotes on a distant knoll.

Sarah told herself that this was what she had wanted most, what she had needed. She lay down again, the cradle hard against her body, and the blankets drawn more closely around them both.

She shivered in the chill of the September night and was all at once desperately alone.

But morning was good and gay. When the men opened the baking pit near the ranch house, it sent up a great breath of corn-fragrant steam. Laughing and joking, the family and friends pulled back the hot moist husks from the ears and ate. Aunt Polehongsi had besides plenty of coffee, and fat prairie dogs roasted whole and tasting like young pork. Bennie was always near Sarah, and always offering her the choicest bits he could find. He joked a great deal.

"You must eat good," he would say, ceremoniously passing her the *pota* of *piki*. "We wouldn't want you getting so thin that you have to stand twice in the same spot to make a

146

shadow." Or, poking out his chin to indicate a stretch of smooth sand near the housewall, "Have this nice soft seat on the sofa, why don't you?" Or, bringing her a joint of prairie dog, delicately brown and so tender that the flesh dropped from the bone, "You like some fried chicken, maybe so?" He had been longer at school than some, and was more familiar with sofas and fried chicken; but his humor was typically Indian.

Sarah thought of him when she had returned to her mother's house. Kirk's English had been perfect. Bennie's ungrammatical speech lifted tingling nerves all over Sarah's body. And Kirk had not joked. Even his nickname for Sarah, Poky, had been copied from someone else, and there was no laughter in his treatment of her. Bennie joked with everyone but most with her, Sarah, though with an anxious air, as if under the fun lay a stratum of worry because she was so thin and so silent.

Sarah thought of all these things during her nights alone with Missy in her mother's house. It took her a long time to get to sleep, and she was often wakened. She would hold her breath, wondering what had roused her, sure that her door had been stealthily shaken, or that soft feet had paused at her door. Sometimes she had found that it was only cats, racing and yowling on the housetop, and then she could go to sleep comfortably. She did not try to embrace the Hopi beliefs about cats, though Aunt Kawasie had little doubt that a cat on her housetop was one of her neighbors in the Witch Clan, seeking to work her a harm.

It was not according to sound Hopi custom, either, to let the thoughts dwell on the dead. Yet Sarah often sat in her house and deliberately peopled it with her father and her mother, and with memories of those days when everything was whole and good and steeped in sunshine. It was not Hopi

147

to stay much alone, but Sarah often shut her door and locked it from the inside and did not answer even when people climbed the ladder and stood calling. She liked them better when she did not have to be constantly with them, she found.

But she had another reason for shutting herself away. She was trying her hand at pottery. First Mesa was the only one of the three to make pottery, the others concentrating on basketry. Sarah's mother had been a good potter, and the child had watched her work. Aunt Kawasie was as skillful, and now Sarah watched her. But there was a great deal to the craft. The right clay must be gathered and purified and tempered before ever the modeling was begun. Thus far Sarah had only experimented, ashamed of her stumbling fingers, of her lopsided pots, of the regularity with which they broke when she fired them. She fired them in her fireplace, making a kiln of dried dung stealthily gathered, and separating and supporting her feeble jars with old tin cans. Aunt Kawasie discovered her secret when she was crushing a batch of spoiled pots to add to her next clay. Sarah would have better luck, she reminded her, if she sang to her pottery as she worked with it. A pot was a made being, she must remember, and every made being had its own soul, which was much more likely to sit quiet and docile if it were kept happy. Otherwise, it felt imprisoned and broke itself to get loose. Aunt Kawasie spoke argumentatively, her eyes sparkling angrily at Sarah, as if she expected mockery from this mingling of sophistication and ignorance who was her niece.

Sarah assented politely; but she could not sing to her handiwork. It made her feel silly, she told herself. And gradually she succeeded in bringing a few pots out of every batch to a good birth, though perfection was still a long way off. One afternoon she sat with the cradle across her knees, raising one leg and then the other to joggle it lightly. Even this was a thing that required a knack, a technique, more than riding a bicycle, she thought. She surveyed her latest pottery with a feeling of partial satisfaction as she sat there, looking forward with mixed hope and reluctance to the next step, the painting. Her eyes went on around the floors and walls of her house. She must soon replaster and whitewash, for the feast of Powanmnu. Perhaps she could find some of the rose-red clay. She smiled at the memory of it: in her childhood the older girls had mixed that clay with tallow and used it for rouge. And her mother had used it to tint the powdered white gypsum, so that the rooms were always as if sunset or sunrise were shining pink through the windows.

But first the mending and the plastering. Through the storeroom door she could see a bit of crumbled plaster. Her eyes passed over it and then returned. It was a hole, and yet no light shone through it. Why not light, when there was a hole? A little longer Sarah sat puckering her brows over the riddle. She peered down at Missy. The baby's lashes made a charcoal black crescent across her cheeks, and Sarah loved to look at her so, when no one would guess about the hidden eyes. Missy's breathing puffed her soft lips rhythmically. Sarah slid the cradle from her knees, cautiously, not to waken her, and ran to inspect the crumbled plaster.

It was a hole through into darkness. Sarah enlarged it and laid her face close, flinching from the bite of the masonry. Gradually the darkness grew gray, a gray laced with threads of light. Sarah was looking into a small, dark closet of a room. It lay between the storeroom and the end of the living room, walled up and unknown.

All that she could see of it was empty. Still, those few frail skeins of light near its top left the lower part of a well of blackness which might hold anything. A long time Sarah stood there, searching with eye and mind. Finally she stepped back from the wall, rubbing her face where the rough stone had bitten into the skin. She leaned out backward to study the contours of the outer rooms. Incredible that she could have lived out her childhood there without even guessing at this hidden chamber. It extended back from the broad low steps between the living rooms, beneath the higher of the two. The loss of that vacant space, maybe eight feet by five, was not noticeable. Besides, Hopi houses were irregularly built. Here a room was added, and there a crumbling, disused part was walled away. Doubtless that was all this was, an unneeded and dilapidated space which her father and mother had never happened to mention to Sarah.

She stood back beside the *piki* fireplace and surveyed the storeroom wall. Was it only a shadow that drew a faint vertical on it, head-high? Or had an old door been plastered over there? She rummaged in a heap of oddments for a stout oak boomerang, and began to push ineffectively at the hole she had first observed. And when Missy summoned her with an imperative howl, she had accomplished nothing.

The first time she could go down from the mesa she borrowed a spike and a hammer from the Water Witch's shop, with a vague explanation that explained nothing. She returned eagerly to attack the puzzle with these more effective tools, and soon succeeded in enlarging the hole. Once a large stone had been pried and pushed out, to thud to the floor inside the secret room, it was easier to push other stones after it. And when the constricted space became visible, Sarah stood staring in astonishment. Though the room held little, it was not a mere emptiness. It contained a great storage jar and other objects so deep in dust and sand that Sarah could not make them out. The sand had half buried them. Cobwebs lay thick across them, with dust deep on the webs.

There might be things here that were old enough to be valuable to the whites. Not long ago Sarah had heard of a hidden room being brought to light, rich with treasures, *ollas* and *potas*, boomerangs and *kachinas* and weaving tools, bows and arrows.

Eagerly she set to work attacking the stones until she could wriggle through the aperture she had made.

Her feet sank deep and soundless in sand and dust as she went over to the group of mysterious objects. First the tall jar. Its mouth was sealed with clay, but the seal broke under her fingers. She stared down into the shelled corn which filled the jar brimful. She took up a handful, her flesh creeping with awe. The kernels were small and stony-hard, but they still retained their variegated color. She had heard the old ones tell of the early law: a part of every good harvest was to be sealed away against a year of famine. Even jars of water, made tight with pitch, had been thus stored away.

Probably these other objects were household equipment likewise. She pushed at the sand and dust, scooped it away with both hands, lifted out a figure perhaps a foot in height. Blowing off the residue of dust, she sat back on her heels and contemplated it. It was the figure of an animal, crudely wrought from stone as black as her *piki* griddle. Mr. Loring had told her that the stone fetishes of her people had usually been eroded by sand and water to a semblance of human or animal form, often pointed up by additional chipping and graving, surreptitiously done. This figure had turquoise eyes and nostrils marked with cannel coal or jet. Sarah knew that her people valued such things because the gods had made them.

For some time Missy, in one of the living rooms, had been making soft, tentative mewings, expecting the usual quick response: hands unlacing her from her cradle and making her dry and comfortable; or a soft fountain pressed to her groping mouth. Unanswered, the whimpering settled to a wail and worked itself up to a roar before Sarah set down the stone figurine and crawled back out of the dim past.

Before handling Missy, Sarah washed her hands carefully with soap, and went to the door to shake off the dust from her clothing. Self-consciously, she prayed a little prayer to the Hopi gods, as she did so, asking them not to hurt the child if she, Sarah, had done wrong in handling the old, precious things. She finished with a prayer in Jesus' name, uneasy at the thought of omitting it. As for the washing, she recalled reading in one of the Ramsays' magazines that archaeologists, excavating in old Indian ruins, had had to wear masks, to keep out of their lungs the ancient dust. As she thought of those archaeologists, Sarah coughed, and was stabbed with fresh fear.

Her anxiety did not prevent her from continuing the investigation. She nursed Missy and dried her and threw a cloth over her cradle bow, not only because of the few large blue flies that buzzed and clung, but to guard against the dust that might sift out from the hidden chamber. Then she went back, eagerly, to her search. Again she murmured an awkward prayer as she pressed in: "Masau'u, make my way good and pleasing," and again added, "in Jesus' name, Amen," as she dropped on her knees beside the treasures.

There were masses of fiber, apparently wrappings, within which Sarah's slim fingers probed delicately. Potsherds were embedded there, like an orange peel opening outward, as if a jar had broken away from its contents. More probing revealed a few objects: a grotesque mask, its bright colors hardly dimmed; another stone fetish, headdresses of twigs, parts of them still holding together. Sarah set them all out in a row. She looked at them for a long time before she crawled back, shook herself free of dust, washed herself, and went once more to Missy, who was indignantly accusing her.

During the next few days Sarah stayed much by herself, wondering what it was best for her to do about this discovery. Gradually vague memories had emerged from limbo and linked themselves with the worship paraphernalia she had found. Her mother's house had been a clan house. Long ago some of its treasures had disappeared, never to be recovered. That was all she could remember.

The Hopi would consider the find an important one, a piece of good fortune that would benefit the whole clan, even the whole tribe. Her good luck ought to bring her more fully into the life of the community, give her the sense of belonging that she craved.

It was not a matter to be hurried. Should she tell Aunt Kawasie? Aunt Kawasie had no connection with this clan house. Should she tell Uncle Abraham? He was hereditary priest, but he had discarded all his rights when he became a Christian. Should she tell Miss Dayton? She left that question unresolved. Certainly she could not tell Miss Lundquist. The Mission Mary would deny these old precious objects any value. All such gear of worship she called "the accursed thing," and read prophetic denunciations of it from the Bible.

Another reason Sarah did not venture abroad was that an early snowstorm swept the mesa on a sharp, raw wind. She did not want to expose Missy to the unaccustomed chill. She flinched from it herself, shivering and coughing, for it was not Missy who fell sick, but Sarah. On the third day

Missy's crying dragged Sarah out of a heavy sleep into a strange cloudiness of fever shot through with pain when she drew her difficult breath.

She suckled Missy, wondering hazily whether her milk would infect the child with her cold. She crept about dizzily, making up the dead fire and drying the baby. She pulled herself to the opening she had made and drove pegs into the wall, swaying and sickened by the effort. She hung her coat over the hole and collapsed again on her hole pallet.

She did not know when it was that some of Aunt Kawasie's and Bessie's children came to see the baby. She dragged herself to the door and unlocked it, and told them to go for their mother, or for the nurse.

After that she sank back again, so deep that even Missy's crying could not pull her up. For a while she simmered softly in a fever that was sweet and only gently warm. Then it grew prickly with pain and fearful with leering masks, and matted with fibers that stuck to her fingers like cobwebs and caught in her throat and tangled the air in her lungs. One of the masks was a likeness of Aunt Carrie.

People began to do a dance through the feverish dreams: Aunt Kawasie and Bessie, Miss Lundquist, Uncle Abraham and Aunt Polehongsi, Miss Dayton. Miss Dayton jabbed her arm with a hypodermic and after a while the mists cleared at intervals. It was influenza, Miss Dayton said, and right at the edge of pneumonia, but with the new wonder drugs she might escape more serious illness. Sarah was wondering how the miracle drugs, being so modern, could have power over such ancient germs as hers, but then her thoughts, clearing, brought her feebly to her elbows and she looked for Missy.

Miss Lundquist had taken Missy home with her, Miss Dayton said, pushing her gently back and drawing the cov-

154

ers up to her chin. So Missy was safe. If only the cobwebs and the fetishes would have let her alone, Sarah could have been content to sleep. Sometimes, in minutes of clarity, she would believe she had only dreamed the hidden room. Then, from her pallet, she would see her coat hanging where it had not hung before, and she knew it was no dream. She wondered whether she had cried out about the discovery in her delirium. Was that why Aunt Kawasie and Uncle Abraham both looked at her so strangely?

Neither of them mentioned the matter, and the coat still hung where Sarah had placed it. Days passed, and nights, and Sarah's fever diminished to nothing, and she began to eat the foods that were brought her. Miss Dayton took off the pneumonia jacket. She had used it as an extra precaution. "There's been no flu like this on the mesa," she said. "Anyway not since nineteen-eighteen. Where you could have picked it up is a mystery to me."

Aunt Kawasie tightened her lips knowingly, and flashed a glance at Uncle Abraham. Sarah thought that both her uncle and her aunt had been there a great deal since she was sick. They both stayed today, after Miss Dayton had departed. Kawasie sat on the floor, her bulk, as usual, supported by the wool-stuffed sack under one hip, her teeth and pudgy fingers busy with strips of yucca which she was plaiting into a flat utility basket. Her eyes rested often, consideringly, on Sarah's face. Uncle Abraham paced restlessly back and forth, across the higher room, down the broad shallow steps, across the lower room, pausing before the grinding bin to stoop and look out through the peephole, retracing his steps. He never went into the storage room, nor looked toward it.

At last Sarah could keep silence no longer. "Did I — talk?" she asked in a frail, husky voice. "When I was delirious?"

Uncle Abraham was midway of the steps, his back toward them. He stood still. Aunt Kawasie sighed through her teeth, not letting go the yucca until she had stripped it to the right width.

"*Owi*," she said, as soon as her mouth was free. "You speak much. You say 'Aunt Carrie.' You say 'Kirt.' You say, 'No, no!' and fight the air."

"And was that all I said?" Sarah whispered.

Kawasie twisted her short neck to look over her shoulder toward the storeroom. She shot out her chin in the direction of Sarah's coat. "No," Kawasie whispered in return, "you say, 'The lion dog!' You say, 'The cobwebs!'" Aunt Kawasie waited, her eyes intent.

"And you saw?" Sarah addressed the question to Uncle Abraham's back as well as Aunt Kawasie's watchful face.

"*Owi.* When I take down your coat to spread it over you because you are shaking with cold."

"You went in?"

Aunt Kawasie thrust out a deprecating lip at her own bulk. Then she indicated the slight Abraham, who had turned and was approaching them. "He went in."

Uncle Abraham dropped down on the floor, cross-legged, beside Sarah's pallet. His kind face was grave. "Do you know what they are?" he asked her, tossing his head toward the coat.

"Worship things of the clan, of the priesthood? Things that had been lost since my mother's grandmother?" she faltered.

"*Owi*," Abraham agreed.

"How do you think —"

"I do not think. We can never know. How the door of that chamber came to be walled up —"

156

"And the things?" Sarah's hands shaped themselves as if holding the fibrous bundles which had so plagued her delirium.

"Medicine bundles of a priest, I think. Perhaps with hollow reeds inside, holding corn and water and other matters sacred to the Hopi."

"Yes, daughter, sacred, sacred!" hissed Aunt Kawasie, her hands spread stiff upon her thighs, her eyes wide and awed. "In the keeping of your clan from the beginning."

"The priest must have kept them in a sealed jar." Even Abraham spoke softly, as if his lips touched the untouchable. "The other things, worship objects used when altars were set up for ceremonials of the clan."

"In the keeping of your clan from the beginning —" Sarah dimly considered the stories of that Beginning, when her people had climbed from the Underworld and made their way painfully to the mesa country. Here, where white men would have starved among the dry rocks, the burning sands, the Hopi had lived and multiplied.

"What am I to do with them?" Sarah said.

"They are in your house," Uncle Abraham said haltingly. "But on the other hand — my daughter, you would perhaps have forgotten that I was the hereditary priest —"

Aunt Kawasie's eyes were quick to stab at him, as if she had been waiting for his words. "You were the priest," she snarled, "until you sold yourself to the mission. I suppose you would likewise sell these precious things. To the *Bohannas'* museums. But I have told John," she broke off triumphantly. "I have told the *Kik-Mongwi*. He is coming as soon as Sarah is well enough."

"That is well," Uncle Abraham said mildly, after a momentary silence. "John will do right."

157

John, the *Kik-Mongwi,* came a day or two later. He opened the door a crack and called, and then slipped in on quiet moccasins. He sat down on the low plank stool, elbows on knees, hands hanging relaxed. He talked and laughed a little with Sarah, who was sitting up against the wall, and asked her about Missy. Miss Lundquist still had Missy. The baby was doing well on a formula given the Mission Mary by Miss Dayton. Sarah said it wistfully. A bottle was now Missy's fountain of life and joy.

John was showing his years. His hair, bound at the brow with a red silk scarf and clubbed in his neck, was gray. Still erect, his body was stiff and dry like a withered plant, instead of slim and pliant. His hands began to show the veins, and his face was wrinkling deeply. But his eyes still looked keenly from under their folded lids, his mouth still sat patient within the enclosing lines that had become slashes. Looking at him, Sarah lost herself in thought, as she had done much since her return to the mesas: thought not moving clearly but groping for things out of reach. *John walks a path marked out for him by the centuries. He walks not alone, but with thousands who have gone before and hundreds who are with him now. He is sad, but he is whole, and he has direction.*

At length, out of a musing silence, John asked, "You sent for me, my daughter?"

Sarah said, "My aunt — and Abraham — should they be here also, do you think?"

"Perhaps you should tie a handkerchief over your nose and mouth," Sarah suggested diffidently. "The dust. I think it was the dust that made my sickness."

As John, with stiff fingers, knotted a bandanna like a mask, Sarah was gesturing toward the aperture, still covered by her coat. The coat looked strange there, with its pale fleecy wool and its lustrous fur collar.

John studied the fur as he removed his moccasins. "What animal, do you think?" he asked with his unwearying interest in everything he saw.

"They call the fur kolinsky," Sarah said doubtfully.

John shook his head. "Ko — ko — I do not know that animal."

He was a long while in the little chamber, and silent. At length he returned, leaning against the wall to put on his moccasins, and came and squatted near Sarah. His face was gravely happy.

"*Lolama,* beautiful," he said. "It is good when the old precious things come back to us from behind the years. It is good for our people." He was quiet awhile, staring at the floor. "I think it is not only beautiful for my people, but for the whole world."

The words carried Sarah back to the day in her childhood when her father took her to the *Kik-Mongwi's* house. John had recently visited the Canyon de Chelly for the first time, and had seen a waterfall made by the torrential rain. It had cascaded over the high wall of the canyon like a great veil covering the white cliff house, and a rainbow had arched across waterfall and ruined dwelling. With this same deep tranquillity John had said that it was a good omen, a good omen for the whole world. The child Sarah had accepted his words readily, since to her the Hopi tribe was bigger than the rest of the world. Now she thought what an insignificant handful they were, not more than four thousand, and maybe less, in all the four villages. John was good; but he was not practical; he was a dreamer.

"Uncle Abraham says they belong to him."

159

John's expression did not change. He tapped horny nail with horny nail, still contemplating the floor.

The tranquil silence had been disturbed by padding feet, by a door's opening and closing, by a wheezing breath. Aunt Kawasie had entered, and she stood there with straight back, round stomach out and large, portentous face reared back. "Did I hear you say Uncle Abraham?" she demanded irately. "Uncle Abraham! What right has he to the things of the Hopi religion when he has gone over to the *Bohanna* God? What would he do with them? Sell them to one of the museum men who is forever coming here?"

Without moving, John lifted his eyes. "Hakami, my sister?" he saluted her politely. "No, Abraham would not sell the valuable things, I think. Have you forgotten his anger against those men who sold the masks and the medicine bundles of the clan that had died out? Have you forgotten what he said of those others who sold things from the graves of our people?"

Sarah stirred inquiringly. "I did not hear that."

John moved his bright old eyes to Sarah's face and let them remain so, but his vision seemed to pass through and beyond her. "It was a long time ago," he said. "Some of our number went to a big fair at the city Chicago. They were paid money to live there in a piece of pueblo built to look like a real pueblo. Just to live there, weaving, making pottery and baskets, making hard goods. So that the whites could see how proper people lived." He spoke detachedly, but with a mild amusement. "One of the men went to a museum. He wanted to see one of those places, since *Bohannas* have so long been coming here to buy things for them, old Hopi things. And coming to ask questions." John's smile wrinkles deepened slightly. "We have given them a thousand answers, and all different."

Aunt Kawasie had let her round body down on the adobe near the two, and was moving her tongue over her teeth and listening with some impatience.

"Well. This man found in the museum a blanket which he had last seen when it was wrapped around his uncle and carried off to the burial place. The uncle was still in it, there in the glass showcase. And he found old articles of our worship. So he went to the boss of the museum and inquired. And he learned the names of some of our men who had sold these things. He found even what these men were paid.

"It is too long a story to tell now, but the news leaked out after that one returned."

"And my Uncle Abraham?"

John's face widened in a silent laugh. "Your Uncle Abraham is not an angry man, but now he was angry. True, the uncle in the blanket was Abraham's own father. But it was not this that made him angriest. It was about the old valuable things of our worship. I remember what he said. He said, He, even he who now followed the Christian way, would never sell for money the things that were sacred to his people. Those were his words, and I remember them still. 'I, even I,' he said, 'who now follow the Christian way, would cut off my right hand before I would sell for money the things which were sacred to my people.'"

Again John sat silent, eyes still fixed and staring through and beyond Sarah, so that she felt more than ever that she was something that did not really exist.

Kawasie snorted, and John returned to the present and regarded her mildly. "This you must say for Abraham. Although he did great wrong in leaving the religion of the Hopi, and the more because he was hereditary priest, still he always tells the truth." He sighed, and his eyes went covetously toward the ragged stones of the aperture. "I

161

think we have no right to keep the old precious things from Abraham. They are his."

Aunt Kawasie grumbled and muttered. She heaved herself up on her short legs and went rocking around the room, picking things up and laying them down, doing unnecessary tasks. John sat unmoved by her protesting bustle. At length he, too, rose to depart.

"I will send word to your Uncle Abraham," he told Sarah.

Uncle Abraham came to Sarah's house by night, so that fewer should see him take away the old valuable things. The news of Sarah's find had made its way through the villages, stirring them to a restless excitement. The mood of some had grown ugly. So, with great care, Uncle Abraham wrapped the things in a blanket, that he might carry them down inconspicuously on his back, as his people had carried burdens for centuries.

While he worked in the hidden chamber, Sarah sat thoughtfully silent. Aunt Kawasie, who could not keep away that night, plaited another utility basket, jerking the strips with angry vigor. She looked up at Abraham hotly when he emerged from the secret room, shoulders bowed under his load, hands grasping the earlike ends of the blanket.

"What will you do with them?" Sarah asked breathlessly.

Uncle Abraham stood silent. He, too, was growing older, Sarah thought, and this affair was hard on him. It bowed his spirit as it bowed his back. "I don't know. I got to ask God," he said simply, speaking in English.

Aunt Kawasie sniffed scornfully. "I suppose you do like that Johnson," she burst forth. "I suppose you burn them and break them till there is nothing left. I suppose you preach a sermon at all the Hopis who come. I suppose you tell us all how much better you are than the rest of us."

She turned to Sarah, who was gaping from one to the other. "I guess you never heard about Johnson," she said, her tone deprecating Sarah's ignorance. "Maybe you were too young. Maybe it was when you were with the *Bohannas*. I forget. Johnson, over at Oraibi, he, too, found old lost valuable things of his clan. And he made a bonfire and burned them for all to see. Calling us devil worshipers."

Sarah listened, lips parted. She knew Oraibi a little. The missionaries there were of a different church from Miss Lundquist, and even more afraid of the devil than she. Sarah thought they were as much afraid of the devil as the Hopis of witches and the Navajos of *chindeh*.

"Would you — burn them?" she asked Uncle Abraham, waving her hand toward the things he carried.

He shifted his burden wearily and looked out into the darkness. "I don't know. Not yet. This is a hard thing," he said, and went out.

Aunt Kawasie muttered to Sarah that it would be only right if someone were to go after the old fool and take the precious things away from him. There was no knowing what he would do. So namby-pamby he seemed, sticking to Pole-hongsi as if there was not another woman in the nine villages, even now, when Polehongsi was old and grown into a mountain of flesh. Why, the man was so chicken-hearted that he would not even crop the ears of the burros who trespassed in his cornfields. Yet stubborn. Abraham was as stubborn as a mule.

The "burning of the idols," as Miss Lundquist called it, was not much publicized, yet a crowd gathered to watch the event. Word had gone on circulating, during the time when Abraham was talking with his God. The Tribal Council had waited on him, arguing that he should give over

163

his inheritance to the tribe. Some of the Council were young men who had seemed to hold their religion lightly, or only as a social system, until it was thus threatened by a Christian. They even muttered against John, the *Kik-Mongwi* because he had surrendered the treasure to Abraham. Several of Uncle Abraham's small windows were shattered by hurled stones. His sheep were loosed from the corral.

Someone sent word to a museum man who came often to the mesas, and just as Uncle Abraham set out the old valuable things beside his bonfire, the museum man drove up. His car wore a plume of steam and his breath came as hard as if he had been running.

"Stop, man!" he panted, dashing up and laying a hand on Abraham's arm. "For God's sake, stop! These things are worth money to you and your family." The light of the bonfire picked out the objects on the sandy ground at their feet, objects respectfully spread on a handwoven blanket. The museum man's face worked as he looked at them. "For God's sake —" he repeated.

Beside the big museum man Uncle Abraham looked very small, but he spoke quietly. "Yess, mister. For God's sake I destroy the accursed thing."

Swiftly the museum man revised his approach. "For your church, then." He waved toward the little meeting-house, for Abraham had chosen a place in sight of the mission buildings. Not on the Hill-Where-We-Spread-Our-Rabbit-Skins, because the government people had asked him not to. They thought it best for the agency to remain neutral in this destruction. "A fine new baptismal font," the museum man offered, "for your holy water."

Abraham smiled faintly, the flickering of the fire deepening the shadows of his amusement. "You got the wrong

164

brand on us, mister," he said. "We got no holy water: just a holy God."

Miss Dayton, standing beside Sarah, tittered uncontrollably. "All the same, Abraham's got a screw loose," she said under her breath. "I don't blame the professor for being wild over this."

Even in the dim light the man's face could be seen growing deeply crimson. His chest pumped and his mop of gray-blond hair quivered. He breathed noisily through his nostrils. "Man," he managed at length to say, "this is an outrage. It's depriving the world of knowledge, and for no sane reason." He gave up, peering about him. "Isn't there anyone here who has authority?" he demanded.

Sarah looked, too. Miss Dayton was the only government worker in sight.

"Two of our policemen," Abraham offered, pointing at them with lips and chin.

The Hopi policeman stood resting his weight self-consciously on one foot, the Tewa with arms folded high on his chest. Both surveyed the flames steadfastly. Other Hopi milled about through light and shadow, some merely curious, others dour. The firelight picked out the lustrous, uncomprehending eyes of children. Off to one side, solemn-faced, the church people were gathered. All the Second Mesa deacons had come, and a few Christians had ridden over from Oraibi.

Uncle Abraham cleared his throat and his voice came thin. "I like it if now we all join singing Holy, Holy, Holy. Please sing it in the Hopi words."

After a moment's hesitation, when none of the Hopis started the hymn, Miss Lundquist began, nervously beating time with her crooked hand, faintly seen in the shadows. She pitched the hymn too high, and it struggled along feebly, while the non-Christians listened in a thickening silence.

When it was finished, Abraham once more cleared his throat and spoke. His thin voice gathered volume.

"Fellow Hopi," he said in English. "A thing has come to me that is a duty. I don't look for it. I don't like it. But I ask God to tell me. He don't tell me plain, but yet he lay it on my heart.

"You remember long time ago when Fred Johnson find the old lost things of his clan. For the worship of false spirits they been used, so what else could Fred Johnson do but sacrifice them?" After a brief pause, Abraham put the words into Hopi, for those who had not understood the English.

The crowd shifted and murmured, and the museum man folded his arms like the Tewa policeman's, as if trying to get a grip on himself.

"Oh, gosh, why do they have to be fanatic about it?" Miss Dayton mourned. "Understand, I like your uncle, Sarah. But I wish he wasn't so narrow."

Miss Lundquist's round gray head was nodding solemnly, the light flashing from her spectacle lenses. Her hands, tightly clasped before her, moved up and down as if keeping time to Abraham's words.

"I will not preach no long sermon," Uncle Abraham said.

Someone in the crowd clapped, and a group of young men hooted.

"But I remember what Fred Johnson say, long time ago." Abraham stood still and straight, and Sarah thought that Fred Johnson's famous act had marked a path for her uncle, one which he could not evade.

"Fred Johnson talk of the Hopi religion," Abraham went on, raising his voice to be heard above an angry, remembering babble. "You know how it was. In them old days we don't know nothing better. We reach out for something to send the rain so that our corn grow and our children live. We can't see nothing but the big sky and the big earth and the wind and the sun and all like that. So we pray to them and we dance to them, because that was the best thing we know.

"Fred Johnson, he say our religion was like a horse that carry us in them days. Because all men been made to have religion, and they die without none. But by and by priests come and tell about a Father God, bigger than the sky. And by and by the Mission Marys come. They tell about his son, Jesus. We learn to follow the Jesus road, and it is a religion that carries us better than the old one. That old religion dies when we hear the better one."

Abraham drew a deep breath. "It is a dead horse, and it been dead so long it stinks. A dead horse can't carry us nowhere. If we stick to it, we are carrying it. And the stink of it."

There was a renewal of the angry muttering, when Abraham put his words into Hopi. A stone whizzed past Abraham's head. Miss Lundquist cried out into the shadows from which the missile came, "Shame on you! Shame!" The Hopi and Tewa policemen came to life and loped around the edges, gently hustling a few of the glowering listeners.

Unconsciously Abraham laid a hand along his cheek, which the stone had grazed. "Some of our old people," he went on, his voice gentle to tenderness, "they do not know that the horse is dead. For them perhaps it is not." Miss Lundquist moved uneasily. "But you younger ones, you who are so careful that the right feather and the right color be used in the ceremonies, you who drink and gamble and do other such things — is the horse still alive for you? Or do you carry a dead horse because so many folks would be mad if you didn't?"

The museum man could no longer restrain himself. "Come, come, man," he interrupted, his heavier *Bohanna* voice easily drowning Abraham's light old one. "It is only ignorance that shuts its eyes to the good in other religions. Why, in the United States alone, with its one hundred twenty million people — one hundred twenty million — there are hundreds of different religions."

Abraham listened and Abraham answered. "Yes, sir, you are an educated man and I am ignorant, like you say. But this I know. When you get past a religion, when you find a better one, then the old one is dead, and it stinks. And all this —" he pointed to the collection on the blanket before him — "all this is part of the dead religion."

Without more words, he struck a match. It seemed to Sarah rather ludicrous that he struck it on the seat of his blue jeans. Stiffly he leaned over and touched the wavering flame to the fibrous masses of the medicine bundle. Native unspun cotton, Sarah had learned the coverings were, yards and yards of the stuff. Swiftly, in the breath-held stillness, he lighted another match at the spurting blue flame, and touched it to the tinder-dry headdresses, the chalky color of the mask. He had come now to the black stone lion dog and other figurines, and the people waited, craning their necks, to see what he would do with them.

The museum man grasped his arm. "These, at least," he urged in a strangled voice. "You can't burn these. Isn't that a sign that your God will be satisfied with the priceless treasures you have already sacrificed to him?"

Abraham shook his head. "These I must bury in a secret place, so deep that they can't hurt nobody no more."

As the crowd slowly dissipated, some hoping for more excitement, Miss Dayton brushed her hands together and sighed. "Well, that's that. A piece of outrageous pigheadedness. I'd hate to be in Abraham's shoes. Everyone will be down on him after this performance."

"Yes, it's bad for Abraham, and just before Powanmnu, the way it is," Sarah agreed.

She was not thinking much about her uncle. It was a mild December night, and she was going to take Missy home. Miss Dayton had offered to drive them up, with the bottles and the formula which Miss Lundquist had made up that evening for the next day. At the moment the return of Missy obscured all other considerations for Sarah.

Even though she could no longer nurse the child, it was a quivering delight to cradle her in her arms, to feel the soft, trusting warm weight of her, to sniff her clean, milky fragrance. Missy was at the stage when she primped her toothless mouth delicately, cooing and murmuring to the face she could not see.

But when Miss Dayton had chugged away in her car, and Sarah was alone with the child in her own house, her thoughts returned to the events of the evening. She could not come to any clear judgment of the actors in the drama. It seemed a little silly to her, to destroy these objects. What harm could they have done behind glass in a museum?

More important to Sarah were the angry glances that had flicked her, herself. Those glances had touched John, the *Kik-Mongwi*. The Hopi had lost some of their reverence for age. They were saying that John was getting soft; that it was time for a young, new chief. As for Sarah, hadn't she found these things in her own house? Then why had she not given them into the care of the Tribal Council? Or to the present heads of the clan?

Perhaps, Sarah thought wearily, the finding of the treasure had been bad luck rather than good. Perhaps it would further hinder her in her search for oneness with her people.

Next morning Aunt Kawasie was short with her, although she could not allow herself really angry thoughts, since she, herself, was a keeper of fetishes.

"It would have been better if you had let the things stay where they were," she grumbled. "Then, anyway, Missy might have had them, or your son when you get one." She stood with hands on hips, looking down at Sarah and her grinding, and her impulse to instruction got the better of her wrath. "Take the *mano* like this in your hands," she said, illustrating, "and work more with your arms and less with your back."

Sarah was grinding fine meal for the ceremonies almost upon them, and finding the simple operation hard on back and knees, hard on arms and hands. There was a knack to it, and Sarah had by no means acquired the knack. She sat back and flopped the hair out of her eyes, sighing. "I'm so clumsy about it," she apologized.

"All the schoolgirls are the same. They come back with their hair bobbed and their lipstick — You didn't grow up as we did, learning from our mothers. You don't know how to sit right, or lift or carry. You don't know how to do any of the important things. You even hold yourself funny. You aren't Hopis. You're *Bohannas*."

"We're not *Bohannas*, either," Sarah muttered.

Aunt Kawasie dropped down beside her. "You are doing the right thing now," she commended her, still in Hopi. "You go ahead and grind lots of meal for Powanmnu. Bessie will come over and help you make *piki*, too. You got to learn about *piki*, or you blister your hands on the griddle. But you do the proper Hopi things, and maybe you can pick

170

a good man at the dances," she ended with a high chuckle.

Sarah cast a frowning glance at Missy, a speculative glance. She had stood the cradle up against the wall near the grinding bin, and Missy smiled and gurgled and blew bubbles at the voices, and at her mother's occasional tickling finger under her soft chin.

"Oh — you are thinking of Missy." Kawasie pleated her lips and shook her head commiseratingly. "But there's plenty that won't mind Missy. You take that Henry, in Sichumovi. His wife has just put his things out on the doorstep. He's looking for another girl, a nice, comfortable one."

Sarah kept her eyes on the millstone and on the small pile of meal accumulating at its lower end while she worked. "Who is Henry?" she asked faintly.

"Henry?" Kawasie asked on a note of high astonishment at such ignorance. "Talayesva, you know Talayesva. Fern's son."

"Fern's son? He must be pretty old."

"Well —" Kawasie's lifted brows and flirt of plump hand said, "You can't have everything. Not when you have Missy."

"What does he do? I mean for a living?"

"Do? He has a good flock, and two or three fields that usually make a crop." Kawasie clucked absently at Missy and brushed her cheek with the fringe of her squaw belt until the child crowed with delight. "If Henry doesn't suit you — well, let me think. There's Samuel. Samuel's wife died."

"Sehepmana?"

"Oh, no. Sehepmana died five years ago. She was bewitched. This one was Louise. Well, of course Samuel might be a little too old. He is older than I am. But there's Tony. Tony wouldn't be too particular."

171

"Tony?" Sarah's voice broke on a high note of protest.

Aunt Kawasie did not answer. She was gazing thoughtfully through the peephole, and blinking faster and faster. "I know just the one: young and educated. Frances says that Robin Adair said you were the prettiest girl on the mesa —" Aunt Kawasie's eyes came back into the house to appraise Sarah's slenderness disparagingly. "Maybe he wouldn't mind about Missy."

Sarah sat back from the grinding bin, and her face grew hot. *Mind about Missy indeed! After the scrapes he's been in, and the girls he's —* "What kind of husband would he make?" she asked in a flat voice.

Aunt Kawasie shrugged and summed up his husbandly qualities with a matter-of-fact freedom of speech. "And if he didn't stick to you after the new wore off —" she made a mouth and threw her hands wide — "you'll find it's easier to get another husband when you've already got one, my daughter."

Resentfully Sarah bent to her grinding, but her thoughts did return, speculatively, to Robin Adair. His name stood out among the many that were incongruous. Sarah knew that it was funny because she had sung the Scotch song in school at Finch. When the government people had moved in upon the Hopis, one of their first acts had been to take a census, and for a census names had been necessary. There was little they could do about the old people, and they found themselves bogged down in Sehepmanas, Talayesvas, Cinquakabusers and the like. So when the new year's crop of babies was harvested, they moved to simplify the problem. They decreed that each child should have an American name. Either government people or missionaries had to supply the names, with results like Matthew and Mark and

Reuben and Joseph, Robin Adair, Annie Laurie, Brunhild. The task was not easy, for with everyone knowing everyone else in nine villages, repetitions must be kept down. After there had been Oraibi Mary, Shupalovi Mary, Walpi Mary and Sehepmana's Mary, further Marys would be confusing. So, after the more familiar names were exhausted, the Deborahs and Ezekiels, the Platos, the Reginalds and Montmorencys, the Imogenes and Hildegardes were brought out.

Robin Adair. He was one of the loiterers who whistled at Sarah. He was one who had stared most arrogantly, looking her up and down as he might scrutinize a wild mare which he might try his hand at lassoing. Sarah thought despairingly, *Is this the only way to fit in?*

As if answering the unspoken wail, Kawasie put in a sneering word. "Unless you want to go down and get ducked by the Christians. Then they'd forgive you. If you live the rest of your life like Miss Lundquist, they'd forgive anything."

Sarah tightened her lips. She had felt more sympathy with the Christians and the Mission Mary before Abraham burned the relics. The act had seemed to her faintly ridiculous. Uncle Abraham had taken himself too seriously. Miss Dayton's laughter had made Sarah's unsure spirit prickle with shame.

She was lonesome. She was young and she was lonesome. She would enter into Powanmnu as Frances entered into it, and Maude. She would see whether participation made her feel different. She would see what came of it all. Even a Robin Adair might be better than no one, forever and ever no one. She smiled reluctantly at Aunt Kawasie. "Well, we'll see," she muttered.

173

The fun at Powanmnu was swift moving and high keyed, even raucous. Good things to eat were served in abundance, among them fresh, tender green beans and onions, there in midwinter. These were supposed to be miraculous growths, though the Hopi knew well enough that they were forced in *kivas* kept steamy hot for the purpose, and that in many Hopi houses boxes of them sent up pale yellowish green tops.

There were, besides the feasting, many dances, many clowns, many races. Deliberately Sarah worked herself up to an activity almost feverish. At length there came an evening when she even left Missy locked in the house alone. She fed the child her bottle, made her clean and dry, teetered the cradle on her knees until Missy slept deeply.

Even then Sarah kept turning back for one more look at Missy, one more scrutiny of the room, of the windows, of the fireplace, with the fire carefully put out, of the stove, burning quietly. What could possibly happen, worse than Missy's waking and crying a little? Sarah locked the door and went out into the exciting night, to stop at Kawasie's house for Frances.

One of the ceremonial races came early in the evening festivities. Feeling that she was taking a long step toward her purpose, Sarah contended with Robin Adair in the race. She had found him in the crowd, and looked at him under her lashes, her heart beating thickly. Robin had laughed noisily with the other young men, had stared boldly at Sarah, had snatched at her in the shadows.

"You got him hooked," Frances whispered excitedly, nudging Sarah. "They say he's tired of fooling around and wouldn't mind being married for a while. If you play it right, Sarah —" She looked at her cousin curiously, half enviously —

Sarah turned a blank face toward her. "Do you hear a baby yelling?" she asked uneasily.

"Gosh, yelling kids aren't any treat to me. My Vincent was howling his head off when I left, but if he thinks I'm going to give up all my fun to nurse his stomachache —"

Sarah was still straining her ears through the noise of merrymaking.

"It isn't Missy, if that's what's eating you," Frances snapped. "You couldn't hear Missy as plain as that even if you were right outside the door."

Sarah stiffened.

"I have to go home," she said abruptly.

"Sarah, my gosh!"

But Sarah was already darting away from the noise and clatter of the plaza into the shadowy streets and lanes that led to her mother's house.

She was not unobserved.

"Hi! Hey, you Sarah!"

Robin Adair was shouting at her. Sarah muttered something and shook her head. She ran on.

"Hey, kid! What's the rush?"

The voice followed her, and Sarah's heart lurched. The only thing she wanted now was to get home, unescorted, to Missy. It was not going to be easy. Certainly she could never outrun Robin in a straightaway race. Even with her small head start he would come up with her. He would come up with her while she was unlocking her door. He would never believe that she had come home to Missy — He would think it a device —

Desperately she changed her course and led toward another quarter of the village. Already she could hear his quick breath. She turned and doubled again and again, with the cunning of a frightened animal. When she reached a short tunneled way between outer street and court she flattened herself in the deep shadow and stood shaken by her own held breath until she was dizzy and faint.

When she was fairly sure that Robin had plunged well past her, back toward the dance plaza, she peered out with fearful caution. No one was in sight. She took to her heels and ran toward her own house. When she reached it she was hardly able to make her way up the ladder.

Gaining the door, she pulled the key from around her neck. *I must not drop it. I must not drop it.* It fell with a clatter that seemed loud enough to summon the village. Sarah stood frozen. She retrieved it, and her fumbling fingers inserted it upside down. All the while she was listening for sounds from within, for sounds detaching themselves from the general merrymaking in the village. Such silence. Could it mean disaster?

At length the door creaked open on complete black quiet. Sarah whirled to lock the door and then ran, shaking, to the cradle on the floor and dropped down beside it.

Soft smackings told her that Missy was sucking in her sleep. Sobbing with relief, Sarah ran swift fingers over the child's face. Missy woke and roared a protest.

Sarah sat rocking her child for a long time, and looking into the blackness. She couldn't follow this way. She could not. To marry Robin Adair was unthinkable.

Presently she undressed and stretched herself on her sheepskin, hoping for sleep.

Frances looked her up next day. Though she was plainly disgusted, she had other matters on her mind. "That Robin got off the hook, I guess. I was sure you really had him."

"How is your Vincent? Stomach all right?" Sarah asked hurriedly.

"No, I guess he's the kind that yells a lot, though. But I got news for you, Sarah. Uncle Abraham."

"Uncle Abraham?"

"Yeah. Bad hurt. Awful bad."

Sarah stared at her, thinking of the burned objects and the buried fetishes, thinking of the hurled rock. "Did somebody — ?"

Frances shook her head almost regretfully. "No. It was an accident. The old folks say it was the gods. But it was just an accident, if you ask me. He had to go with a gang of men to work on that bridge that got washed out. Over Weepo. Seems like he fell. He fell on his arm. He broke it real bad. The bone stuck out through the skin in two places, and —"

Sarah shivered, envisioning the ugly injury. "But if they got him to the hospital quick, surely they could —"

"They didn't, though." The girl's voice had a moist relish. "He asked Luke to take him in his truck, and Luke said he didn't have no gas. He asked some of the others, but there wasn't nobody would bother. So Uncle Abraham had to hoof it to Keams —"

Again Sarah shivered, thinking of her father, thinking of those rough miles.

"He's awful sick now," Frances finished complacently.

Uncle Abraham weathered the acute infections. He praised God, he said, that there was this new stuff to keep off the lockjaw, and these other wonder drugs like sulfa and penicillin. As soon as he returned from the hospital, Sarah went in to see him. Again he lay on the floor, where he liked best to be when ill, his head at an angle against the wall. The life of the house surged noisily around him.

The break had been at shoulder and forearm, and his arm

177

was held upward in a formidable metal stirrup. Abraham surveyed the contraption with grim pride.

"They say maybe I can use it a little," he said. "Maybe never much."

"And your right arm, too." Sarah's pity flamed into anger. "That Luke: he had a lot to do. I suppose he's satisfied now."

"We-ell," Abraham said pacifically. "Luke thinks I been doing wrong all these years. You maybe can't blame Luke so much. Though I kind of didn't feel that way at first," he admitted.

Sarah blinked the tears away and busied herself setting Missy's cradle on end against the wall beside Uncle Abraham. He clucked at the baby, reached over his good hand to tickle her under the chin. She wrinkled up her round brown face and turned her head this way and that, gurgling and blowing out moist lips at him.

"*Bas sonel mana! Bas sonel mana!*" Abraham crooned, his eyes misting. "She sure is a smart baby," he added with a delighted chuckle. "Now would you look at her try to talk to Uncle Abraham!"

The baby was primping her lips deliciously, thinning them to a flower-petal line and uttering esoteric syllables.

Sarah's eyes darted resentfully toward Bennie. He was the only one in the room who was not focusing an admiring attention on Missy. He was lounging on a straight chair, heels hooked over the rungs and chin in hands, listening to the radio. It was not even worth listening to, Sarah noticed indignantly. Reception was poor in the desert in daytime, and only a series of faint words and squawks issued from the loudspeaker. But Bennie had not even a glance to spare for Missy.

178

"What are you doing around here?" Sarah snapped at him. "Every time I see this place, here you are."

Bennie said defensively, "Abraham, he couldn' get along so good without a man around. Now that's he so bad crippled up."

Sarah looked about her questioningly. "Well, my goodness, where are your own boys, Uncle Abraham?"

Uncle Abraham went on amusing Missy, tickling her with a straw from a handleless broom that lay on the floor. His eyes turned with mournful triumph to his niece. "You didn' heard? Those boys gone down to Parker."

Sarah lifted astonished brows. "Working down there for somebody?"

James was a good carpenter and Joseph a mechanic. Both had tried their luck out in the world before this. They had worked in an Indian community in Nevada, and down at the Railroad. It had never seemed like home to them, and the wages which had looked so rich sifted through their unaccustomed hands like cornmeal, paying for rent and groceries.

Aunt Polehongsi's large face quivered. "They go down to work. Cleaning the ground. Mending up the houses where those Japanese stay. But if they like it they say they come back and get their families and take land for themselves."

Sarah stared at her stupidly. "You don't mean — move away? Not to make their homes there? Hopi people?"

Uncle Abraham gazed out of the window toward the edge of the earth, where Herkakkaway and the other Black Buttes stood remote in their misty purple. His smile was that of one who sees far. "Sometime it got to come," he said.

Sarah's gaze was fixed. Sometime it had to come. If the Hopi learned to take care of the babies, so that the enormous

179

infant mortality did not keep down the fecund population growth as it had always done in the past, then, obviously, the ravaged desert could not sustain the people. For decades it had been overgrazed. Millions of sheep, shearing away the vegetation with their efficient lower teeth, had consumed even the roots. When the rainy season came, there was no binding root-mass to hold the topsoil, and year by year it wasted away. Year by year the violent rainfall gouged out arroyos. Even during Sarah's absence new gullies had been made, and she found waste gulches where fields had stood.

"But I didn't think anything could take the Hopi away from the mesas," Sarah said faintly.

"No, it always seem that way, don't it? Washindon try and try, and no luck. When I was young, they put up windmills and then they build houses for us, handy to the windmills. Long ago those houses all —" Abraham wafted them away with a turned hand — "they try to get the children so use' to white ways at school they won't come back. But the children homesick. And like they say, it too hard for them to get away from the beating of the drums.

"But now, maybe so, the time has come. Washindon lend a Hopi three thousand dollars — three thousand, you understand? — to get started. It take him and his family and his things down there, two hundred miles. Three — four crops a year, they say, alfalfa, garden truck. Pretty soon they can pay it all back. Three thousand dollars."

"Joseph says those houses, they are all built together, like a Hopi village, only none of them but one story high," said Joseph's wife.

Sarah nodded, turning unseeing eyes upon her. Poston. On the old Mojave Reservation. She remembered pictures of the old army barracks, set there, naked in the sand.

The Hopi were used to having scanty room, slight privacy, no running water. To be able to get a stream at a hydrant down the block, that would still be luxury; and the community bath and toilet house, and the community laundry, would be nearer than any had ever had on the mesas. The heat would bother them, in those thin shells of houses; heat without the relief of cool nights, without the refuge of thick walls of stone and adobe, cool as caves.

"They will all come back, you'll see," Sarah said uneasily.

"Maybe I will go, too," Bennie said with a touch of bravado.

"You?" Sarah asked cruelly. "What would you find to do in Parker — in Poston? Have they got a newspaper down there?"

Bennie had learned the trade of printing at the government boarding school.

"You like for me to build the brush shelters in the near fields tomorrow?" Bennie asked Abraham the question abruptly, and slipped away without waiting for the answer; slipped away without another look at Sarah.

Uncle Abraham eyed his niece with bright, gentle eyes. "Bennie is a good boy," he said.

"Oh, Uncle Abraham, he has no backbone!"

"Well, maybe so." Again Abraham contemplated distance. "Bennie isn't so strong as some. You know how it was with Bennie. He got pewmony and his grandmother, Lena, up there on top, she just let him lay on the sheepskin, getting thinner and thinner. Lena was mad because he was a Christian. So Miss Lundquist, she brought him down to the mission. She set up a cot in her house and kep' him there. She fed him up real good. All winter she kep' him and nursed him, and he got well."

"Why didn't he stay at the mission?" Sarah asked scornfully.

Abraham shrugged. "Lena, she send for him. She say she got nobody else to bring her wood and tend her garden. He need a good smart wife, Bennie does."

Sarah thrust out her lower lip, lifted expressive shoulders.

Joseph's wife entered the conversation, from where she sat on the bed nursing her baby. "No foolin', Sarah, for a girl like you I'd say Bennie was the best catch on the mesa."

Sarah yawned elaborately.

Aunt Polehongsi, who understood the drift of English conversation, though she used none herself, launched into a complaint in Hopi. "You're going to just sit and let some of these little schoolgirls get Bennie. Maybe you do not see how they make eyes at him and giggle. In church last Sunday night they were acting like *Bohanna* girls."

Joseph's wife bent above her baby's round dark head as the child released the nipple to laugh up at her, but she still regarded Sarah thoughtfully from under her brows. "Maybe you forget, Sarah, that Hopi girls always did propose to the boys."

"Why, they were dropping that old way even before I left here."

"They picked it up again. When the agent said tribal marriages were OK. And anyway, well, it seems like it's the Hopi style. I guess some of the boys never would come to the point."

Uncle Abraham interrupted the conversation. "Miss Lundquist!" he greeted her, as she knocked and entered, a towel-covered plate in her hand.

"We're trying to get Sarah to encourage Bennie, Miss Lundquist," Joseph's wife said, grinning at her companionably. "We tell her that some other girl's going to get him if she doesn't look out."

Nodding vehemently, Miss Lundquist said, "Some of my

182

johnnycake that you like, Abraham. Polehongsi, you give him
some right away, while it's hot. I split it and put butter in
between — not margarine: butter." When Polehongsi took
the plate from her, she perched on the bed beside Joseph's
wife and turned bright eyes on Sarah. "Yes, Sarah, I hate
to say it, but our boys do need a little pushing."

"If Bennie has to be pushed, some other girl can push
him," Sarah said sulkily, wondering which schoolgirls they
meant. Sandra Marie, maybe, with nothing in her empty
little head except boys; or Alice, who had a temper as fiery
as chili peppers.

Miss Lundquist clucked absently at the nursing baby,
whose wide-mouthed answering smile lost it the nipple
again. It grabbed hastily for it, eyes still on the round, pink
face.

"It's too bad. I really think it's too bad. But some things
you almost have to take as they are, Sarah. There are times
when I do get out of patience with our boys. All they seem
to think about is tearing around on a horse or in an old car,
with those ten-gallon hats of theirs. And girls," she added
delicately. "I don't know why our girls stand for them,"
she said vehemently. "But Bennie's not like that. Bennie's
off another shelf."

"Miss Lundquist, what's so wonderful about Bennie?"

"Sarah, if you wait for a boy with as good an education
as you, and as much get up and get — I don't know why it
is — and excuse me, Abraham, present company is excepted
— but the Indian girls beat the Indian boys four ways for
Sunday. Look at Ruby, from Second Mesa, head surgical
nurse in a hospital; and that Navajo nurse back there now
getting her master's degree. A girl, sure it's a girl. What
boys do you get to match them?" She went on more indignantly, "Surely you've noticed how all the Indian girls that

183

train for nurses get snapped up the minute they've graduated. Looks like the boys want a meal ticket for life, so they can just keep on riding to the races and the dances and living the life of Riley on their wife's salary." Miss Lundquist was snorting over her own words, her hazel eyes sparkling wrathfully. "No, seriously, Sarah, there isn't another one like Bennie, and you might be sorry later on if you don't make it a little bit easy for him to ask you."

Sarah pinched her lips together and leaned over Missy, carefully loosening the cradle straps and then as carefully tightening them again. "I guess Missy and I better go home now," she said. "I want to stop at my aunt's and see how Frances is by this time." She would steer away from the subject of marriage, since she could not say what she was thinking. She would have liked to ask Miss Lundquist why she, Sarah, should not make a life without a husband, as Miss Lundquist herself had done.

Mention of Frances diverted all thoughts. "Such a stout, strong baby!" Miss Lundquist said. "Frances feels real bad about it. I went in right away, as soon as I heard."

"*Okiway*," Polehongsi was murmuring sorrowfully. "They say it was melons that killed him. But all Hopi babies eat melons."

"Well, all Hopi babies better quit eating melons," the Mission Mary exclaimed.

"It was an old melon, too, stored all winter," said Joseph's wife, gazing tenderly at her own child.

Trudging up the trail with Missy in her arms, Sarah's own thoughts reverted to the earlier talk, to Miss Lundquist's spinsterhood. It was not the same for a Hopi girl. These bold, roving Hopi youths would give her no peace, no safety, until she married. Ella, at Second Mesa, had lived and died

184

a spinster; and Silas was still a bachelor at fifty. But these were Christians, and the Christians could do things no one else could.

And even if she could have remained unmarried, Sarah was less and less sure that she wished to. Even Missy did not fill the emptiness in her life. She hoisted the heavy cradle higher in her thin arms, for the first time wondering why Hopi women always lugged the baby baskets thus awkwardly, instead of swinging them from their back as most Indians do. It was hard work. She was tired. Yes, she was tired, but much more poignantly she was lonesome.

She had not noticed the light footfalls behind her, but now she heard the quick breath of a runner who was overtaking her. She kept her head stubbornly bowed above her baby. She would not turn to see who it was who followed her.

Hands grasped the cradle, took it from her arms. She whirled about, startled. Bennie was smiling at her, half abashed.

"It is heavy for you," he said, "and I am going up."

Sarah felt suddenly humble. She hated the feeling, and opposed it stubbornly. He might be a paragon among Hopi boys, this Bennie, but wasn't he spineless? Wasn't there something weak about coming after her when she had spoken so contemptuously to him? His look had been almost worshipful, as he took Missy's cradle from her. She guessed maybe he was in love with her. And he set her high. There was healing in that reverence.

They went climbing on, his stride only a little longer than Sarah's, his boyish arms stretched clumsily around the big flat basket. Even the slight change in gait registered with Missy, and she turned her head this way and that, with small, questioning murmurs. She seemed to decide that she liked the steadier arms, for she cooed and gurgled enchantingly and blew little bubbles. Bennie glanced at her no more than as if she had been a basket of laundry. He was carrying a load for Sarah: nothing more.

They were climbing the great flight of irregular stone steps that hung on the side of the mesa. It was a relief not to have to lug Missy up those steps, and the trail shortened remarkably with someone beside her — with anyone, Sarah reminded herself sharply. She stole a glance at Bennie, and away again because his eyes were upon her hopefully.

He was not bad looking, though maybe nothing very special. His aquiline nose was finely modeled, and so were his sharply undercut lips.

At the top they had to press through a loitering crowd of boys, Andy among them. There was a chorus of hoots, and frank remarks in mingled Hopi and English, about the baby in Bennie's arms. There were perfectly audible speculations, and jeers, and laughter that was not exactly malicious, though it was insinuating. Sarah held her head proudly high and tried to laugh with them. Not until they had passed through the little mob did she look at Bennie. Again he was looking at her, and again there was hope in his eyes.

Sarah could not repress a warm rush of gratitude. She smiled at him.

Bennie took a quick breath. "It's too heavy for you to lug back and forth," he said huskily, thrusting out his chin in a pointing gesture at the basket. "I could — on Sunday morning, Sarah, why don't I stop by and carry it for you? We got a nice class. Young folks."

Sarah parted from him at her own door, taking the baby's basket from him and dismissing him unmistakably. But her defenses had gone down with a rush, and she knew it. Nothing so formal as a proposal was needed. By the time the yucca was lighting its waxy white candles far and near across the desert, by the time most of the planting had been done, Miss Lundquist was delightedly planning a church wedding. They could trim the bare white chapel with yucca, if only Sarah would let it be early enough. Yucca would look beautiful and make the whole place sweet with its fragrance. And if Sarah could not appropriately wear a veil, she could have a perfectly lovely white dress, and be as bridy-looking as anyone. Miss Lundquist was sorry that Sarah would not consent to leave her mother's house and come down to live in the one little stone house that was not being used. If you didn't break loose, you didn't break loose, the Mission Mary reminded her soberly.

Other people than Miss Lundquist and the mission community were agog with the news of the approaching marriage; others than Aunt Kawasie and Bessie and Frances, with her sulky face still sometimes swollen with weeping. Bennie's grandmother, Lena, was as much concerned as anyone.

She was one of the old matriarchs. "She boss everybody," Bennie summed up the case. "Always my father say she put a spell on my mother. My mother get sick and die without no reason. My father say Lena don' like her, because my mother have a strong will, too, and don' give in to her."

Lena was one of those elderly Hopi women who remained spidery thin and quick. She was dressy in the old-fashioned way. Her wife-locks always curved up just so in a shining fan against the bronze of her cheeks, and the coils that lay over her shoulder were long and heavy and well brushed. The best blue turquoise shone from bright silver on her ears and wrists and fingers, and her squash-blossom necklace, which came out for festal occasions, was the biggest on the mesa.

Lena had flown into a rage when she heard the first definite gossip about her grandson and Sarah.

Sarah commented stormily the next time she met Bennie. "I hear your grandmother doesn't like me. She doesn't think I'm good enough. I suppose it's Missy, maybe."

Bennie reddened, and stumbled over his excuses. "I told her she's got no call to hold it against you, Sarah. You couldn't help it." — He had never before referred to Sarah's misfortune — "But you know what an old-style Hopi Lena is."

"So am I an old-style Hopi," Sarah said jealously. *If they could guess all the ease and cleanliness I have given up, just for the sake of being an old-style Hopi —*

"Well, you know how they say it when a boy marries a girl who's been married before — or something like that — how they call him a basket-carrier."

Sarah blinked uncertainly. The term was not familiar to her. "Basket-carrier?" she asked suspiciously.

Bennie shifted from one foot to the other, there outside the post office. "There isn't no sense to it, it's just old Hopi talk. They say the boy will have to carry a heavy load even after he's dead. Because — well, because —"

"Because he was such a darn fool to marry that way," Sarah flashed.

"Now listen, Sarah. I tol' Lena I don' care. I tol' her, there isn't no girl on the mesa better than you are. I tol' her I got my mind set on it and she might as well quit fussing." Though he kept his voice low and his head down, Bennie was inspired by his own unusual fluency. "I say to her, you better be good and glad I don' marry inside my own clan, or such as that. I would if I wanted to. So she simmers down. She give up, I think."

Bennie's face wore the triumphant expression of one who has won a struggle with unexpected ease. Sarah eyed him dubiously. "I wish I was as sure as you are," she said, going on into the post office to ask for the mail that did not come.

That afternoon the latch of her door rattled up and rattled down. The door did not open, being locked from inside. "Who is there?" Sarah called.

"It is I."

Sarah scrambled to her feet and stood considering. She had recognized the insinuating female quality of the voice. Reluctantly she turned the key in the padlock and creaked the door open. Lena stood there, wrapped in her summer shawl of white cashmere with printed roses and deep fringe. Smiling coldly, Lena stepped past Sarah into the house, her eyes darting busily around the shadowy place.

"You keep house nice and clean," she complimented her. "But I'm surprised you didn't got no bed and table."

"I like the old style," Sarah said defensively, motioning toward a sheepskin on the floor.

Lena sat down with a grunt. *I don't trust that shine in her eyes. She's up to something.* The old woman was chirping at Missy, bare except for her diaper, whom Sarah was getting ready for bed.

"Fat," she said, prodding her with an appraising forefinger. "I suppose you wash her every day like a *Bohanna*. It takes their stren'th. Too bad she's blind. She'd be a real nice baby."

Sarah slipped the nightgown silently over Missy's head. She wished she had got Missy to sleep before Lena came. She wished she had hidden her pottery. Having disposed of

189

Missy, Lena had turned to that pottery, her disparaging gaze returning to it again and again. The ghostly gray shapes stood defenseless in their imperfection under the stove. They were drying out, to be ready for polishing, painting and firing.

"You try to make pottery," Lena said with an amused twist of thin lips.

Sarah said nothing.

"I think I must tell you that Bennie is a great boy for his *piki*. Bennie say, 'Even when I am sick, the good old paper bread make me well again.'"

Sarah stiffened her softening defenses, remembering how long Bennie had lain feverish and untended, on this grandmother's adobe floor.

"Of course you haven't learned to make nothing so old-style as *piki*," Lena went on. "But maybe so you can learn. And there is a trick with the *somoviki*. Bennie, he eat the *somoviki* like a pig. If you feed a man good, I always say, it make up for other things." Lena let her lids droop meaningly. "But maybe so you are like all the other schoolgirls. You will be new style and buy store bread and canned peaches and have more time to go running about."

"I am learning all I can of the old Hopi ways," Sarah said tonelessly, replacing Missy on her cradle. The cradle was already too short for the baby. It was almost ready to be discarded. Sarah tried to keep her eyes and thoughts on safe matters like cradles, but she could see the stare of Lena's half-veiled eyes without looking.

"I always tol' them you had more sense than you looked," Lena went on. "I tol' them, Sarah isn't fooled none by the *Bohannas* and their ways. She already got a stomach full of *Bohannas*. I tol' them, they think they got her tight, down there at the mission, but you wait and see. She'll fool them.

She'll leave them cold, soon as she's got a good husband out of them."

Still Sarah said nothing. The lacings of Missy's cradle were often a refuge, for they could be endlessly adjusted.

"It would be a good joke on Miss Lun'quist if you was to run out on her before the wedding, when she's got the church all messed up with flowers like she does." Lena loosed a malevolent cackle. "I tell you, Sarah: you come and have a real Hopi wedding here on top. I'd like to see her face."

Sarah moistened her lips. "Miss Lundquist has been good to Bennie," she said. "She is good to Missy and to me."

Still refusing to look at Lena, she could tell by the edge on the woman's voice that the implication had angered her. "She has had her reasons. But of course I know how you feel about her taking Missy like she did. Babies, they sicken so easy. They die so easy."

It was not the words that jerked Sarah's eyes up to the woman's face, it was the tone. In the white world this business of witchcraft had seemed foolish, fantastic, but here — Not the cats on the housetops, nor the dogs that were not dogs, but the mysterious illnesses which even the doctors at the hospital could not explain, the many who sickened and died after a fellow villager had set the seal of hate upon him. In high school a class had discussed the voodoo of the Haitians, and Sarah had wondered then whether it was not akin to the things that happened on the mesas. Maybe her own mother had died of TB and not of witchcraft. But what if she had not? Sarah's mouth filled with hot saliva, and she swallowed, clutching the cradle convulsively to her thin body.

"Oh, do not frighten yourself," Lena crooned. "Everything will be all right if you are a good Hopi. And you are a good Hopi, aren't you, Sarah?"

Lena's eyes had the dull shine of beetle wings in their yellowed whites, under their fleshless folds of lid. Sarah could not get her own eyes loose from them.

Startlingly, Lena chuckled, as if she and Sarah were cronies indulging in a pleasant conspiracy. "How would it be to fool the old Lundquist good?" she asked in her normal tone. "I tell you, Sarah: right now you come with your basket of meal to say to Bennie that you want to marry him. Right now we have the marriage and get ahead of her. That way she don't have all the bother of fixing for you at the church. I was fooling about that."

Again Sarah swallowed the hot, salty saliva that continually welled up in her mouth. "Bennie wants a church wedding."

Lena showed small shallow teeth and pale gums in a mirthless laugh. "Bennie wants a wedding," she said significantly. Swiftly she got to her feet. "I think tomorrow night would be good. Kawasie will take care of her." She tossed her head toward the sleeping Missy. "Tomorrow night. I'll get ready for you."

On her way to the door she paused and leaned low over the cradle, and Sarah had all she could do not to snatch it up and shield the child with her own body.

She would not say anything to Bennie about his grandmother's visit. They would go ahead with the church wedding, not because she wanted a church wedding, but because it was only fair. Otherwise she would prefer to follow Hopi procedure. Why not? Why not, when her one aim was to ally herself strongly with her own people? But it would be letting Miss Lundquist down, betraying her who had saved Bennie's life and helped Sarah and Missy even against Sarah's will. No, they would go ahead with the church wedding. Afterward she could gradually stop going to the mission. Other husbands and wives lived on for years like that, one Christian, the other pagan.

Next night when Bennie came to see her, her resolution had faltered.

"Somebody say Lena came to see you yesterday," Bennie said uneasily.

"Yes. She pretends to like me now, but — Bennie," she broke off, "just once look at Missy. Doesn't she look funny to you?"

Bennie's eyes slid over the child and away again. "She sleep nice," he demurred.

Missy did sleep quietly, her lips pursed with her softly blown breath, but Sarah frowned as she leaned close above her, listening and laying light fingers on her cheek and in the deep creases of her satiny neck. "To me she looks — someway," she said, catching her breath. "And she feels hot. Oh, Bennie, maybe it would be better if we had just the Hopi wedding. The agent says it's all right. It's perfectly legal."

"My grandmother been working on you, too."

Sarah could not bring herself to say to him what she was saying to herself.

"Miss Lundquist — she plan — " Bennie argued, his face angry and his eyes hurt — "And me, I belong to the mission —"

"Miss Lundquist would get over it. She always does. And you'd only have to go before the deacons and be disciplined — And it wouldn't really be your fault: it would be mine."

Bennie stood at the door, lips compressed, fingering the padlock and keeping his eyes away from Sarah's.

"Really, it would save her a lot of trouble — Miss Lundquist. And we'd be married, Bennie. Nobody could change that."

Sarah had left Missy and stood close beside Bennie, reaching up to touch his hair, coaxingly. She hated wheedling women. She hated herself. Bennie's face flamed and he breathed hard, but he shook his head. "Better we have the church wedding like we plan," he said hoarsely.

On her cradle Missy stirred and coughed. Maybe it was only fuzz from her light blanket, tickling her throat; but Sarah's heart tightened with fear. "Tomorrow," she murmured breathlessly. "Tomorrow night we could make it, Bennie."

8

THE MONTH of the Hopi wedding stretched interminably for Sarah. She hated Lena's house, where she must stay until the necessary amount of cornmeal was ground, and until her own wedding garments were made by Bennie's male relations.

The house was neither white nor Indian. The floor of the big room was covered by three nine-by-twelve linoleum rugs from a mail-order house, their colors bright and varnished except where a roughness in the adobe had broken and worn the linoleum. Lena had a bedstead, with a mattress which she had made down at the government community center. If the mattress had no sheets, it did have a shiny rayon spread, smooth over the quilts. There were also straight chairs and a table.

Sarah, kneeling in the small room adjoining, still inexpert in scrubbing out the cornmeal, yearned for the untouched Hopiness of her mother's house, so serene, so right.

But as the days passed and her back ached more and more miserably with the continued stooping, the continued push and pull, it was Miss Dayton's rooms she thought of: the davenport and soft chairs; the cornmeal ready ground and stored in the kitchen cabinets with the wheat flour; the shiny tub; the hot water. Her thoughts even reverted to the plushy comfort of the Ramsay house. This half and half lacked both ease and beauty.

Her chief solace, as she worked and ached under Lena's merciless driving, was that Missy was all right. The morning after she had first stayed at Bennie's house, she hurried to Kawasie's to see her child, and found her perfectly well.

Bennie was a mixed comfort. Even his young ardor could not keep the somberness from his hawk face, and she knew he was ashamed of what they had done. His brooding made Sarah's temper more variable. She flung herself into the wedding celebrations with high laughter that alternated with moods of sullen withdrawal.

Lena stood watching her as she ground, brows knotted and lips locked. "Girls are always sulkier than boys," she scolded. "Many's the time, they say, that a Hopi girl has made up her mind to die, just because she didn't get her own way. Yes, and gone ahead and died, for spite and nothing else. But I sure got a pair of you. What for is Bennie so sullen and black, tell me that, Sarah?"

Sarah kept her eyes down, for fear Lena should see the hatred in them. "You should know why, if anyone does," she muttered.

The long wedding was noisily gay. Even the grinding had its spots of excitement, when it was a race between Sarah's friends, especially between Maude and Frances, to see who could grind the most, shrewdly egged on by Lena. The mud fight was hilarity unleashed. Sarah's relations and Bennie's sloshed each other with soft wet masses of clay, with railery and shouting that sometimes held a harder core — like the mud itself.

Finally there was the feast. Everyone came laden with corn, with meal, with *piki*, with dried peaches and dried meat. Everyone feasted, in a house ebullient with grown people coming and going, with young people, with children milling around among their elders.

Sarah was dressed in her bridal finery and felt a temporary elation when she viewed herself piecemeal in Lena's small looking glass. Miss Lundquist's wedding gown could not have set her off half so well. The snowy whiteness of this heavy handwoven cotten was slashed by the boldly colored wool embroidery. The small white moccasins were even smaller below the bulky white leather leg-wrappings. Sarah seemed to have no feet at all. Lena had not grumbled much at Sarah's *"Bohanna* paint," for the girl needed color. With cheeks and lips glowing, her eyes were enormous and feverishly bright. She was beautiful, with a loveliness that brought back her part in the senior play at Finch, when her life had begun accelerating until it crashed. *If Kirk could see me now —*

Then, luckily, she was caught up in the dramatic climax of her wedding. The crowd hilariously escorted Sarah and Bennie home. They were escorted to her mother's house and left at last alone.

9

Sᴀʀᴀʜ's ʟɪꜰᴇ ᴡɪᴛʜ Bᴇɴɴɪᴇ began in early summer. Bennie was busy with Lena's fields, scattered wide across the desert. He must start with first dawn, jogging from one to another, seeing that all was well: that the field mice had not eaten the seed, that the mulch of sand had not drifted over the tender young plants and smothered them. The young family did not move out to Sarah's small ranch house, for it had fallen into decay. Later they might have a work party and repair it.

Sarah had hoped that everything would be better when they had left Lena's house and her presence, as pervasive as musk. Their days did hold moments of warm and tender happiness. For the most part, Sarah thought, Bennie was too tired. He came home in the dusk, fagged by the long day, and silent. They would go early to bed, to be rested for the early rising. Sarah would hear Bennie turning on his pallet and turning again, so that she knew he had sleepless hours as long as hers.

Not till midsummer did he go to the mission or mention it. Then, on a Sunday morning when they sat at a good breakfast which Sarah had instituted for Sundays, Bennie spoke of it.

"Why don' we go down to the mission this morning?" he asked, roughly, to hide his emotion. "Miss Lundquist, she ask me yesterday. And I like to go. We already wait long enough."

"Well," Sarah agreed. "We have time, if we hurry."

It was an ordeal. They set out presently along the trail, clothes clean and hair well brushed, and Missy on her cradle fresh as some exotic tea rose or the brown blossoms of the sweet-shrub.

"It is a fine morning," Bennie said with sober hopefulness, "to make a new start."

The morning was warm with June, but it was not oppressive. The high, clear air was dry and sparkling, and every spot of shade as cool as spring water. From their work on housetops and in the houses with their wide open doors, the villagers greeted them, staring.

"Lena will know we've gone before we get there," Sarah muttered.

"Lena is not our boss," Bennie said thinly.

The mission knew that they were coming before they arrived, too, and some of the young people met them at the foot of the trail and walked with them over to the church. No one said a word about their defection, and their forebearance fretted Sarah.

Throughout the prolonged services of the morning, Sarah watched for evidence of resentment, of disappointment. Only once, as Miss Lundquist led the singing, beating time as she always did, with an enthusiasm that jerked her small, high-keyed body, did Sarah surprise a revealing look on that cheerfully round face. For that moment, as she looked at Sarah, her hazel eyes were rounded with wonder, her smooth brow a little puckered, as if she were trying to comprehend the incomprehensible. Sarah dropped her eyes quickly to the Hopi hymnal. That pained question was too hard to bear. Why had not Miss Lundquist's thirty-odd years here given her a hornier callosity? Surely she had encountered ingratitude a hundred times more heinous than Bennie's and Sarah's. *I cannot come here again. I cannot stand it.*

When the classes were at an end, and there had been a brief recess for the sake of the children, the worship service began. "You want I should sit with you?" Bennie asked in an undertone. Though Sarah did want it, she shook her head. "We'll do like the rest," she said.

With the women and girls, she and Missy edged into the left-hand side of the little box meetinghouse. Polehongsi, her hands clasped across her stomach, nodded and beamed and nodded again as Sarah slid along toward her. From beyond Polehongsi another of the women leaned forward to stretch out a hand small as a baby's, almost losing her balance as her feet reached for the long wooden foot bench, like prie-dieus, placed on that side to ease the discomfort of the short-legged women.

Bennie had taken his place in a pew directly opposite. Sarah's infrequent glances toward him showed him smiling and nodding and stretching out his hand to receive the welcome of the other men and boys. When everyone had settled down, except for the inevitable procession of fathers or mothers taking the children out and in again, Sarah found herself looking toward her young husband oftener than she wanted to. Sometimes he was looking covertly at Sarah. Oftener he sat with his eyes downcast and his hands hanging between his knees. She looked hopefully sidewise as they sang. Bennie loved to sing, and lost himself in singing. Now he held to his side of the book, but his lips were tightly compressed and she did not once hear his voice, surprisingly low pitched and strong.

I cannot come again and see Bennie like this.

The next Sunday morning Sarah did not wait for her husband's suggestion. "Bennie," she said as they ate, "would you mind going to the mission alone? I have a headache this morning."

Bennie went, but he came home dejected.

Sarah tried to make talk about the church. "Who is on the list to keep the church swept and mopped this week?" she asked as they sat eating their dinner.

"I think Abraham and Jason, and I forget who else."

"And to lead the singing?" she asked brightly. "You maybe?"

Bennie choked on his bread-that-bubbles-up. "Not me. You know it couldn't be me. Not now."

Sarah said nothing, for she could think of nothing to say. The church discipline was important. As Sarah had said earlier, he would only have had to come before the deacons and confess that he had stepped aside into the pagan way. He would soon have been reinstated. But Bennie made no move toward this reinstatement. Sarah was surprised by his apparent feeling. Bennie seemed so mild, so soft, she had not expected his pride to stiffen itself against the humiliation. Perhaps there was a little aquiline firmness in his spirit and will, as well as in his nose and lips. He sat smouldering darkly and breaking the rest of his bread into pieces without attempting to eat. The only heed he paid Missy, who was free of her cradle and had crawled over beside him, was to flush deeply as she pulled herself up by his arm. Sarah bit her lips and sprang to lift the child away, holding her, cooing to her, tickling her, until Bennie got up and strode outdoors, leaving his dinner hardly tasted.

So soon as the next Sunday Sarah had a fair excuse for sending Bennie alone to the mission. It had already become evident that she was pregnant again. The nausea,

201

the dizzy misery she had felt when she doubled her body above Lena's grinding bins had meant what she had incredulously feared.

As long as possible she kept her condition from Bennie. On a hot July morning, when the mesa was noisy with preparations for the big *kachina* dance of the year, he stood looking at her when he was ready to go off to his fields to work.

"Sarah," he stammered, "you look someway."

"It's hot," she said, smiling at him.

"You mean it's just only that you're hot?" he persisted, dropping down on one knee beside her where she sat on the floor mending.

Uncontrollably Sarah's face contorted with a spasm of nausea. "Oh, well," she said, "I suppose you have to know. You're the daddy."

He had never moved her so deeply as he did at that moment. His surprise and delight had so boyish a quality, such a shyness mingled with his pride, that she smiled a mother's smile and leaned close for a quick, un-Indian kiss.

During Sarah's first pregnancy, Miss Dayton had taken good care of her and watched to see that she did not overwork. This time was different. The months dragged by without relief. Increasingly they seemed to Sarah the pattern of her Hopi life, a design made up of winds, hot sun, sand, heaviness and nausea.

Sarah pulled herself about the house or huddled limply on the floor watching Missy. The wind squealing around the mesa became the voice of her misery, and wrapped itself about her like stinging cobwebs. The morning sky would be bare of clouds, the sun coming up brassy and insolent. When a few clouds took shape and veiled the pitiless blaze, laying blue shadows on the desert, Sarah hoped against hope for the relief of rain.

"Surely," she said on an August day when Frances had sauntered in, "surely those clouds mean something."

Frances patted a yawn. "No. Mother says nothing but wind. My gosh, Sarah, don't you wish there was a movie round the corner? Or a ice-cold Coke someplace?"

Maude came up from her house to join them, her boy slung on her back. "What's new?" she asked with a brittle cheer. "No, you don't need to tell me. There ain't nothing new. What do you say we ought to have our heads examined, living out here when we could be somewheres lively?"

"I thought you were going to be so gay from now on," Sarah rallied her.

Maude lifted her shoulders and made a face. "Gay. Hmm. I guess I'm just nuts. If I'm gay I don't feel good about it. If Conrad's gay I'm mad. Good land, Sarah, isn't it time you was getting over this morning sickness?"

Sarah was covering her mouth to hide her weak retching. When she could speak she shook her head wearily. "It's all-day sickness this time. Seems as if I'd never get over it. The heat. And the smells — You'll have to excuse the way this house looks —"

As soon as the girls had gone, she flew at the house furiously, shaking with weakness. Missy was minding the heat and wanted nothing but to be held and amused by her mother. She crept as fast as Sarah could walk, and was always underfoot, so that Sarah stepped on her fingers and had to sit down and comfort her, or barely caught herself from falling as the child clutched at her dress and pulled herself to her unsteady feet.

It took Sarah much of the day to bring the dusty disorder to clean serenity. Then she must bathe Missy and dress her in fresh clothes. Cleanliness was a problem, for water could not be lightly used, when it must be carried up from the spring. And when Missy was clean, Sarah must hasten to cook the evening meal.

Supper was not yet ready when Bennie came in from the fields, carrying a fine load of brush for the fire.

"Oh, can't you be a little bit careful how you track that stuff in?" Sarah flashed at him despairingly. "Missy likes nothing better than to get into it — and look at her this minute, not an hour after I had her bathed and dressed."

The adobe dusted up quickly, and Missy's knees and hands looked like molasses cookies well floured.

Usually Bennie took Sarah's fuming stoically. This time he flung the hard-garnered brush violently out at the door, together with a handful of mustard greens that he had brought. "Other women keep their houses clean without so much whining," he said bitterly. "And your Missy isn't some doll, is she? You fuss over her like a speck of dust would kill her. If you spent half as much time on anybody else —" Bennie's eyes were hard and bright in a thin, hard young face.

He did not speak to Sarah again that day. He ate supper staring in front of him and not even pulling away when Missy crept over to him and dragged herself upright, crowing with delight. Sarah thought jealously that the baby paid more attention to Bennie than to her mother. *And it's no good, this marriage of ours. It was only because I was so lonesome, and we're both young, and that isn't enough.*

She had no answer for Bennie next morning when he paused at the door in the early light and said gruffly, "I'm sorry I was mean, Sarah."

He came home early that afternoon, riding a pickup truck with an iron bedstead and a mattress on it. Andy helped him carry them up the ladder to their door, and the two maneuvered for a half hour, with laughter and joking, before they got the springs through the small door. Sarah stayed out of sight in the storeroom until Andy had gone and Bennie came looking for her.

"You see the su'prise I bring you?" he asked boyishly.

Sarah longed to respond to the boyishness, but her anger leaped to her lips as if against her will. "Where did you get it?" she asked stiffly.

Bennie's smile faded. "I ask Miss Lundquist if she knew where is a nice one nearer than the railroad. She had this one stored away." His face warmed again, softened. "Sarah, you do look someway. I don't think you ought to sleep on the floor when you're like this."

"I always told you I wouldn't sleep on a mattress without sheets," Sarah said implacably.

"Even if it's got no sheets it's softer than the adobe."

"I won't sleep on a mattress without sheets. It's a dirty trick."

"Oh, all right!" Bennie shouted, bringing his hands from behind his back and hurling a package onto the bed. "There's your sheets, and you can have them all to yourself. I bought them off the Mission Mary, and I sure wish I hadn't."

They both slept on the floor that night as usual, though pride had forced Sarah to make up the bed with sheets and blankets. She didn't want it standing naked to the eyes of callers.

Next day she felt even more drained and useless than before. For days after that she could force herself to do little more than get together the food for their meals, and watch

Missy. She rigged up barricades at the door, but Missy pushed and wriggled her way through with patient ingenuity, grunting and scolding and chirping.

One morning when Sarah had been convulsed with a long and violent nausea, she looked through streaming eyes at her barricade, and found it opened. Shaken with fear, she thrust her way through and ran across the housetop. Missy was creeping as fast as hands and feet would carry her, crowing with delight at her escape, and she was aiming straight at the roof's edge. Sarah threw herself at the child as a football tackle, barely in time to pull her back from the brink.

Missy set up a howl of disappointment at first, and struggled in her mother's arms, but as Sarah rocked herself to and fro and cried, the child wriggled about to pat her face with gritty little hands, and coo and plant wide-mouthed, wet kisses on her mother's face.

Miss Lundquist found them there, when she came panting up the ladder. Missy held out her hands joyously to her friend, and Sarah struggled to her feet, shamefacedly wiping her tears away with the back of her hand.

"Whatever is the matter, Sarah, dearie?" Miss Lundquist demanded, breathlessly, trotting the baby as she talked. "You do look so tuckered out. Just stretch out on your nice new bed while we talk. I'll put this paper across the foot so you won't soil your nice clean blanket."

Though unwillingly, Sarah stretched herself for the first time on the soft springiness of the bed.

"Don't try to tell me now," Miss Lundquist went on, sitting down on the edge of the bed with Missy on one arm. "Just lie there and get your breath. I brought the baby a dress." With one hand she held it up against Missy to see if the size were right, while Missy giggled and pranced and then, smelling the fresh clean cotton, tilted her head and wrinkled up her nose and laid her cheek against the smooth crispness.

"She is the smartest little thing!" Miss Lundquist cried exuberantly.

"Too smart," Sarah agreed, laughing weakly. "Miss Lundquist, when you came I'd just saved her from pitching off the roof."

"Oh-oh." Miss Lundquist's attention sharpened. "And it didn't do you a bit of good, plunging after her. You'll have to get Bennie to make you a half door. And high enough so that she can't reach the hook. You'll smother if you try keeping the door shut, these hot days. Oh, lie still. You look like a little ghost."

But Sarah struggled up determinedly and lifted Missy out of the caller's arms. The clear white cotton with its pink and blue flowers made Missy's soiled and faded dress look still dingier. Even Missy's nose was not clean, and a clean nose had always been a badge to Sarah. Sarah lugged her over to the wash basin and washed her face, Missy jerking and pulling and howling. Sarah spatted her cushiony hands down in the water and polished them off, and combed her frowsy hair till the child shrieked with protest.

"Seems as if I can't keep her clean," Sarah mumbled. "The house, either —" She had been too sick and aching to see that house clearly, but now, through Miss Lundquist's eyes, it leaped at her in all its stickiness and staleness, with blue flies buzzing around a litter of soiled dishes on the floor. *She will be saying. Eight years in a spotless Bohanna house, and then this.*

"I always say," Miss Lundquist defended Sarah, "that it's pretty easy to be clean when you have everything to be clean with. Especially water. I recollect," she rambled on determinedly, "when I used to be at the mission at Second Mesa. You know there isn't any well there, because they say a well would have to be put down so deep that it would cost two thousand dollars. Well, after I'd gone through a few summers at Second Mesa, I was a lot slower to criticize the Hopi ladies." She gurgled with laughter, taking Missy from her mother and dancing her.

"She's wet, Miss Lundquist," Sarah cautioned her, "and the diapers aren't dry yet."

"Since when did wet babies scare me? — The cistern would get so near empty that the bucket would come up with a cupful of water. Then we'd go to the windmill — you know, on the Polacca road, four miles or so — and haul back a drum of water. And then wouldn't we nurse it along! Try to wash dishes clean in a pint, and clothes in a half tub. Use the suds to scrub the kitchen floor. Take a sponge bath with a cupful. I never have taken water for granted since then."

Sarah smiled dutifully, but as soon as Miss Lundquist had gone, led by a procession of small boys and girls who had been sent to fetch her to their mother's house, Sarah attacked the unkempt house with feeble fury. *Maybe it won't be so bad when the rains come and lay this everlasting dust and wash the stickiness away.*

When the rains came, they came furiously. Again they turned the mesa dust to filthy mire. It tracked in over the adobe floor. Missy was walking now, wide-legged and unsteady and immensely proud of herself. She still went on hands and knees when she wanted speed, or hitched herself around sitting. Her hands and knees, her diapers, were black with the tracked-in mud, and she transferred much of the dirt to face and clothes. And when the sun came out after a storm, the mesa steamed with rank fetor that increased Sarah's queasiness.

"Looks like you'd be over all this tetchiness," Kawasie remonstrated, counting the months silently on her fingers. "Maybe if you ate more it would settle you. You have to remember you're eating for two."

"It won't stay down when I do."

"I'll fix you a dose of herb tea," Kawasie said, shifting her eyes away from Sarah's wan pallor. "Mormon tea. It's good for what ails you."

Lena was there at the same time, talking with Bennie in a far corner, while Sarah strained her ears to keep track of what she was saying. She could catch only a few words in Lena's conspiratorial undertone: "I told you . . . puking around . . ." Bennie's raised voice filled in the gaps: "She can't help it. The poor girl's sick." The unnatural bullying lift of his voice robbed the words of conviction, Sarah thought.

When the callers had gone, Bennie said, "Lena says if you'd try to get out a little more — get your mind off yourself. Maybe's she's got something there, Sarah. Anybody gets to feeling someway if they stick in the house and don't get no exercise."

"Well. I'll go right now," Sarah said, expressionlessly. "I'll walk over and see how Bessie is doing."

She carried Missy on her back down the ladder, and went laboring along the deep-rutted stone streets carrying her. That mode of locomotion did not suit the active Missy, and she flailed her mother with heels and fists until Sarah stopped and set her on her feet. Independently Missy pulled free from her hand and staggered joyously along the street, so that Sarah had to labor after her and get a firm grip of her skirts. She was so spent by the time she reached Bessie's house that she sat overlong in Bessie's golden oak rocker. As she struggled homeward again she thought in a panic that she must hurry to build a fire and cook the supper, and the task looked like an impossible effort. The house was empty when at last she reached it, and it was still empty when supper was ready. Bennie did not return until after she had fed Missy and settled her to sleep.

"I have kept your supper warm for you," Sarah said, trying to keep reproach from her voice.

"I ate at Lena's." *Because he was sick of a cluttered house and a nagging woman; sick of Missy; sick of food out of cans.*

"You oughtn't to have waited to eat," he said in a clumsy suggestion of apology. "You feeling pretty bad?"

"When you don't get any good out of your food — Seems as if I never get rested — " Before she could control them, the tears spilled over in Sarah's eyes.

Bennie dropped on his knees beside her, shoving Missy not ungently aside. "Look, Sarah," he said. "You got to sleep on the bed tonight. I'll sleep like usual on the floor, so you have plenty of room. This time I say you got to, Sarah."

It had been a long time since he had looked at her with such pity, spoken to her so gently. If only he had not put Missy aside. Never had he voluntarily picked her up. His own baby he would love: Sarah hated the baby she was carrying, thinking how Bennie would love it, because it was his, and because it was not a blind burden. Hopi men lavished love on their babies, and Bennie loved all children. Except Missy.

Sarah said nothing, only sat with bowed head and dried her tears with the edge of her apron.

"And in the morning," Bennie said wistfully, "I'll ask

210

Miss Dayton if she won't come in and have a look at you, next time she's up on top."

"You sleep in the bed, too. There's no call for you to lie on the floor," Sarah conceded.

Miss Dayton clucked deprecatingly when she came in a day or two later. "Bennie isn't beating you or anything?" she asked with false heartiness. "You look awfully done in."

"Seems as if it crowds my breathing so," Sarah said. "And when it kicks it hurts plenty. But it doesn't kick very often. It's been so still now for a few days, I'd hardly know it was alive." She looked with quick concern at Miss Dayton.

Miss Dayton frowned and then smiled a half reassurance. "Sometimes it's just because they're quiet babies; not nervous. Maybe it won't be such a lively piece as its sister," she added, poking at Missy's fat stomach as the child went edging around her chair, listening to the forgotten voice. Then Miss Dayton's voice lost its cheer. "You were grinding, weren't you, Sarah? Doubled over in that gosh-awful posture. After this baby was started, I mean."

Sarah nodded, half comprehension in her eyes.

"I bet that old hell-cat of a Lena kept you at it good long hours, too. Little she cares, so long as she gets some extra work out of it."

Sarah was pulling out her memories and reading the nurse's meaning. At one time a survey had been made of the mothers on First Mesa. The field matron had queried every mother in the three villages, Walpi, Sichumovi and Tewa. She had found that not one of them had borne a first child that lived. The long-continued grinding —

Sarah proved no exception to the rule. After Christmas Miss Dayton hurried her to the hospital at Keams Canyon, and Bennie's little boy was born dead.

211

Bennie cried like a child, and Sarah was not surprised at his grief. "My firs' chil'," he apologized, lifting his distorted face from his arms. "My poor little Sarah —"

What did surprise Sarah was her own emotion. All along this had been Bennie's baby, and she had hated it, resented it. When she saw it, small and finely shaped and lifeless, irretrievably lost, it was hers, too. She would bear no more. There was a curse on her motherhood. Twice she had borne the long burden, twice she had brought forth in pain, and she had only a single blind baby to show for it.

Little as she had looked past the misery of her pregnancy, bitterly though she had resented this child she had nevertheless vaguely glimpsed a different world once this baby was born. Surely, she had felt, life would have to be better, with Bennie happier, and with a normal child to vindicate Sarah.

Still, there were good moments. The hospital had kept Sarah until she was in better health than she had known for a year and more. Bennie was depressed by the loss of the child, but his wrath was directed wholly at his grandmother, and his raging was a catharsis for Sarah's resentment.

Once he broke out abruptly, "If I hadn't let Lena boss us — If we had been married at the mission, with none of that — that crazy grinding."

Sarah said thinly, "I guess we'd better excuse each other and begin over."

It was one of those February mornings when the mesa country was at its best. They were standing together at their open door, before the villages were thoroughly awake, and looking out across the desert miles to the sunrise and to the radiant buttes and distant mesas. The wind had not

212

begun, the air was clear and sparkling, and keen with burning piñon and cedar.

Sarah's heart softened and expanded. She felt for kinder words, to say that she had been as much to blame as he. Before the words could shape themselves, Missy came stumbling out, newly awake and warmly crumpled like a rose in the pink nightgown Sarah had made for her. She steered straight for the dangerous roof edge.

Sarah darted after her, and Bennie turned sharply away. The moment had passed. In a little while the wind began to blow again, and the same old pattern had set in.

Uncle Abraham came to see Sarah soon after her return from the hospital. The shock of his injury, and the long idleness to which it sentenced him had aged Abraham, yet his face still held its cheerfully upturned lines, his eyes their serenity. He carried his injured arm as if it were a child, and let it down cautiously on his knee when he had seated himself.

"Uncle Abraham, does it hurt all the time?" Sarah asked pitifully. "Missy, you keep away from Uncle Abraham. Poor Uncle Abraham hurt. Missy might joggle him."

But Abraham caught the child in his good arm and smoothed her hair with horny fingers. *"Bas sonel mana,"* he crooned. "Uncle Abraham's own Missy-*hoya.* — Sarah, it don't hurt too bad. Only it keep me awake at night. I got plenty time to repent of my sins, these long nights," he added, smiling.

"Your sins, Uncle Abraham!" Sarah scoffed tenderly. "Who's taking care of your fields?" — Now that Bennie's here on top with me, her mind accused her — "It's time to put in the brush, isn't it?" That was the brush which would hold down the mulch of sand.

"Well, you know how Bennie has kep' doing all he could."

No, I didn't know, and Bennie was afraid to tell me. "And young Aunt and I maybe can manage the rest. I got a good left hand yet, and maybe the right hand get so it can help some —"

"Isn't Joseph coming back, though? Or James?"

"No, they decide to stay in Parker. For good. They come home this summer, maybeso, but just to pack up what they got here and move."

Sarah was making pottery. She paused with a snake of gray clay between her palms, and her mouth made its silent childhood "O" of negation, her eyes wide with unbelief. "For good, Uncle Abraham? Oh, you can't mean they're going for good."

He nodded, his hand playing with Missy's contented one, as she nestled, relaxed, in the curve of his arm. "Maggie and her husband go, too. And the children," he added wistfully.

Sarah still stared, incredulous, the roll of clay moving, forgotten, in her hands. With these things happening, the great stone mesa itself seemed to lose solidity. "Our people, do you think they do so well when they try it in other places?" she asked stumblingly.

Abraham lifted quizzical eyes from Missy's glossy black head. "Do you think us Hopis have done so good here?"

"I don't know but they're happier than white folks out in the world," Sarah protested. "And I'd much rather be here than where the poor whites live in the cities. Awful places."

"But here it is hard to keep clean. And decent," Abraham said soberly. "And anyways, it can't go on forever, not the way the topsoil washes off and blows off. Sometime it has to come, my daughter, the going away."

The afternoon was bright and warm. Sarah had both doors open, with the half doors fastened securely for Missy's safety. The air flowed through the house, gently cool and sweet.

Sometime it has to come — Sarah shook a rebellious head.

"The climate down there," she said. "Can they stand it, do you think? They've never been used to heat and dampness."

"We jus' have to wait and see. There been other pioneers: Dan'el Boone; the Bible Abraham. Maybeso our childern strong enough, got willpower enough. Maybeso they can break up what's held so tight all these hundreds of years."

"How many are going?" Sarah asked, laying her coil of clay carefully around the upper edge of her growing bowl.

"I don' know — fifty — maybeso a hunderd, counting the childern. Anyways, there's that many talking it up to go nex' summer. Miss Lun'quist, she say it won't leave nothing much of our church. Just us old folks."

Sarah widened her eyes at him. "You don't mean it's all families from the mission?"

"Well, the others, they say they can't get away from the beating of the drums. Looks like us at the mission had to stand a lot when we come down from on top. Now those mission young folks can stand some more."

Sarah's fingers pinched viciously as she pinched the clay in place, pinched rebelliously. "They won't like it when they get there."

She was recalling how many boys and girls had suffered from the climate when they went to the Indian school at Phoenix. They had been unable to sleep in the sticky, heavy nights. They had soaked their bedsheets in the bathtubs and wrapped themselves in the clammy muslin. They had come home with tuberculosis, to die slowly on their sheepskin pallets.

"They do say six crops of alfalfa a year," Uncle Abraham

went on, "besides the gardens and the grain. Horace was one of the first to try it, and he already paid off some of the three thousand he borrow from Washindon. Take care of his family and pay off a hundred dollars cash money already."

Cash money. Cash money, which the Hopi had hardly known the meaning of, no, nor their neighbors the Navajos. Corn and beans and peaches to dry for their larder; melons to store, and squash; mutton from their flocks to dry; mutton and sheepskins to trade for sugar, flour, coffee, canned goods; driblets of money for the women's pottery and baskets, hardly enough to buy shoes, underwear, Pendleton blankets — That had been the Hopi economy, ever since the white man came.

And now, three thousand dollar loans. A hundred dollars cash money, paid off before the first year was half spent —

Bennie had come in and dropped down on the other stool, listening to Abraham.

"How big are those farms?" he asked.

"Forty acres each. All in a piece, not broke up and scattered like ours. And they say you never seen the like of the soil. And more than enough rain."

I need not worry about Bennie. Lena is too strong for him. I, Sarah, am too strong. And he is no pioneer, no initiator.

"And they really take up land, your boys?" Bennie asked. "Don't they just work for some man down at Parker, like before?"

"They take up land. All. Like I tell you, they get that money from Washindon for tractors and seed and all. Tractors. I never think my boys go from the planting stick to the tractor." Uncle Abraham spoke with melancholy pride.

Bennie stirred restlessly and glanced toward Sarah. "It

216

so dry we got to get the brush in quick or the seed all blow off someplace, isn't it? Maybeso I take tomorrow to help you with yours, Abraham."

Spring passed into summer, and summer swelled to its fullness, and still it was windy and dry. The chiefs held their prescribed prayer retreats. The old man offered the wind his gift of eggs. Still every morning dawned clear and bright, and every morning the wind came up and resumed its ceaseless harrying of desert and mesa. Its long whine beat a pain into Sarah's head, and the eddies of dust and debris churned her stomach as if in memory of the past two springs. The corn which normally rustled like silk, this year rattled like paper.

August came, and the Snake Chiefs were busy. Unless they could bring rain the Hopi were in for a bad year. They would make it the best Snake Dance in a decade. All day the road across the desert was set with plumes of dust as cars hastened in from the white world. Dust spurted up under the little hoofs of the sheep, and the desert vegetation crackled and broke under the feet of men.

On the last day of the Snake Dance the rains fell. They came so violently that even the Hopi muttered. Dangerous to question the amount or kind of rain which the gods sent you, but this was too much. Some of the old men and women said darkly that the young people were to blame; the young people who were planning to abandon the mesas and go down to Parker. It wouldn't be the first time the gods had shown their anger and their power. It was usually when these puny mission people had grown bold. Years ago when the Hopi had listened to the Spanish long-coats, the gods had shattered Corn Rock and sent part of it crashing down. Then they had sealed up the skies and the earth and let no corn grow. The Hopi had died of hunger. They had died like flies. The Hopi priests had warned them that next time the gods might overthrow the rest of the sacred rock, and turn the earth and the sky to stone, and let the Hopi perish from the face of the earth.

On this last day of the Snake Dance, the rain poured out as if an ocean had broken through the sagging sky. The air was a stormy sea. Rain rebounded from the mesa floor, the ascending water fighting the descending. It plunged over the edge with a deafening roar, a waterfall arching over every abyss. The Hopi women huddled their shawls over their heads and scurried to their houses, where the rain entered only in spots. The visiting *Bohannas* had crowded the one tunneled street full, and flattened themselves against housewalls, gasping as the deluge struck them. Others blindly fought their way into the grudgingly opened houses, while the Hopi laughed behind their hands at their discomfort.

The rain stopped almost as suddenly as it had begun, stopped with no moderation. The sun came out and a great double rainbow arched across the clearing sky. Steam rose from the stone streets of the mesa. They had been swept almost clean by the furious onslaught, their filth beaten down onto the ledges below.

The Hopi surged out of their houses, chattering excitedly. The *Bohannas* emerged from the tunnel, from the houses, which were glad to be rid of them, and stood about, exclaiming over the rainbow, staring at the villagers, talking about them as if none of them could understand English.

Sarah had run home with Missy in her arms. Now she ventured out again into the clean-washed air. Missy was as exuberant as in her babyhood. She was stimulated to excitement by the freshness that followed the storm, and by the many voices thronging the village streets which were usually so sparsely peopled. She capered and danced at the end of her mother's arm, squealing with delight. She hung full weight from Sarah's hand, begging to be whirled as her mother sometimes whirled her. Missy did not retreat into a shell in the presence of *Bohannas* as so many Hopi children did. Invisible to her, they did not yet impress her by their strangeness.

Keeping a firm hold on the little hand, Sarah walked along the outer street of the village, at the back, where there were fewer loitering whites. The keen cool air exhilarated her, also, and she lifted her head and drew it in deeply. Mechanically she skirted the puddles of rainwater caught in shallow depressions in the rock, drawing Missy close. For the most part the rock street looked almost scoured. "But there is mud, Missy. Here is more mud. Keep close to Mother —"

Mud rimmed one of those shallow pools, and Sarah was edging past it on the shelf street when she was halted by voices in the angle of the next house. Some of the *Bohannas* who had taken refuge from the storm still stood there, watching the mesa steam off, watching the cloud shadows dissolve upon the desert. Like most of the whites, they were talking freely — *as if they were at a zoo and we were the animals.*

"Looks like their corrals are right down here over the edge," the man was saying. "Down here, fifteen feet, maybe, on a ledge."

"Seems mean to keep horses there, with no fence at the edge." The girl was emerging from her shelter to peer over, "My goodness, it goes down miles, it seems like."

"Weird people," the man said casually, "I'm glad we're not Indians. Especially when I look at their women."

From his first word, Sarah had stood breathless. It could almost have been Kirk's voice. When he stepped out from the wall the sight of him did not dispel the sense of likeness. She could not see his face, but he was tall, and his wavy hair was ruddy gold where the sun struck it.

Sarah stood in a vacuum, the past three years blotted out. His words came dimly to her ears, as through rushing waters.

"Notice the women we've seen today? Meal sacks. Or else dried fish."

Sarah's eyes dropped to the pool of water at her feet, so still that it was a bright blue mirror, holding only sky and Sarah, slight, small, stringy —

In a panic she turned to hide as the young man swung toward her. She had known it was not Kirk. She would never see Kirk again. This man's face did not resemble his at all. This man's face — but why was it so shocked and white? At the same instant Sarah felt the emptiness of her hand —

"Missy!" she screamed, leaping toward the edge of the shelf street. "Missy — Missy — Missy!" and then, not knowing that she screamed the name, "Bennie! Oh, Bennie!"

She had dropped there in the muddy margin of the pool and lay staring over with straining eyes that could not believe what they saw. Twenty feet below, the frightened horses milled around a huddle of pink frock.

The young white man was grasping Sarah's shoulder, jerking her back. "No — a sheer drop — you'd scare the horses and then —"

But Bennie was already there. Bennie was swinging himself down with the sureness of long use.

Sarah watched, frozen, until he had lifted the little form and was making his way toward an easier ascent. Then her body settled together where she knelt, and she stared fixedly at the puddle, at the mud that rimmed it. The story was written in the mud. A small footprint, clear and clean, was filled now with water from the puddle and mirrored the sky. It was a child's foot carved from turquoise. The print beyond it was smeared and broadened, showing where Missy had slipped and gone sliding over.

The end of Missy's story. The end of Sarah's. There was nothing left.

She was only dimly aware of the surge of people, of excited voices and hands. None of the voices made sense until one said, "Sarah," and she looked up into Bennie's face, with tears streaming down it.

She looked wordlessly at the stained pink bundle in his arms. The legs dangled, and one arm, with brown baby fingers delicately spread and motionless. Convulsively Bennie clasped the child closer to his body. Sarah's eyes widened, unbelieving. Was Missy stirring under that tight pressure? Missy whimpered and flung up the delicate arm —

Sarah could do nothing but crouch where she was, whispering, "No — no — it can't be —"

It was Bennie who reared back his head and gazed down at the child with the color flooding into his blanched face. It was Bennie who stretched Missy across his wife's knees and felt her over with shaking fingers. "Sarah," he gasped, "she opens her eyes. Sarah, she is maybe all right. The mud, it was so deep —"

Hopis and *Bohannas* crowded in upon the boy and girl and child. They jostled them, curious and kind, they helped them up, helped them to their own house, their own ladder. Sarah was unaware of them. She and Bennie and Missy were alone in the midst.

"Gosh, that old ladder's going to bust —" *"Okiway, oki-way!"* — "Don't crowd them so. Can't you give them room?" — "I go quick for the bone doctor." — "Say, lady, you ought to carry her flat, in case her back is hurt —"

The crowd pressed into the house until it was full. Hopis

221

were used to thronged houses in times of sickness, and while Sarah held the child, Bennie clumsily stripped off the filthy garments, reached backward for sheepskins to make a soft pallet where Sarah could stretch her. When the child began to roar lustily and thrash about, Sarah drew a deep, believing breath.

"If you'll pour the water from the teakettle — into that pan —" she said to Frances in a rusty voice —

"Hardly any in the kettle," Frances chattered, pouring —

Sarah left Bennie to watch the child, and scrambled to her feet, her body shaking. Expertly she thrust sticks into the embers, reached for the dipper in the old pottery jar, half filled the teakettle. By that time Maude had come breathless up the ladder again, carrying warm water from her own stove.

It seemed to take hours to get Missy clean of the mire, to see what hurts there were. They were still touching the small brown body with incredulous fingers, finding no evidence of anything but bruises, a scraped knee, when the bone doctor came pushing his way through the neighbors and tourists.

He was a very old Hopi, and in his time he had seemed to hold magic in his touch. "Sssso," he muttered, looking at the lingering white people with eyes flat and yellow as a hawk's. To Missy, in their own tongue, he mumbled, "There, little girl — there, little girl —" as he dropped down beside her.

After the first frightened gasp and clutch of arms around Sarah's neck, Missy let the bone doctor examine her, only jerking and sobbing when he touched the bruises and abrasions in manipulating the small limbs.

After a few minutes the old Hopi sat back on his heels, and

his benignant survey moved from the child to the two young people. "The child is unhurt. Frightened, but unhurt."

Slowly the house emptied out. After a long time the three were alone. Bennie spoke abruptly out of a stillness.

"Don't you think we should take her to Keam's Canyon? To make sure?"

"How would we —?"

"I will get someone to take us." Bennie sprang up and raced for the door as if inaction were too heavy to be carried any longer. "You be ready. I get someone quick."

Almost at once he came back, running up the ladder, dashing across to the bed where Sarah had laid the child. When he had lifted Missy and carried her out and down the ladder, Sarah, following, drew a quick breath. It was Andy's car, and Andy, pale and grave, was fussing with brakes and pedals.

Sarah could find no words. Silently she climbed in the back and held out her arms for Missy.

"Everything set?" Andy asked.

The ten or twelve mile ride to the hospital was long, though Andy drove fast. In the front seat the men talked a little, about the rain, the crops, the sheep. In the rearview mirror she met both pairs of eyes, scrutinizing her, scrutinizing Missy.

For a while Sarah cradled Missy and played with her dimpled fingers to keep her quiet. Soon, however, Missy pulled herself upright, her feet cudgeling her mother's knees. She stood with arms outflung, and squealed with pleasure at the feeling of swift motion. Sarah, looking quickly toward the mirror, saw the eyes again dart to her child and cling. Sarah felt a surge of joy because there was no likeness that either could trace. Missy was her mother's

223

child, the broad, low brow, the short nose, delicately aquiline, the full lips, the eyes — the poor eyes — set deep, with large lids.

When at last they reached the hospital, Bennie helped Sarah out and took the child from her, running ahead of her up the double flight of steps. The nurses welcomed them with exclamations of quick sympathy. Sarah had gained their friendship in the weeks after her son's birth. The doctor's hooded eyes, too, were warm when he came hurrying in. Missy was stripped and ready, and wriggled with pleasure when he whistled to her and gave her a gentle spank of greeting.

"Twenty feet, you say? Sure you're not stretching that? We'll X-ray her, then, but it will be just routine."

"You don't mean —? Doctor, you really think —?" Bennie was stammering —

"I mean this child's all right. Must have nine lives, like a cat. Yes, I'd be willing to gamble on it that she's all right. Officially, of course, I won't say a thing till I see the X-rays. It's a marvel to me that your mesa babies live through what they do."

Tired as Sarah and Bennie were that night, sleep came hard after the excitement of the day. They had stopped at Abraham's, and Miss Lundquist had come skittering over, and Miss Dayton had hurried to join them, for the news of Missy's fall had reached the last house in Polacca. Nothing would do but that Polehongsie bring what was cooking on her stove, and they all eat together at Miss Lundquist's before Andy took Sarah and Bennie and Missy home again.

The hour, the two hours, were bright and dim, they chattered with sound and fell quiet, eddied around Sarah in half reality. Miss Lundquist had pushed her gently into the high-backed oak rocker, saying that they certainly didn't need any more help to get this pick-up supper on the table; she and Polehongsi and Miss Dayton were tumbling over each other as it was. When Missy fell asleep in Sarah's arms, Bennie took the child and laid her on the old sofa behind the stove; drew chairs up close along the outer edge so that she could not fall off. Then he stayed, perching on the end of the sofa, leafing through an old copy of a magazine that featured color photographs of Arizona. Andy was as apparently absorbed in the Geographic. Sarah just sat and let the room rise and fall around her.

At last the meal was over, and Miss Lundquist was shooing them out. —"Stay and wash these dishes? I should say not. It does me good to get my hands in hot water. And if Polehongsi or Miss Dayton wants to dry them, there's plenty of fresh towels. But you young ones go on home and get some rest."

In their own house at last, they went thankfully to bed. Sarah found herself too tired to sleep, each inch of her body asserting a will of its own, refusing to let the mattress and springs hold it, but trying to hold up the bed. Between Sarah and the wall, Missy jerked and trembled with bad dreams, and cried out when her turning hurt the bruises.

"Why couldn' I make a crib for her?" Bennie said out of the restless dark. "It would be pretty made — how do they call it when they make it of branches with the bark on, like her cradle basket?"

"Rustic —"

"Yes, rustic. And what do you think for springs? A hide? Abraham knows how to tan a hide right. And then couldn' you go to the community house and make a mattress?"

"Yess."

Bennie lay on the far edge of the bed, not to disturb her;

225

yet he did not seem so far away as he usually did. She slept.

The room was lightening to gray when next Missy woke her. That cool, still gray paled until not only the windows were visible, but the *vigas*, and the shapes of *potas* and *kachinas* on the wall, and Missy, beside her, turned now on her stomach with arms and legs thrown wide, and her silky black hair fanning out from her head. Bennie, too, was visible, lying on his back with chin high and mouth and eyes strained shut as if he might be feigning sleep.

Missy was unhurt. That was a miracle. Yet what hope was there for Missy? She, Sarah, was living in her mother's house, and it had never looked more serenely beautiful, not even to the homesick dreams of her years in Finch. Yet she was like one camping overnight, and if she were to stay here for days or months or years, there would be no difference: they would be makeshift days or months or years.

Somewhere a cock crew, but otherwise the silence was as absolute as the silence of a graveyard. It was like living in a graveyard. When Bennie swallowed audibly, and stifled a yawn, the interruption was a relief.

"Bennie?"

"Oh, you don' sleep? What is it, Sarah?"

"Bennie, maybe it isn't so good for us to live here."

He spoke after a long silence, haltingly. "You mean go down to Polacca?"

Sarah in turn was silent, and he waited. She could not bring the words out. At last she said, "Maybe not Polacca —"

"But I thought you were so crazy for Walpi," he said.

Still Sarah had no answer.

"And if we went off somewheres — to the railroad, you mean? Winslow or Holbrook? — Well, do you think we'd do so good? The print shop — I don' know if they would —

226

and I don' like it where the girl is the one that earns the living —"

Sarah said, "Bennie, I didn't thank you. You were good about — about Missy today. You were good. And when you — never liked her very well, too —"

Bennie stirred abruptly, turning his head away from Sarah, so that she had to listen hard to hear his mumbled words. "It — it isn' like that, Sarah. I couldn' not like Missy. It was only —" he breathed hoarsely before he could get out the words — "it was her father. I hate her father so."

Sarah lay looking at the back of his head, sorting out her thoughts and feelings. "He isn't worth hating, I guess," she said at last. "He's just — nothing. And he — I suppose he really thought I was — fooling when I — fought him —"

Bennie's voice was still muffled. "You — don' like him at all, Sarah? Then why — ? Why don' you like me much, either?"

Sarah sat up cautiously and put Missy's hand and foot carefully down from her own body. She reached over and touched Bennie's turned cheek with one finger. He lay tense.

"No, I certainly don't like him, Bennie. I never did like him." She felt for more positive words, but she could not find them. She drew a deep breath. "Bennie, if you want, I make another baby. For you." *If I can,* her thoughts nagged her. *Because there doesn't seem any way out. Not for our generation. Only for our children. So, if I can . . .*

Bennie turned his head toward her, his face flushed and childlike, only his lashes wet, glued into points like a baby's. "You like to go down today and say goodbye to Joseph and his wife?" Bennie asked. "This week they go to Parker."

They smiled at each other, shyly, only half their thoughts on their words.

"How do they go?" Sarah asked.

"A lot of trucks, and three cars, and a bus, all together." Bennie sat up, too. "They're going to Keams Canyon early in the morning. The school say they give them a good breakfast, so they start off happy. Then up to Jeddito, and out to Holbrook, and back to Flag. They got to stop and sleep there, they say — And then down through Oak Creek Canyon —"

Sarah put her tumbled hair back from her face. "It will be hot — hot —"

Bennie sighed as if his enthusiasm were leaking out.

"Bennie, do you think we could go with them? Could we arrange it even this late?"

His mouth had fallen open, and he was gaping at her. "You — you just kidding, Sarah?"

She shook her head. "It might be the right way. Like Uncle Abraham said, it's got to come sometime."

Bennie leaped from the bed, shaking free from the swathing quilt. He stood waving his hands and chin at the meager furnishings. "Could — could we get ready so quick?" he stammered.

Sarah looked around her, too, and achieved a careless shrug. "Lucky we haven't got a Frigidaire and a washer to bother us." Her eyes were touching the pole-and-brush ceiling, the soft adobe walls, the peephole above the grinding bins, where now the early sun was streaming in.

They would turn the key in the lock. After a few years, coming back for a visit, they would find that a storm like yesterday's had battered its way in, damaging the place too badly for repair. Again a few years and only the *vigas* would remain above them, so that the sun indifferently poured its splendor through the skeleton roof, as it did now at the house just beyond, at the tip of the mesa.

"It will be hot there, Sarah," Bennie was saying, his voice shaken with a growing excitement. "It will be hard. I can farm. That is a thing I can do all right. But for you, Sarah —"

Sarah could remember newspaper pictures of that camp, with nothing beautiful or restful to the eye: old military barracks. Could the Hopis make it homelike? The satisfying loveliness which they had possessed through the centuries had grown slowly, out of a way of life. They would be unskillful in transplanting it, if indeed they could transplant it at all.

"We don't have to have it so pretty," Sarah said. "And we are not too old. Twenty and twenty-two — that is not too old. We have time."

Bennie seized his battered suitcase from the corner where it was stored, flung it open. He snatched a boomerang from its pegs on the wall, and laid it in, carefully. "Let's begin, Sarah," he stammered. "What are we waiting for?"